DEVIL
YOU HATE

USA *TODAY* BESTSELLING AUTHORS

J.L. BECK &
C. HALLMAN

1

CELIA

arriage. A legal bond of love and the union of two people becoming one. For many women, it's the greatest moment of their lives. It's something they've dreamt about; the beautiful dress, the gorgeous venue, and a handsome prince charming who would swoop in and sweep them off their feet.

When I was a little girl, I had those same dreams. I thought I would marry for love. That my future husband would be my fierce protector, my knight in shining armor. It's too bad that was all a lie.

As soon as I was old enough to realize that my life was never really mine, I let the idea of marrying for love go and accepted reality. Which leads me to my current predicament.

I have to marry this stupid man. It's the only thing that echoes in my head as my fiancé sits beside me in my family's dining room at dinner. Like always, no one speaks. The only sounds are the scraping of forks across porcelain and the occasional tinkle of ice when my mother lifts and lowers her whiskey glass. Her third since dinner began, if I'm counting correctly.

She'd gone all out for tonight's meal. It was a rare occurrence that we ate dinner together. I spend most of my evenings propped against the kitchen counter as the chef tosses things on a plate for me to scarf down between my local volunteer appearances. I've never even seen this china set before. In fact, I didn't even know we had any.

I glance over at my soon-to-be husband from under my lashes. He's handsome enough, with high cheekbones, a sharp jawline, and soft black hair, but looks aren't everything. At least not to me. We've only spoken a handful of times since my father cemented the Ricci and Gardello alliance a couple of weeks ago. An agreement hinging on me marrying Marco, the dumbest of the five Gardello brothers.

As a second son, he won't be heir to his own family, but as the only child left to the Ricci's, I suppose he becomes the successor to mine.

The thought causes bile to rise into my throat, and any appetite I had evaporates into thin air. My sister should do this—my beautiful, smart, brave older sister.

Pain slices through my chest at the reminder, and I spare a look at her empty chair on the other side of my mother. The one we've all been dancing around since her suicide six months ago.

Blinking back tears, I suck a breath into my lungs. I won't cry in front of these people. It will only enrage my father and cause my mother to drink more. Then again, maybe I should. Marco needs to know what he's getting himself into.

He blots the sides of his mouth carefully with a napkin and spins his own whiskey glass (neat) on the tablecloth. I'm stuck in a trance, wondering why my sister had to take her life. Why isn't she here right now? Out of nowhere, Marco boldly turns to me. I feel his penetrating gaze on the side of my face. The heat of his stare traces the scar that bisects it from my mouth to my eyelid.

Usually, I couldn't care less about my scar, but the way he gawks at it like it's a two-headed dog, I hate it. I shift forward a little, letting my long brown waves slide into place. Like a curtain, it obscures not only my face but also the pink tinge in my ears, if the burning in my cheeks and neck is anything to go by.

"By the way, you look lovely tonight," Marco compliments, while continuing to stare at me.

I barely keep from squaring my shoulders and preening under his gaze. He spoke louder than necessary, telling me he's trying to show my parents how nice he will be to me once we marry. Once he has my trust fund. *My life.*

I'll be like a dog, collared and cared for but never free. It's hilarious that he even attempts to show interest, as if my father would change his mind. Maybe he cares, or maybe it's just a ruse?

"Thank you," I choke out, keeping my eyes trained in front of me.

"Celeste," my mother hisses from across the table.

She's the only person in the world who calls me by my full name.

My father simply calls me *Girl*, as he did my sister. No doubt, even twenty-odd years later, he's still disappointed we aren't boys.

Boys get names, girls get... well... married off to cement alliances.

I know what she expects from me, and I hate that in the next instant I turn in my chair and offer Marco a smile. As the only daughter left, I need to be good, to be *here*. Even when I want to be anywhere else. I have a duty to fulfill, an obligation, as my mother has called it many times over. I owe this to them, my parents, and family name.

"Thank you, I chose this dress because I thought you would like it."

An outright fucking lie since my mother chose the almost indecently short red A-line dress with cap sleeves and a low-cut neckline. I prefer my slacks and silk blouse combo when I need to dress up. Not Marco, he likes his girls leggy, and since my five foot three frame didn't lean toward leggy, my mother opted to show as much of my legs as possible and hope for the best.

As I sit here awaiting my fate, I feel like a head of cattle at auction. Any minute now, he will pin a tag to my ear and haul me off to the slaughterhouse. The thought makes me laugh, but I hide it behind my hand as I return to my dinner.

Marco clears his throat and continues to draw my parents into conversation. It's hopeless, but I like to watch him flounder.

"How are the wedding preparations going? Is there anything I can help with?"

An actual conversation at dinner is a battle twenty years in the making for me. My parents don't speak to each other unless absolutely necessary, and even then, it's always to the point. There is no joy, no love, or happiness. Everything is stiff and cold. A family that is anything but a *family*.

Nevertheless, my mother has no problem speaking to Marco. "The planning is complete, my dear. As long as you two show up at the church on time, everything will be perfect."

My mother plans parties like the CIA plans covert missions. By the end of the thing, someone's likely eviscerated, and everyone wonders how it got pulled off. I knew my wedding day would be the same. Sadly, I wasn't asked to pick flowers or even the cake. My mother did everything, even though it was my wedding. I try not to be bitter about it since, technically, this isn't a marriage, but a business transaction. It's easier to stomach if I think of it that way.

Marco reaches out and takes my hand from my wine glass, cupping it in his like a parent might hold a child's. He gives the room a shining smile, and I want to puke. "I'm so glad you ladies have everything in order. I know my mother has been up to her ears in decorating the home we'll move into once we are married."

I fight with the urge to rip my hand from his. Each of his clammy fingers digs into mine, applying pressure, and laying claim. Why he feels the need to do so here with only my parents watching, I can't figure out.

I lift my chin and look up at him again. *Oh.* The pressure of his claim is for me. I was hoping, once we married, we might be friends. That I could go about my business, and he his, and that we would meet up for dinner on occasion. Sure, he'd have other lovers, something I wouldn't be allowed, but we'd be on the same page. It would be more of a partnership than a decree.

But I can see by the look in his eyes, he won't be happy until he has my complete submission—my money, my family name, my life as his own.

A tiny thing inside of me dies because, for the very first time since my sister's death, I can see a glimmer of why she did it. Why she'd take her own life when she always had so much to live for. It wasn't Marco they had betrothed her to, but his older brother, Antonio. Who walked away completely unaffected and was now engaged to the only Marino daughter. At this rate, the five families risked more cross-breeding than the royal families of Europe.

Marco stands abruptly and buttons his black suit jacket with a smirk. He saunters to the bar on the far side of the dining room like he already owns the place. I drop my gaze to my food once more. I should eat more, but I can't stomach it right now. A moment passes, and he returns to his seat, grabbing my hand and pressing my fingers around an old-fashioned. I try not to cringe. I fucking hate rye whiskey.

Something he should know by now, since I declined his offer to make a drink for me when he first arrived. Not to mention I've told him at least three times since our marriage contract negotiations began. I'd much rather toss the drink in his face and retreat to my room, but that's not an option. I don't want to risk another scolding from my mother or a beating from my father, so I lift the drink to my lips and take a sip. I try to hide the sour face I'm making with a smile, but I can't imagine it looks good.

I watch as he finishes his drink, and I abandon mine, placing it on the table next to my still partially filled plate of food.

"Would you like dessert, Marco?" My mother's gaze flashes with disapproval as she looks down at my plate and back up at me.

"Oh no, I'm stuffed," he declines and pats his stomach like a child.

Thank the lord. If I had to endure one more stiff minute of this meal, I was going to explode. Turning to me, he says, "Walk me out, Celia."

Finally, something I am more than happy to do for him.

"I look forward to having you as my son-in-law," my father says, shaking hands with Marco. Marco leans into my father's ear and whispers something low. I shove from my chair and move to stand near the entrance to the dining room. Men's conversations aren't meant to be heard by women, so it's best to stand and act like you hear nothing at all.

Once Marco pulls away, it's a short walk through the foyer to the door, and I open it wide, resisting the urge to shove him out and slam it closed. I'll have to get used to his presence since, in a short while, he'll be my husband.

With a finger, Marco tilts my chin up, painfully, since he has almost a foot of height on me. For a moment, I think he might kiss me. *Please don't. Please don't. Please don't.* I chant in my head. His lips tip up at the sides, almost like he knows what I'm thinking.

"I really think you could be exceptionally beautiful, Celia. Once we're married, as my wedding gift to you, I'll take you to this plastic surgeon I know. I'm sure they can do something about, well..." he breaks off, and I can feel the heat of his stare on my scar, "well, that."

I blink because anything coming out of my mouth might spew lava along with it. It takes a bit of willpower to stop myself from lashing out at him, but somehow, I do. Forcing the corner of my lips up into a smile,

I say, "I hope you have a wonderful evening, Marco. I'm sure without this scar, I will be much more beautiful."

"I can't wait for you to become my wife." He smirks and then grabs my hand, placing a chaste kiss against the top. I stop myself from pulling away and merely nod, knowing that, if anything, I would wait a million years for us to marry.

Marco leaves a few moments later, and I shut the door behind him, nearly sagging against it. I take a couple of deep breaths and gather my wits. I'll allow myself this one reprieve before I'm forced to mask my pain and put on a smile.

I suck one last calming breath into my lungs as I scrub a hand down my face and lift my chin. I might be drowning, but as long as a part of my head is still above water, I'll continue on. I tiptoe past the dining room, hoping to escape without further notice. As soon as I reach the stairs, I race up them, stripping out of the itchy dress as I go. By the time I reach my bedroom door, the dress is off. I leave it in a heap near the door and slam the heavy wood behind me.

There, if one of them wants to come speak to me after that, at least they know what they are in for. The heels that I hate just as much as the dress fly across the room in opposite directions as I kick them off. Each of my toes ache, so I sit on the edge of the bed in nothing but my underwear and slip and rub some of the pain out of them.

It's then that I notice the lights across the room in my bathroom and closet are on. The maids must have finished the packing they started yesterday and forgot to switch them off. The fireplace between the two doors is lit, the flames casting a soft warmth through the room.

The memories I made here with my sister threaten to bubble up, but I try to swallow them down with the rest of the people I have lost... too many in this life.

.   .   .

I EXPERIENCED my first loss fifteen years ago. As I sit, my thoughts drift to the boy I thought I'd one day marry—Cici. The son of my father's friend and business partner, of the now decimated Costa family. Cici had been my best friend for years, and then when I was only nine years old, he disappeared from my life forever. One day he was there, and the next, his entire family was targeted by a rival family and killed.

My father used it as a reminder to my sister and me of how quickly we can be taken away and why we should always listen and let him keep our family safe.

His safety net meant nothing to me, not after my sister died. Deep down in my heart, I knew if anyone should stand beside me in two days' time at that church, it should have been Cici. It wasn't going to be him, though; it was Marco, and I would just have to be content with settling. It's the right thing to do, or at least that's what I keep telling myself.

I close the little spot in my mind where I keep him. With my sister's death so fresh, and my marriage looming, I can't afford to indulge in frivolous fantasies. My childhood ended years ago. It's time to move on. There is no point in dwelling on the past when there is nothing there to dwell on.

My head aches from the pins at the top where my mother's stylist coiled some of my curls. I tug them out, massaging my scalp as I walk to the bathroom to wash my makeup off. One step inside, and I find it's bare. The maids have already packed most of my toiletries away. The only things left on the sink are my toothbrush, toothpaste, mouthwash, and facial cleanser. It feels empty, and I'm reminded that my time here in this house is ending. It wasn't always great, and there were a lot of horrible memories in this house, but this was the last place my sister was alive. Once I leave here, my life will never be the same.

I make quick work of washing my face. Each slide of the rag reveals another sliver of the real person beneath. With the makeup gone, I stare at myself in the mirror. Usually, I hate looking at myself, the scar being the only thing I see, but tonight, I see deeper than that.

Tears glisten in my eyes, and I blink them back. To dive into the water of my own personal issues and matters, no one has time for that, and even if I did, I have no solutions. I toss the rag in the sink and walk out of the bathroom to find a nightgown.

Most of my clothing is packed, as well as any other belongings. The only things left for me are a couple outfits, some underwear, a nightgown, and my wedding dress—a giant tulle thing hanging off the closet door on the far side of the bedroom. I wish I had the balls to light it all on fire. How fast can a ten-thousand-dollar dress burn? I'll bet mighty fast. That is, if I were the betting type.

Another stack of items lay on the bench at the end of the bed. I lift the items, the fabric so soft and luxurious. It's the handmade white lace lingerie my mother insisted I'd need for the wedding night. It would burn faster than the dress. I eye my fireplace and consider throwing it in, if only to cheer myself up.

A knock on the door breaks my concentration, and I call out, "Come in."

Maria, one of the maids, enters carrying my discarded drink from dinner. I've known her my entire life, and in many ways, I consider her to be like a grandma.

Her smile is warm, and her presence always brings me joy.

"Your mother sent me to give this to you. She told me to tell you to finish it. That your fiancé made it for you, and you will show respect."

I take the glass from Maria and stare down into the honey brown liquor. Another test of my resolve and commitment to the marriage my father agreed to.

I look from the glass and to Maria and find her face is a mask of guilt and shame. Now would be a good time to start practicing how to hide my emotions better.

"I'm sorry, Celia. Sometimes we don't get to make choices in life. Sometimes they're made for us. You can only do with what you're given. I will miss you greatly, child," she whispers the last part.

"I'll miss you too, Maria. You're probably the only person I'll miss from this god-forsaken house." I smile and wrap my arms around her middle.

Her sweet scent washes over me, and I suck a thick breath into my lungs. We hug for a moment longer, and when she pulls away, I see tears in her eyes.

"You're only given one life. Make the best of it." She clears her throat and backs out of the bedroom slowly.

My heart clenches in my chest like someone is squeezing the blood right out of it. There's no point in trying to fight the inevitable. There are no other options for me. There never was. I'll have to make do with what I've been given.

Shifting gears, I sip the drink and drag my attention back to the lingerie again. I try to imagine Marco taking it off of me. The image in my head leaves me cold. Marco won't care about what I want in bed. He'll strip me, use me, and then leave—a piece of ass he paid for with his family name.

I should find the worst granny panties in the world to wear on our wedding night. Maybe he won't be able to get it up and instead seek out one of the many girls he keeps on his roster. That will set the precedence early that I won't welcome him in my bed.

Could I even set that boundary?

Or would Marco take by force what I deny him? He seems like a man who would take it and enjoy stripping me of my dignity. I throw back the rest of the drink in a couple gulps and set the tumbler on the fireplace mantle. The alcohol burns all the way down my throat and settles deep in my gut, radiating warmth and taking a smidge of the coldness in my bones away.

I return to the bed and wiggle my bra out from under the champagne silk of my slip. No use putting on my nightgown when I can sleep in this. With the whiskey finally working its way through my system, a warmth swirls in my belly and radiates out toward my limbs. It's like being wrapped in a heated blanket.

Thoughts dip in and out of my brain hazily. I lie back on the bedspread and let the liquor gently lead me into oblivion. Maybe this is why my mother drinks? To numb her of the absurdity called her life.

I can't imagine after twenty years with Marco what I'll look like by the end. Spirit broken, and of no more use than to plan parties and entertain his guests. Most of the men in the five families want a trophy wife. There aren't many daughters in the pedigreed lines that make up our own little world here in Chicago. The sons of these families can take one of the daughters as a wife and have a hundred mistresses on the side. No one cares. The second one of the wives takes a lover, well... I'd seen the grave of one of their wives with my own eyes.

Are their mistresses held to the same standard of conduct? I need to get my brain to shut off. The questions are compounding, and I don't have any answers. I'm wasting my time thinking about things that don't matter.

I close my eyes and picture my sister's face in my mind. Her beautiful silky black hair I always envied. The gentle curve to her brown doe eyes. I can feel her ghost nudging me along, giving me the strength when all I want to do is rip my hair out and scream until someone listens to me. Until someone hears me.

Undoubtedly, no one cares. I'm alone in this. In two days, I will become Mrs. Celeste Gardello. All the dreams I have as a person will be gone. Stripped away to unearth new desires, all of which must center on my husband and his needs. It's the way things are done, my mother told me after we signed the contracts.

"If you be kind to him, show him that sweet heart of yours, how can he not fall in love with you?" she'd said with her liquor-laced breath and tears swimming in her eyes.

They weren't tears of joy. She was weeping for me, for my loss.

My mother loves me. But not enough to save me.

No one can save me now, not even myself.

2

NIC

$\mathcal{T}$he problem with the five families today... every one of them has gone soft. They consider holding their territory and keeping it tucked tight in their fat fucking fists beneath them. Which is why, when I'm done, I'll take it all. Every fucking thing will be mine. Every man and woman will bow to me or face death. I don't make idle threats, and I'm anything but soft. I've clawed my way out of hell and back. I'll make them all pay for their sins.

As for holding my territory... I revel in it. I delight in showing every dickhead who steps into my lane exactly who's boss. Starting with the three idiots kneeling on the pavement of my parking garage before me.

I sit in front of them on a stool, my trusty *Desert Eagle 50AE* clutched in my hand, resting on my thigh. With thick cloth bags over their heads, they can't see the gun. It wasn't necessary when they had nearly pissed themselves the moment I put them on their knees.

"Do you know why you're here?" I ask them.

The question is rhetorical because they know why they're here. Plus, they are all shaking so badly, I doubt any of them are going to volunteer an answer.

They fucked with me. Now they'll pay the price.

I keep my voice level and calm. An easy trick considering these assholes will be dead in five minutes or less. "Will any of you tell me where the gun cache you hid in my territory is?"

I don't need to tell them who I am. Every single criminal on the streets knows where the boundary lines to my domain are. The moment they shift, you better believe it's learn quick or die fast.

I slide off the stool and step up to the first dickhead. He visibly quakes as I crouch in front of him. Not that he can see me through the sack. Though I'm sure they can feel the slight stir of air, feel death breathing down their necks.

"How about you, Big Shot? Want to tell me where the guns are?"

"Will you promise not to kill me?" His voice wobbles. I can imagine his bottom lip is trembling, his face a mask of pure horror. I wouldn't even be surprised if he had tears running down his cheeks. The number of times I've seen grown men cry is astounding. There are never tears when they're doing wrong, only when they're caught in the devil's clutches.

I glance back at my second-in-command, Soo. His shoulder-length black hair is already in a bun at the base of his neck, ready to make a move the moment I ask. I shake my head with a little grin. "This one wants to know if I'll promise not to kill him."

Soo just shrugs, matching my smile, knowing damn well that begging never works with me.

I turn my attention back to my captive. "Sure, I'll promise not to kill you. Just tell me where the guns are."

The man visibly sinks into himself, thinking I've given him a reprieve. Immediately, the other two dickheads speak up, talking over themselves to save their own skin.

"Fifth street..." one says, and the other finishes his sentence.

"Near the warehouses, across the railroad tracks."

I almost laugh, it's funny what people will do once they think there are no repercussions. What they don't realize is that there is always a repercussion. For every good and bad thing you do in this world, there is a consequence, and this is there's.

Without delay, I press the barrel of the gun to the middle guy's temple and say, "Thank you."

I pull the trigger, and he falls back onto the sheet of clear plastic, waiting for easy cleanup. The other two men immediately huddle into themselves. *Why?* I stare at them, genuinely trying to figure out how cowering will help keep them alive. Their fear only feeds my rage, and without even blinking, I pull the trigger again and then hand my weapon, barrel first, to Soo.

As he takes the hot metal in his hand like it's nothing, he says, "It's time."

I turn toward the SUV idling nearby. The sound of the gunshot behind me causes the sides of my lips to tip up into a sinister grin.

Never make a deal with the devil.

He always wins in the end.

I climb into the car, and Soo takes the driver's side. Already, my men are gathering the plastic, rolling up the dead bodies for easy disposal. There are very few people on my payroll. But every single one of them I trust implicitly.

Every bond I make is forged in blood. Nothing less will do to ensure my men stay loyal. Paying them well and giving them a cut of my product doesn't hurt either. The gangster's retirement plan, they call it.

As if any of us will make it to retirement age. That's laughable. It doesn't matter, though. I don't care if I die as long as I finish my plans first. Death is inevitable; it will catch you in the long run and even more so in this job. I've come to terms with that, and when my time comes, I will greet death with open arms.

We ride through the city, and the closer to my destination we get, the higher the buzz under my skin climbs.

Today begins the end of it all.

Soo glances at me, his hands clenched so tight around the steering wheel his knuckles are white. "Are you ready for this?"

Of all the people in my life, only he and my brother could question me without earning a bullet to the temple.

"Do I not look ready?" I counter, staring straight out the windshield.

The familiar upscale neighborhood is where one of the worst crime families in the world hides out. They pretend to stay beneath the radar, but everyone knows the darkness that circles them. There is no hiding evil. It's best to wear it like a badge of honor.

Soo doesn't comment on what I look like, so we lapse into silence. The side-gate for a large mansion stretches out in front of us. Two figures dressed in black, one carrying a small form over their shoulder, rush down the driveway. The prospect of getting revenge gives me an all-new excitement; not even the thrill of murdering my enemies gives me this kind of high.

Once Soo comes to a stop, he unlocks the vehicle, and the men bolt through the gate and into the backseat of the SUV. The small feminine body lands in a heap flat across their laps, her arms flayed out over her head.

I gesture at the girl. "Put her in the fucking trunk."

Mic climbs out and drags the girl, belly down, into his arms. Then he opens the back of the SUV and tosses her inside, none too gently. I'm not particularly happy about it but it's better than having her on their laps.

Once he's back in his seat, Soo takes off the way we came. I check the rearview mirror and smile. No one is rushing out. No one seems to be coming to save her—all the better.

Soo remains quiet as we drive. Mic and Archy, if that's their actual names, aren't on my payroll, and once we get back to my house, I'll pay them, and hopefully never see them again. I don't like the way they were manhandling her or how they tossed her into the back. I can feel the desire to kill them rising with every beat of my heart. I have half a mind to cut off their balls and feed them down their throats when we arrive at the house. Yes, it's an irrational thought since I asked them to grab her for me, but I don't care. Rational thinking is for men that care what others think. The only one who gets to touch or hurt her is me... for now, at least.

We make it back to the house before I let my anger ruin a perfectly adequate working relationship. Soo enters the gate passcode, and we drive into the underground garage we'd been in only a half-hour earlier.

Once Soo parks, everyone gets out, and Mic takes it upon himself to gather up my newest possession from the trunk. I narrow my eyes at him, but he ignores me and follows Soo down a corridor and into the basement. I'd set up a little room just for her. We file in, and Mic drops her down onto the mattress. She bounces and then settles; the slip she's wearing is under her breasts, leaving her panties and legs exposed to everyone.

I grit my teeth hard enough to crack them and march across the space to inspect her. The second daughter of the reigning Ricci family sure grew into a beautiful young woman. Her dark brown hair lies around her head in a halo, some obscuring her features. I crouch beside the mattress and lift the strands from her face, smoothing them away so I can get a better look at her.

Her eyes are closed, and she looks peaceful, like an angel that's sleeping. Too bad she's been given to the devil. My gaze lowers, roaming over her creamy flesh. The blood in my veins becomes molten lava when I notice the red scrape on her cheek. It looks fresh. *Too fresh.*

Gently, as if she is made of glass, I brush my thumb across the wound, lingering where it is flayed across the scar that runs diagonally on her cheek.

Her scar does nothing to hinder her beauty.

Rage already a low simmer in my gut reaches a boil. I quickly cup her head, feeling down her exposed skin until my gaze lands on her chipped fingernails. Blood is caked under two of them, and as my gaze lowers, I notice a bright purple bruise in the shape of a handprint across her thigh, only inches from her lace-covered pussy. My insides burn, and I've never felt the need to inflict pain on someone so badly.

I stand casually, a storm brewing inside of me. Soo moves behind me, no doubt attuned to my shift in mood. The two men I paid to bring her to me huddle near the door, waiting for their money.

I approach slowly, a predator sizing up his prey. "I'm sure I instructed you not to harm her."

Mic speaks up first. "She woke up when we nabbed her. I had to hit her over the head to get her out of the house quietly."

I turn my attention to Archy. "And you? Did you decide to cop a feel while your partner here subdued her?"

An awareness enters his eyes. He can see his death at my hands, and I let him take a good long look. "In the hallway, now."

The men precede me, and Soo follows me out, leaving the door open so he can lean casually in the frame.

I force air into my lungs to calm the fuck down before I put my *Eagle* in their eye sockets and blow their brains out. I'm not bothered by death, and I have no problem killing.

"Tell me what happened. Every single fucking detail, like your life depends on it."

Mic, of course, takes the lead, his mouth open like a fish out of water. "She was passed out on her bed like we were told she would be. Except when Archy went to grab her, she woke up and started to fight." He pulls down the neck of his shirt, revealing a set of claw marks across his skin. "She's a hellcat, if you ask me. I had to knock her out so we could get out of there before she started screaming."

I shift my eyes to Archy. "And you? What's your excuse?"

His gaze shoots to Mic and then back to me. Obviously, not the brains of the operation here. "I just carried her, Boss. Promise."

"Promise," I whisper.

Soo presses the *Eagle* into the palm of my hand behind my back. Once I have hold of it, he shifts down the hallway. No doubt to get the cleanup crew ready to take care of these dickheads.

I bring the gun out and press it to my temple as if I am figuring out a problem. "So how did she get that bruise on her thigh? Is one of you not getting laid enough at home and need to put hands on what's mine?" My voice remains calm, but inside, everything roils to waste these idiots.

Mic, suddenly realizing they are in a lot more trouble than he thought, raises his hands up in surrender. "We didn't know she was yours, Boss. Honest. Archy just wanted to see what she was hiding under her nightgown."

I glance back at Archy, who stares at Mic like he just got himself killed. To be fair, he did. "I'm sorry, she just... she looked so soft. All I did was touch her a little bit."

I bring the gun down in front of me with a nod, like visions of their imminent death aren't pinging around in my head. Call me a monster, but I even give them a grin to set them at ease. "Her skin does look soft. It's because she's a pampered princess."

Both men smile back, nodding, thinking maybe, just maybe, they'll walk out of here alive.

I continue, "I hear she's a virgin. I bet that sweet little pussy is going to be so good when I claim it."

Mic shifts back, his smile placating. The smile of a man praying to keep on breathing. Archy, the goddamned idiot, only grins wider and nods.

"Did you look at it?" I question Archy. "Check it out for me? Is she clean-shaven?"

Archy swallows, his grin turning lecherous. "I couldn't see because of her panties. Mic wouldn't let me take them off her."

Back to the brains of the operation who slowly shifts away from his friend, too stupid to realize he's gone from the lion's gaze to his mouth.

I lean in and nod conspiratorially. "I don't know about you, but I like a little hair down there. Makes me feel like I'm fucking a woman and not a child."

Archy shrugs. "Don't care as long as the hole is wet."

Oh, he seems the type to not give a shit. While I don't give a shit what my possessions want or don't want when it comes to their bodies, I *do* care about some trash gangster nobody putting his eyes, and worse, his hands on what's mine. The boiling anger in my gut rises, and I let it level to the surface, finally allowing them to see the predator beneath the mask.

I wrap my arm around his neck and squeeze him to me, his head underneath my chin as I whisper down to him. "No one, and I mean, not a single soul, touches what's mine. Period."

I press the gun to his temple and pull the trigger, smiling at the splatter of brain matter and blood that coats my face, the wall, and his twitching dead body.

Once he hits the floor, I turn to Mic, who has already made a run for it down the hall. He doesn't get past Soo, though, who holds him on his knees where he's caught.

"I'm sorry, Nicolo. Please, please let me live. I have children, and a wife. They need me." Mic begs tirelessly for his life. There's no point. I've already decided to kill him.

I crouch down in front of him. "You should have chosen your partner better, Mic. You should have known who you were working for and ensured her safety while in your care."

He continues to beg, and I glance up at Soo, who is staring over my head and down the hallway.

The woman is standing in the doorway, leaning out, eyes wide as she takes in the carnage. When her gaze reaches mine, I lock eyes with her, raise the gun to Mic's head, and pull the trigger. Soo releases him to the floor while I stand and hand him back the gun. He'll clean it and bring it back to me later.

I keep my eyes on my prey as I stalk back down the hallway toward her. She finally tracks her gaze up my body, lets out a whimper, and scurries back into the room. I follow and watch as tears pool in her big brown eyes.

"Those men kidnapped and touched you. They're dead now." I don't owe her an explanation, but I offer it anyway.

She hikes her chin up, a small cleft at the center. "Then you saved me. So please take me home." Her eyes plead with me, and I can tell she knows she's not going home. Not tonight. Not ever.

"Oh, *stellina*, you're not going anywhere." I stalk forward and shove her back so she stumbles onto the mattress.

She stares up at me, the tears now pouring down her cheeks. She tugs the slip over her bare thighs to hide herself from me. For now, I'll allow it because I have other business to attend to. But she won't be able to hide from me for long.

I study her carefully, looking for any signs of a concussion from her blundering kidnappers. Her pupils aren't blown, and she seems alert enough despite her terror.

"What do you want with me?" she whispers so softly I barely hear it.

Her voice is gentle, like a soft melody that invites a man to bed, promising carnal delight. She has no idea the damage her family has done, the things that can't be undone, and the people that can no longer be brought back. If she knew what I really wanted from her, she'd be screaming and begging for me to let her go.

I tower over her, letting her take in my tattooed forearms below rolled-up sleeves. Blood coats my face, my slicked-back hair, my shirt—every inch above my navel.

A bloom of blood breaks up the creamy white expanse of her cleavage from where I pushed her back onto the mattress. Something in me uncoils at seeing a mark I made so boldly on her pretty skin. I wonder what she would look like painted in the blood of my enemies? I push the thought away before it can take root.

"Right now, *stellina*, I want you to shut the fuck up, and do what you're told. If you do that, it'll put me in a better mood, and I'll be less inclined to kill you."

She swallows heavily and tracks the blood dripping off me as if it punctuates my threat better than my words ever could.

"That's not my name," she grits out.

She remains huddled up, though, belying the heat in her tone.

I duck down in a crouch again so I can meet her eyes straight on. "I believe I said shut the fuck up, and do what you're told. If I want to call you my little whore, I will call you that. And if I want you to call me Daddy while I fuck that sweet little cunt, you'll do so with abject delight. Am I clear?"

She stares at me wide-eyed, her breaths heavy out of her nose. When she nods, I stand again and leave before I do something drastic, like drag her over my lap, fuck her into oblivion, and ruin my investment.

Because men are going to line up for a taste of her body.

Until someone pays for the privilege, she's mine alone.

3

CELIA

*T*he man's gun is bigger than my face. I don't know why it's the only thought that stuck in my head while he towered over me, covered in someone's blood. No, I do know. It's my brain trying to disassociate, to give itself a hold in reality, so I don't fucking lose it.

Lose it like I am right now.

My hands are shaking as I stare down at them. Shock is setting in, and while my years of home-study psychology should help me, a trauma response isn't necessarily controllable.

I let the images wash through me. The tattoos under the thick layer of blood up his arms. The rich material of his blood-splattered dress shirt. The flint blue of his eyes, again broken only by the blood splattered across his face.

He shot that man while he stared into my eyes, as if killing someone was as easy as brushing his teeth—his straight white teeth, which also sported a few blood droplets.

He'd been smiling when he killed those two men. Heartless and cruel. That's all I could think of him. Who smiles as they end another human's life? I don't want to think that deeply into it, but every time I close my eyes, his face is all I see.

Stellina. He keeps calling me that, and I can't place where I heard it last. It's like the memory is in my mind, but it's lodged deep in the back.

I wrap my arms around myself to abate the cold. A girl can use a knight in shining armor right about now. Just then, I picture Marco strolling through these street thugs, taking them out, and saving me.

It's irrational, considering how short our relationship has been, but he depends on me being alive. If we don't get married, he loses the position in my family, the money, the power, everything. Maybe it would be enough to prompt him to come to my rescue.

One can only hope, right?

I know his guys run more in money laundering than guns, but no doubt they needed them to secure said money. Yes, Marco would come to save me from this nightmare, and once that happens, I can forget I ever saw that hulking brute covered in blood. Some of my panic abates, allowing me to think a little clearer. My head is pounding, a lump at the back of my neck aches, and I can't remember anything since I walked Marco to the door after dinner.

How did they even get into my house to kidnap me?

God, this is a fucking nightmare.

I cup my face in my hands and catch sight of the blood splattered on my clavicle. Staring down at it like a spider waiting to strike, I try not to panic. Quickly, I cup the edge of my slip and wipe at the red mark. Most of it comes off, but a stain remains along with the pink of my abraded skin.

The door opens with a creek, and I scurry to the far edge of the mattress, placing my back in the corner of the room. My eyes land on a water bottle that's tossed into the cell. It rolls across the floor and stops at the edge of the mattress. I look just in time to find the door closing again.

"Wait!" I leap up and rush to the door, intent on talking to whoever kindly gave me the water. "Please, let me out of here."

The door stops a few inches from closing. "Sit down and shut your mouth, or we'll find some better use for it," a gruff voice booms through the small room. Followed by the door slamming shut.

Frustration mounts, and all I can do is lash out. I bang on the door, pounding until my fists ache, but no one comes back, no one opens it again.

The water, wrapped in a blue label, looks sealed up. I scoop it off the gray concrete and inspect the cap as much as I can in the very dim light. Did they drug it? The man's words filter back to me.

If I want you to call me Daddy while I fuck that sweet little cunt, you'll do so with abject delight.

Is that why I'm here? So they, whoever *they* are, can rape me? It seems highly unlikely, given the work it took to kidnap me. I don't know this world like my father, like Marco, like any of the men in the five families. Women in our world are ornamental, not functional. Hell, I couldn't even talk my dad into letting me go to college. It had been one reason I agreed to marry Marco. Hoping, once we married, he'd let me take some classes and get my degree. If I can't get the hell out of here, none of that will ever happen.

I study the water bottle again, crack the cap, and take a tentative sip. It tastes like water, so I swish back a large mouthful and pray I haven't just ended my life.

My hands have finally stopped shaking, and I'm a little calmer, so I look around the room. The hulking beast doesn't seem like the type to make mistakes, but a girl can hope.

The mattress on the floor looks new. It's not stained or scuffed from repeated use, so it makes me wonder, do they replace the mattress for every new captive, or am I the only one?

The entire room is about as big as a small closet. The full mattress in the corner, bare. It's only a few paces to the one window, high on the ceiling. Between the window and the chill in the air, I don't doubt they tucked me away in a basement somewhere.

I try not to think about the dead men as I remember the long white hallway with the same gray concrete floors. No windows or exits that I could see. None of this information helps me escape. Not with a locked door and no clothes or weapons.

Surely, it's still dark outside, which means no one is even going to realize I'm gone for a few more hours, not until the maid wakes me up or I don't show up for my last fitting at the bridal boutique.

Will they think I ran like my sister, Kat, did? Probably, and my father isn't the forgiving type. So, putting positivity in my thoughts, when I make it out of here, I need to ensure I clear my name with my father first. Ensure he knows I was kidnapped and didn't make a run for the border to avoid marrying Marco.

I sit down on the mattress and tuck my legs underneath me to cover as much as possible with my short slip. At some point, I undressed before they kidnapped me, or did they undress me *when* they kidnapped me? Shit. The answers are becoming as bad as the questions.

I rake my brain for the memories. We ate dinner, I walked Marco out... I think. Then I went to my room. Didn't I?

Why can't I remember?

The lock on the door ticks, and I scurry back to the corner, shoving my slip around my ass as I move. The same man from before with the steel-edged eyes and a blood-coated body saunters into my room, rubbing his hands together.

28

I glimpse briefly an Asian man closing the door behind him. And then it's just me alone with the man who will probably end my life.

He walks around the room casually, inspecting the walls and floor, before landing those intense eyes on me.

I meet his gaze head on, even if every inch of my body is recoiling with fear, preparing to shoot a fight-or-flight response to my system and send my adrenaline into overdrive. Fuck. *How's all that psychology reading helping now, Celia?*

He stalks toward me and then crouches down in front of the mattress and studies me. Despite my fear, I do the same to him. His hair is wet, slicked away from his face. Inky black tattoos cover his arms and swirl up his neck at the fringes of his shirt. He's showered, and the scent of woodsy soap wafts off him in waves.

He cocks his head to the side and flicks up the corner of his full pink lips. "You don't have to huddle away from me, *stellina*. I'm not going to hurt you—*yet.*"

I swallow heavily and maintain my position, scooting as far away from him as I can. He shrugs like it doesn't matter to him and folds his hulking frame on the edge of the mattress.

Shit. He draws his knees up and rests his elbows on top of them. His shiny shoes gleam in the low light. Which seems absurd, considering the amount of blood he had splattered on him only a short time ago.

"You must have one hell of a dry cleaning bill," I say.

Obviously, my shocked brain has a death wish engaging this creature.

The slight smile he sports grows the tiniest fragment. "Why dry clean when I can just buy a new shirt?"

"I'm sure your tailor appreciates it then." There is no doubt in my mind he has one with shirts that fit him like *that*.

He continues studying me and then abruptly stands. I jerk back into my corner as he extends his hand. "Stand up, *stellina*."

Can I refuse him? It seems unwise for such a small request. I ignore his hand and ease upright, the mattress buckling under my weight at the corner.

He crooks his finger and points to the floor right in front of him. "Come to me."

Another easy enough task. Why anger him unnecessarily? I position myself exactly where he points. Now only inches from him, the scent of his soap is stronger, as is the heat rolling off his muscular body.

"Good girl," he purrs. I feel the deep, husky scratch of it in my belly.

He circles me like a shark, waiting for the perfect moment to strike.

I hold my chin up, staring off across the room, ignoring him in the hope he might not.

No such luck.

"Take your clothes off," he whispers in that same husky, deep grate.

This time, the flutter in my stomach is nothing but fear. I swallow and look back at where he stands behind me. Slowly, I reach up and grip the strap on my shoulder. But for him, my movements aren't quick enough. He shoves his hands into the back of my slip and rips the silk clean down the middle.

His rough knuckles graze the length of my spine as the material parts, and I bite back a gasp. I shiver and hold the silk to my naked chest. When he comes around to the front, he wags his finger at me to drop the material. So, I do. What else can I do at this point if he's going to rip my only clothing to shreds?

"Do you want to take your panties off too, or should I give them the same treatment? I promise you'll be in here naked until I feel like giving you something to wear. I'm not a patient man, so don't make me wait again."

Before he even finishes speaking, I shuck my panties down my legs and gently kick them to the side of the mattress.

"Good girl," he repeats. "You're a fast learner. Keep it up, and we'll get along just fine."

I don't want to get along with him. I want to bash his skull open and make a run for it. That's a fantasy since I can barely reach the top of his head. But hey, a girl can dream, right?

He makes another circle around me, and I can feel his eyes on my skin. His fingers brush across my hip, and I jerk.

His eyes narrow at me, and I fortify myself to remain still.

The next touch is across the back of my shoulder blades. Then the back of my right thigh. It tickles, but I don't dare move for fear of him doing much worse.

"You're beautiful, *stellina*. But I'm sure in your pampered existence you hear that all the time."

He touched a nerve. Jerking my chin up, I glare at him, then purposefully tip my hair out of the way so my scar is visible. "Actually, I don't." It's quite the opposite, but I keep that part to myself.

His gaze traces the long line down my cheek and continues further south, down to my breasts, flat belly, and finally to the apex of my thighs. He doesn't comment on my admission, and that silence is deafening.

"What do you want from me?" My voice comes out low.

It takes so long for him to answer that I figure he'll simply ignore me, but then he clears his throat, and words tumble out his smug mouth.

"Everything. I want everything from you. And when I take it all, every single bit of you, I'll get my revenge on every member of your weaselly family."

Revenge? On my family?

It doesn't come as a surprise to me that this man wants revenge. My father is not known for kindness or charm. If only the bastard in front of me knew how little my family gave a shit about me. They've only ever cared for the connection I can make when I leverage my vagina into marriage. I wonder if my father ever cared about me at all.

Maybe when I was a child. I have a few lovely memories of my father bouncing me on his knees, or maybe that's just my mind making up stuff that never happened? All my vivid memories are of my parents acting like strangers toward each other.

I don't offer this information up to him since I doubt he cares.

A chill settles over me, and I clutch my arms under my breasts without thinking.

He pounces, shoving my arms to my sides, holding me tight so I can't move while he presses every unyielding inch of his body against mine.

A tear springs free, and I wish I could take it back. Die with a little fucking dignity.

My ruthless captor glares at me and then shoves me back. I stumble, but keep my hands down. When he crowds me again, he tips my chin up, so I'm forced to look into his eyes. A bully, a fucking monster. That's what he is.

"You don't cover yourself until I say you can. Nod if you understand." I nod frantically, and his eyes soften. "Now, tell me, are you still a virgin?"

His question douses my entire body with ice cold water. I want to defy him, lie, be proud and tell him to go fuck himself. I don't do any of those things. Instead, I squeeze my lips together and stare into his eyes.

After a moment, his gaze drops to my lips, and then, like a cobra strike, one hand goes to the back of my neck, and the other between my legs, to cup my vagina. All bravado sizzles out of me as I stare into his eyes.

"Answer me," he grits the words through his teeth, "or I'll part your pretty thighs and find out for myself if you've been touched."

I shiver in his hold, locked against his rock-hard body and his unfailing grasp. The words are in my head, but I can't bring myself to say them.

Yes, I scream in my mind, but all that comes out is a whimper.

He frowns, almost as if he is sorry, and then gently, I feel his fingers probing between my legs. "Is this why you don't answer? You want my fingers inside you, testing you, feeling how tight you'll fit around my cock?"

I shake my head, the lump in my throat still not letting a single word pass. With my fists balled tightly, I shove at his chest and squeeze my thighs together, but he simply kicks them apart and wedges his legs in between mine.

His fingers delve deeper until the blunt end of his index finger slowly slides inside me. I whimper and try to jerk away from him, but he's strong, so much stronger than me, and holds me tight in his grasp.

The soft tissue burns from his intrusion of my body, and I glare my hatred into his face. He can touch me, but he can't make me want it. He can enter my body, but never my mind.

After a few seconds, he pulls his fingers from my channel, brings them to his mouth, and licks the wetness I see coated there.

Once he finishes, he smiles, showing me straight white teeth. A predator's move, if I ever saw one. "You're so sweet and tight. I know men who will pay top dollar for your pretty little pussy."

I swallow and move away from him. This time he lets me go with a chuckle while walking toward the door.

"Don't worry, *stellina*, I don't plan to kill you. But by the time I sell you to the highest bidder, you might wish I did."

4

NIC

I can smell her as I enter my security control room the next day. Since I set up the video camera in her cell, I've banned my usual security from entering. I don't want anyone to see her without my permission.

Soo sits in front of the control panel, his long legs propped up on the countertop.

"So, what now?" he asks. He's changed out of the blood-splattered clothing from last night. But he likely stayed the entire time, not sleeping, so he can monitor the situation.

I don't bother asking if he witnessed what happened between us in her room. I know he no doubt watched it unfold on the screens. Not that it matters. I have nothing to hide, and Soo's opinion on what I do to the woman doesn't matter to me. I shrug and watch her on the monitor. She sits on the mattress, clutching the remnants of her silk slip against her bare breasts. There is no sound but the way her shoulders heave forward, she must be crying again.

I take a moment to watch her, trying to figure out what could be going on in her brain. Crying won't get her out of that room, it won't keep me from selling her, and it certainly won't keep me from touching her again. Even now, my cock is a steel rod against my thigh. Another thing to deal with later.

Soo lingers behind me, and I spin in the chair to face him. "If you have something to say, then say it."

There are no secrets between us, and he knows my moods can be volatile. It takes him a full minute to form his thoughts and say what's on his mind.

"Are you sure this is the best way to get your revenge? Selling a little girl for profit?"

My anger rises, but I let it simmer, tucked tight in my gut. He doesn't deserve my ire for asking a simple question. "One, she is no girl. Two, technically, she has already been sold off. Or do you think what her father was doing with that Gardello idiot is any different?"

He snorts. "Fair point, but I fear this will backfire, regardless."

My eyes narrow to slits, and I turn to face the monitors again. "Noted."

While I watch her, he slinks out of the room silently, only the shift in the air, letting me know he's left. On the screen, she huddles into herself and continues crying, tucking that proud chin into the top of her knees to hide her face.

Since nothing is happening in the room, I queue up the past twenty-four hours of her sitting in the cell. More out of habit than actual interest. I instructed my guys not to go in unless they were feeding her.

Most of the feeds show her crying and attempting to cover herself. She spends a good chunk of time looking for a way to escape. Jokes on her. I designed the room myself, and the only way out is the same way in.

I fast-forward the recording until something catches my eye. She speaks to one of my guys, grabbing his arm.

It's not her clumsy attempt at the coercion of my guy, but the lingering look he gives her as she throws herself back on the mattress. It's common knowledge that her father treated his daughters as little more than chattel. At the very least, she lacks the ability to threaten the way her father did.

I sit back in the chair and wait to see if she will try seduction next. As it stands, I owe the guard a fucking head busting for looking at my prisoner the way he did. Like a man starved for something more.

The guard places a tray on the floor by her bed, still eyeing her in a way that makes my lip curl, and then exits the room. I'm almost disappointed. She didn't try to use her wiles to sway him. Interesting. She may be a Ricci, but she doesn't know how to use her beauty as an advantage, unlike her father, who did in his younger years. There was even talk he screwed men when he needed to get what he wanted. It must have worked, or he wouldn't have built his empire to where it stands today.

I drudge up the guard's name in my memory and shoot Soo a text to find him and bring him to me so we can have a conversation.

The rest of the footage is minimal. Her nibbling on some food, using the small toilet built into the corner, and then curling up on the mattress. She remains still until the monitor beep, and then I'm back in real-time.

I barely have time to come up with a punishment for the guard when her eyes jerk toward the door. The camera angle is diagonally across the room, so I can only see the top of the door cut across the lens. Her eyes fly wide open with panic, and I wonder what the hell is going on. That is until I see my younger brother. Lucas's broad tattooed shoulders come into view as he looms over her.

Well, fuck.

I rush out of the chair and down the long hallway. The scent of disinfectant and bleach burns my nostrils as I make it to the door and hover in the frame. I pause and listen. I'm not here to rescue her, but to ensure my brother doesn't hurt her in a way that will cost me my revenge.

Her soft sobs reach the hallway, and I poke my head inside and spot Lucas crowding her. At this angle, all I see is his broad tattooed back and his disheveled blonde hair at the crown of his head. Would she fight him? I watch them both, curious how much spirit I have to strip from her by the time our acquaintance ends. The more, the better, I suppose.

By the time the auction occurs, she will walk through fire for me and thank me afterward.

5

CELIA

"*D*o you even know what your family has done? I guess the better question is, do you even care?" The man's voice is pitched low, deadly, dangerous.

A shiver runs down my spine but doesn't leave my body. It is as if a permanent chill is settling deep into my bones. One I'm not sure I'll ever be rid of.

"I don't know what you're talking about," I tell him, realizing that even my voice is shaky.

The man charges forward until his boots almost rest against the edge of the mattress. Scooting away as far as I can, I back up until my skin kisses the cold concrete behind me. I cower in the corner again like a trapped animal because that is exactly what I am. A tiny mouse caught in a trap.

"You're part of that disgusting family. The only one with decency was your sister, who knew when it was her time to die.

I flinch at the mention of my sister, and a whimper escapes my lips, even though I try my hardest not to let my fear show.

The man drops to his knees on the mattress, his weight pressing it down enough that I jostle away from the wall just to realize there is nowhere else to go and scramble back to it.

The man's gaze bores through me. "I should kill you right now. Slit your throat and send your body back to your daddy," he spits. The venom in his voice tells me he means every word. He wants to hurt me, kill me in the most painful way he can think of.

My heart is beating a million miles per hour while panic has an invisible grip around my throat, making it hard to breathe.

I shake my head again, not looking up. "I haven't done anything. I volunteer at the soup kitchen. I take my mother shopping—"

"With money earned off the backs of others. Blood-stained bills running red with the blood of your father's enemies. You use it to buy your shoes, style your hair, it's all over you, whether or not you like it. Even this..."

Before I can think about fighting, he grabs a fistful of my already ripped nightgown and tears it off my body completely. Turning my face toward the wall until my cheek rests against it, I tuck my hands around my breasts.

"You don't deserve clothes. You don't deserve anything besides pain, humiliation, and death."

I've never felt so vulnerable, so exposed, and even my drawn-up knees cover little of my body. He doesn't reach out to touch me, but something tells me he wants to.

When I glance over at him, I find him with his hands clenched at his sides, the silk of my nightgown balled into one of his fists.

"What should I do with you, whore? What would hurt you the most? Maybe I'll gather all the men I can find and let them each have a turn."

Biting the inside of my cheek, I swallow the fear threatening to eat me alive. I'm able to hide the sob, but not the tears as they slip from my eyes and run down my cheeks. The bed moves, and I blink my eyes open just in time to see the man leaning in. His hot tongue laps against my cheek, and I flinch as he runs it over the tracks of my tears, licking up the moisture. Distress signals go off in my mind, blinking like a red neon sign.

My hands move before my mind catches up, and I push him away with all the strength I can muster. He captures my hands with ease, shoving them beside my head, banding them tight against the concrete wall.

"You disgust me," he growls into my face.

I try to pry my wrists from his grasp, but I might as well be fighting a bear. I quickly give up struggling, especially when I notice the bulge in his pants.

Of course, this display of power turns him on. I hate how helpless I am right now and clench my teeth, gathering my wits to spit something hateful at him.

It will be worth it, even if he slaps me.

"If I'm so disgusting to you, then why is your hard dick in my face right now?"

He shuffles forward on the mattress, pressing against me now, so his zipper is practically in my face. "Maybe because the idea of putting a bullet in your brain turns me on. It's not your body that turns me on or your innocent look. I'm not interested in all that pretty white skin. I want your blood on my hands and your brains at my feet."

I recoil from his grasp, wanting to scream, to fight, but knowing that I can't. This man won't hesitate to snap my neck. It's best to be docile and hope for the best. When he finally shoves me away, I gather myself into a ball against the seams of the wall to make myself appear harmless and less noticeable.

The man pushes himself to stand on the mattress, hovering over me. "You know your father once killed a toddler. An innocent child whose only crime was being born to the wrong family. I saw the body, the life drained from its eyes."

No, no, no! I shake my head. My father would never. Yes, he is a bad man, who is heartless, but to kill an innocent child? He would do no such thing.

I press my hands to my ears and ignore his voice, ignore what he is saying, because it's not true. My father wouldn't harm an innocent child, would he?

"And what do you think happened to your sweet older sister, whose only crime was to defy him?"

My eyes go wide as I stare up at him, and my hands slide away from my ears. "Don't you dare talk about my sister!"

"Don't worry, there are plenty more dead bodies at your father's feet. Hundreds, men, women, children, entire families slaughtered at your father's whims. You're going to pay for all of it. We will use you, break you, sell you so you can become the whore you were always meant to be. Blood for blood," he sneers.

My hand moves without permission, and I don't even think of the consequences or how badly this could be for me when I lash out and land a slap across his cheek. Not until a second after the hit when his rage-filled eyes zero in on me. His nostrils flare as he breathes through his nose, and his lips curl into a cruel snarl.

In that second, I realize the mistake I've made and that I may not make it out of this cell alive.

6

NIC

*L*ucas didn't realize he touched a nerve, his thoughts so deep in his own internal battles. I, on the other hand, knew she was going to slap him before she even did.

As far as blows go, Lucas has seen much worse, but I know this has nothing to do with his pain and everything to do with his pride. Even if I don't want to, I know that I have to intervene. If only to keep my new property from damage.

I make my presence known and stalk into the cell, grabbing his arm before he causes any damage. Celia's wide eyes find mine, and for a moment, I can see the gratitude in them. Before I can digest how that makes me feel, I tighten my grip on my brother and shove him away from the bed.

Like a bull seeing red, he struggles until I close the door to her room, and he can no longer see her. Then his gray eyes clash with my own, and he huffs out a breath. I can see the hate—the pain and rage burning in his eyes. It's suffocating and reminds me that Lucas has had a much harder time handling what happened than I have.

"Feel better?" I ask.

He shakes his head, turns to the wall, and punches it. *Violence*. It's his vice. When he faces me again, some of his anger has dissipated. Lucas and I have had a strained relationship for years. Our parents were killed when we were young. It was my job to protect him, and I failed. He fell into the same life I did. Not that I expected him to go off to college and get some kind of fucking degree. But I didn't expect him to turn in on himself so much, to become a different person.

I wait for him to speak, but he simply stares at me, daring me to challenge him about his treatment of her. He didn't hurt her, not physically at least, and I don't give a fuck what he says to her. But I can't have him hurting her, not when I need her looking fresh and pretty for my clients.

"You good now?" I ask him again.

His only response is to glare at me, then he turns and stalks down the hallway toward the garage. When he reaches the end of the hall, he turns and says, "You can't protect her every second of the day. Eventually, I'll get her alone, and all I need is one second..."

A minute passes, and I hear the roar of his motorcycle before I see him peel away on it, still shirtless, still angry by the set of his shoulders as he leaves.

With him gone, I relax and stare at the door. My brother took her slip with him, leaving her with nothing to wear. Not that I mind looking at all her creamy skin, but I don't want my men's eyes on her.

In fact, I think I like her better like this. Naked and weak. A so-called innocent princess trapped in a cage. I consider my brother's parting threat and her holding cell. *Shit*. I need to move her to a more secure location where, if necessary, I can hear her screams. I don't doubt if my brother approached her again, she would need me to come to her rescue.

I shove the door open, and my gaze immediately falls on her. She's slumped in the corner of the mattress, her face and neck pink from crying. Her dark hair hangs down around her cheeks like she's made no effort at all to recover from her meltdown.

"He's gone," I tell her.

She glares at me, and I return the look with a smile. Then I unbutton my dress shirt. Her eyes grow wider the further down I go. I can't imagine what she is thinking right now. Actually, I can. She thinks the worst of me, but she has no idea how much worse this is going to get.

When I jerk the shirttails from my pants, she flinches, and excitement rushes through my veins. The way her fear turns me on is sickening, but I came to terms with my tainted mind a long time ago, so there is no shame.

I drag it off my arms, cross the room, and hold it out to her.

She doesn't move from her huddled position, and I huff with annoyance.

"If you don't take it, I'm going to change my mind. Then you'll stay naked until your new owner decides what to put you in."

Her gaze shifts from my hand to my eyes, waiting for a trick, no doubt. I toss the shirt beside her on the mattress and watch as she quickly grabs it and drags it around her body, her fingers slipping as she buttons it up in the front. Of course, the material is comically large on her small body, but I can still see the rosy tips of her nipples underneath.

For some reason, it satisfies me, seeing her in my clothing. Her hair is still tucked under the collar, and the ends of my shirt skim her thighs.

"Why is he like that?" she whispers.

I stare down at her, any warmth in my tone dissipating. "It's none of your goddamned business. If you see him again, don't engage. Don't speak to him, don't look at him, don't enrage him. Pretend as if you don't exist, and you might make it out of this alive."

"He wants to kill me. Because of something my father has done to him?" It's both a question and statement.

"Yes." That's the short version.

"Do you want to kill me?"

I crouch down, putting myself at eye level with her. "I thought I made myself clear. I don't want to kill you, not when leaving you alive will be so much sweeter." I keep her gaze locked with mine and continue, "But don't think I won't put a bullet in your brain if necessary. I'm not a nice man. This isn't a fairy tale. No one is coming to save you. The sooner you realize that the easier things will be for you."

Her lips wobble once... twice... then she nods slowly.

"Good girl." I grab her by the arm and drag her to her feet. She shivers in my hold and closes her eyes like she is trying to escape me.

"None of that." I shake her to force her focus back to my eyes. "I'm taking you to another room as a precaution for now. Don't get too comfortable. The second you step out of line, you'll be back down here, naked and alone. Are we clear?"

She nods frantically, no longer trying to dislodge my grip on her bicep.

"Great." I let go of her, and she flops back to the mattress like a rag doll. Only when I move to leave the room does she get back on her feet.

I lead her out into the hall and up the staircase at the opposite end from the garage. She stumbles along beside me, her feet barely on the ground as we walk.

Once we reach the second-floor bedrooms, I shove one open and toss her inside a guest room I allow the women I occasionally see to sleep in. With a few steps, she rights herself, hugging the shirt tight around her. I follow her into the room, richly furnished in shades of navy and gray.

She peers at her surroundings wide-eyed, and then whispers, "Thank you."

I surge toward her and drag her back into me. "No. Don't thank me. This is only until the auction. Then you're some other assholes' problem, and they might not be as accommodating as I am."

Back to glaring, I cup her around her waist tighter, setting her off balance in my grip. "I'm going to wipe that fucking glare off your face. When I'm through with you, you'll be broken and begging for me to take you any way I want."

"Not likely," she grits out.

Why does she keep challenging me? Have I not showed my ruthlessness multiple times since she came into my possession?

I back her toward the bed. When she stumbles and threatens to topple, I lift her off her feet and throw her effortlessly, face-first, on the iron-gray coverlet. I press my weight on top of her, my hips against her ass as her feet reach toward the floor but never meet the carpet.

"You want to test me, *stellina*? That's fine. I'll give you a demonstration." I keep my hips lined up with hers, letting her feel the outline of my dick against her ass cheeks through my pants.

She shifts underneath me, trying to crawl across the bed to escape. "No, you wanted to push me," I whisper against her cheek.

Her elbows pop up on either side of us in another attempt to dislodge my weight from her back.

When she settles back onto the bed, resigned, I deliver a slap against the side of her hips. The strike isn't hard since we are pressed too tightly into the bed for my entire hand to meet flesh. She still flinches and gasps into the blankets.

I rub against her again.

This time her attempts to wiggle away are half-hearted until she stops fighting altogether.

I soothe the area I smacked and then deliver another blow, sharp and harder than the first. "Just as a reminder," I tell her. "I'm in charge. I want to let someone pay for the privilege of taking your virginity. But if you don't stop fighting me, so help me, God, I'll rip these little teasing panties off your body and fuck you until all you can think about is obeying me, so I give you more of my cock. Nod if you understand me."

She nods against the bed and her back tenses underneath me as I press into her sweet heat one last time.

"Good." The word comes out strained, as it takes a lot of my self-control to release her.

As if she is stunned by what's just happened, she is still for several long seconds before crawling up onto the bed. She turns to face me, her body still tense with fear. Her cheeks are flushed, her eyes bouncing around the room, looking everywhere but at me.

Backing away from her, I open the door to the right of her bed and slam it behind me as I enter my own room.

On the other side of the wall, I hear furniture moving and shake my head. As if a side-table can keep me away from her. If it makes her feel safe for tonight, I'll allow it.

Tomorrow, every revolt will earn her a much worse punishment than a few swats to the ass.

7

CELIA

I hate this man. He hasn't even told me his name yet, and every time he addresses me, it's by his little pet name. He's probably doing it on purpose to get a rise out of me. I know he is. It's merely another step in his plan to break me.

Maybe I should come up with my own pet name for him. The devil would be fitting.

I stare up at the ceiling in the bedroom he so graciously offered me. If he makes one more comment about my vagina or selling me, I... I will...

Ugh. Nothing. I'll do nothing because I know that would only make it worse. It's ironic that he hates my father so much, yet he is so much like him.

Just like my father, he thinks he is more important, more powerful, more worthy than everyone around him. They both don't value women other than for their own gain, and they both like to threaten death when they don't get what they want. Maybe his ending my life now will be better than being forced to play whatever twisted game this is.

The light streaming through the window is muted, pale. I turn to look at the clock beside the bed. It reads six am. I pull the covers over my head for a moment and contemplate screaming. That's probably not a good idea, especially not early in the morning. I take a few calming breaths and then shove back the covers and tug down *his* shirt as I hurl myself off the edge of the very tall bed.

I want a shower, some clothes, and apparently food since my stomach decides then to rumble loudly.

Have I only been here for two damn nights? It already feels like an eternity.

I shiver as my bare feet smack against the cold wood floor. In the room's corner is a bathroom. The lights turn on automatically as I walk in, and my eyes swing around the room, moving from the toilet to the shower, and then to the vanity.

I notice it's fully stocked with supplies, but nothing I can use as a weapon unless I want to squirt shampoo in the bastard's eyes. The image of me shoving a pair of nail scissors in his eyes gives my spirit a little boost as I start the shower.

The soap all appears new. Not that I can be picky about it as I scrub my skin, paying special attention to the still-stained blood splatter on my chest. I can't believe I slept like this, but truthfully, I was too exhausted to care.

After I dry off, I put his shirt back on with my overused panties, but I'll be damned if I go without them, and braid my wet hair. When I exit the bathroom, I find an older woman standing in the middle of the room, holding a stack of clothing. Her mostly gray hair is pulled back into a tight bun, reminding me of a strict teacher. Her face is weathered with frown creases that look to be permanently carved into her face.

The glare she is giving me makes it clear asking for her help in escape is a dumb plan. For some reason, she already dislikes me. I can see it in her eyes.

I stare at her and wait for her to say something. She watches me for a moment, almost like she is sizing me up, then shrugs, drops the stack on the bed, and walks back toward the door. "He expects you to bring him breakfast, and he does *not* like to be kept waiting."

"What?" *Did she just say bring him breakfast?*

"While you are staying here, you are to work as a maid, cleaning the house, doing laundry, and serving in any other way you are required," she explains to me like I'm a misbehaving child.

"You do know I'm not here of my free will, right?"

"And what does that matter? Would you rather be in a cold cell with no food? Staying in the guest room isn't free. Now, hurry before we both get in trouble for being late."

I take a moment to wrap my head around what she is telling me. Only when my brain has caught up with reality do I answer.

"Of course," I grit through my teeth, not even trying to hide my annoyance.

She walks out with a lingering look that's equally curious and challenging. If I didn't know better, I'd think she sees me as a threat. Stopping at the door, she says, "I'll be in the hallway when you're ready."

The clothing isn't much—another dress shirt, still too big for me, and a clean pair of white cotton panties. Well, I'll take it. I strip my dirty clothes and slide into the clean ones. The scent of fabric softener and soap drifts off my skin. For the first time in hours, I take a deep breath. Whatever this psycho wants from me, I can endure. At least that is what I have to keep telling myself, so I don't lose my mind.

I cross the room and open the door. The woman stands in the middle of the hallway, fidgety. I gesture for her to lead the way, but she is already trudging off down the empty hall.

We walk down a staircase, past a few doorways—with guards posted outside—into a giant kitchen. Only two other people are inside, washing dishes or cooking. I stand against the granite countertops and wait. The woman works, and I feel like an idiot for lingering and not doing anything. To be fair, I've never cooked a thing in my life. We always have chefs and maids at home.

"Don't just stand there. Get to work," she sneers at me. "Are you not good for anything?"

"Excuse me?"

"You heard me. Start cooking."

"Okay..." I look around the kitchen like the cabinets are going to give me instructions on what to do. "Can you tell me what he likes to eat?"

She flops the ball of dough she'd been kneading on a wooden cutting board and crosses to the refrigerator. When she returns, she shoves a carton of eggs and a couple of cheese slices at me.

Eggs. Okay, I've seen people make eggs on TV; it can't be that difficult, right? I find a skillet quickly enough, then approach the giant stovetop. Its black metal grates rise above the surface of the stove, and fire leaps underneath at the turn of a knob.

Pan. Heat. I stare down at the eggs, little brown orbs neatly nestled in the gray carton. The other maids are gone now. The only person left in the kitchen besides me is the grouchy lady, and no way am I going to ask her for help. My eyes dart to the knife block, which is in easy reach. Would she notice one missing? Do I even have a chance if I rush out of here with it? I'd most likely have a better chance at stabbing myself than someone else.

I stare at the knife block a little too long, contemplating my next move before letting a sigh escape my lips. No, I can't do it. If I take it, I might have to use it and stab someone in my path, someone simply doing their job. Yeah, I couldn't. I'm a fucking coward. The thought of hurting someone that might be innocent makes my stomach churn.

Slowly, I turn my attention back to the eggs and begin cracking them into a bowl. It takes me ten minutes to get the tiny pieces of shell out before I can even attempt to cook them. I should leave them in there just to spite him, but I'm afraid of what he might do to me if I don't pass this small task.

Strangely, I feel a sense of accomplishment as I watch the eggs turn from a clear runny mess to a white and yellow mess. She didn't specify how he wanted them, so I did the best I could before throwing them on a plate. It doesn't bode well that they really don't look appetizing, but my stomach growls loudly as I stare down at them. And I know if I had the chance, I'd eat them.

The woman gives me a couple oranges when I hand her the plate. "Those are for you. Follow me up to his office and hurry. He's already going to be angry that it took you so long."

Perfect. Can I turn one of these oranges into a strong enough weapon to disable him? Probably not, but it doesn't stop me from imagining it as I follow her through the house. It has to be as big as my father's. Cut crystal and modern furniture throughout, the floors in the halls are marble, the entire house is posh. No surprise considering his clothes and the literal parking garage on his property.

We enter a room down from the bedroom I slept in. The woman sets a plate and a cup of coffee, I never saw her pour, on the desk and rushes out. I turn to follow her, an orange in each hand, but the monster speaks up.

"No, you stay." He gestures at an armchair to the side of his desk against the wall. "Sit."

Even the grumpy lady's presence is preferable to his, but I do as he tells me to keep the peace a little longer. Maybe we can go a day without him touching me inappropriately. *Ha, probably not.*

I arrange myself on the chair, ensuring my legs are covered by his shirt, and stare at him. His dark hair is slicked back, and his eyes are menacing, even early in the morning. I wonder if he goes to bed and plans to be an evil monster every day or if something made him this way?

He's immersed in studying a ledger but points at the plate. "What the fuck is this?"

I lean forward to look at it. "Eggs."

He drags his eyes up to mine, a sneer on his full lips. "Did you cook this?"

Instead of answering right away, I stare down at the fruit in my hand and dig a nail into the soft flesh of the orange. I can feel his eyes on me, and no matter how much I want to deny it, his mere presence makes me squirm.

"Yes, I made it. I don't exactly know how to cook, but I tried."

"Of course, you don't, princess. You've always had someone to do it for you, am I right?"

I blink at him. Every word he speaks is a knife slicing through my skin.

"What do you want from me?" I try to keep the bitterness out of my voice, but it's hard with the way he treats me. "Yes, I've never had to cook before. I'm sorry I grew up the way I did. I can't change that, and forcing me to be your maid isn't going to produce a good breakfast. What's the point?"

He narrows those pensive eyes and shoves the plate over the edge of his desk. It hits the floor with a thump but doesn't shatter. The eggs spill out in an arc around it. "The point is you're a spoiled bitch who needs to learn her place."

He shoves his desk chair back. The strength of it causes it to crash into the wall. My lips press firmly together, and I try to keep my mouth in check as he stalks over to where I'm sitting. Last night, he told me to stop fighting him. No doubt he counts this argument as me fighting. I'm going to die in this place if I don't watch it.

He hovers over me, and I huddle into myself, waiting for whatever fresh hell he offers me today. Dropping to his haunches, he crouches in front of me, a move he seems to enjoy doing, but so far, it only precedes some kind of violence. "Your place is wherever the fuck I say it is." His voice is icy cold, and I shiver at the chill his words spread over my skin.

"Okay," I whisper, keeping my eyes down on my oranges.

When he returns to his desk, I finally draw a full breath and uncoil my tense muscles. How much more of this does he expect me to take?

Silence settles over us, but the room only grows more tense with every passing minute. He has gone back to scribbling something on paper, ignoring me completely.

"You said you are going to sell me. My family has money if that's what you need." My voice is small and submissive, and I hate every syllable that leaves my lips, but I don't think approaching him any other way is going to do me any good.

He doesn't look at me as he waves at his office. "Does it look like I need money?"

"So this is just about revenge for you?" Silence greets me yet again, so I continue in the hopes he will hear me out. "I know you hate my father for whatever he has done to you, but I am not him. Just let me go. If you do, I won't tell anyone anything. I'll go away. I'll never go back home. I can promise you that."

Finally, he glances up at me. "I'm not letting you go, so you can fucking forget that. What I want from you is for you to sit there, eat your food, and shut up."

I flinch back in the chair and drop my gaze. Quietly, I eat the oranges and gently place the peels on the seat beside me. When I finish chewing, I watch him as he scribbles down the ledger, one line at a time.

"I—"

He huffs loudly, annoyed. "If you say one more goddamn word, I'm going to give you my full attention, and believe me when I tell you, you won't enjoy it very much."

His warning is clear, and I slump back again, waiting, but time ticks by slowly as he refuses to acknowledge me. Instead of waiting patiently like a good girl, I cross the room to the mess he made of the eggs on the floor and try to clean it up as best I can with the linen napkin the kitchen lady had placed with his silverware.

After that, I gather the orange peels and pile them on the plate and sit the mess on a table near the door. When I turn to take my chair again, I find he is staring at me over his desk. The pen long forgotten, his eyes on me, intense and focused. Suddenly, I'm not wearing enough clothing for the hungry look in his eyes. My pulse races and my mouth goes dry. Flicking my tongue out, I wet my bottom lip. This is a cat-and-mouse game I won't win.

I cross the room quickly, all but diving for the chair. He closes the book on his desk, the sound making me jump. When he swivels to face me, I know damn well I shouldn't have moved from my seat.

Intent on not drawing his attention further, I keep my eyes on my hands and tuck my feet under me in the chair. I think maybe he'll direct his attention to something else, but it's too late for that.

Shoving away from the desk, he faces me in his own chair. "Come here." He's not asking, he's ordering.

I don't meet his eyes and shake my head. "I'm good. I won't move, promise."

His tone tells me everything I need to know about how much I just fucked up. "You're good?" Menace laces each word.

Shit. Damn. Fuck.

In one fluid movement, he drives himself out of the chair and stalks toward me. His grip is tight as he lifts me by the waist like I weigh nothing. Without a word, he settles me across his lap. I consider struggling, but what good would it do me? He'd just overpower me anyway. He places me in his lap, diagonally. "Let's try this again. When I give you an order, you follow it without question or delay."

I tuck my chin to my chest, trying to paint the picture of a meek submissive even as I chant how much I hate him in my head. "Okay."

He grips my jaw in his huge hand and forces me to meet his eyes. "Try again, but this time with a little conviction, *stellina*, fucking convince me, and maybe I'll let you scamper away unscathed."

I clear my tightening throat. "What's your name? What do I call you?"

His eyes narrow, but to my surprise, he answers, "Nicolo."

"I'm Celia. I'm sorry, Nicolo." I glance up to look into his flinty gaze. "I'll listen to you next time."

He loosens his grip on my chin and drags his calloused fingers down to curl around my neck. My heart shoots into my throat, and I shiver against his firm chest. *Is this it?* The moment he decides he's tired of putting up with my shit. Maybe I should've tried harder. Now I'm going to end up like my sister. Dead.

His fingers remain loose around my throat until I cease shaking. "Why are you so useless? Is there anything you're good at? How about sucking cock? With no sex to offer your little boyfriends, did you spend a lot of time on your knees?"

I know he's baiting me. Deliberately degrading me to draw me into another fight. Another excuse to punish me. He likes to see me angry, but he's going to be deeply disappointed. I won't let him drag me into another fight. Instead of defending myself, I duck my chin again and focus my attention on the floor and let him believe what he wants.

But even my refusal to rise to his prodding angers him.

He coils around me like a snake, his chest pressing against my bicep, and his free hand wrapping around my hip. Hot breath fans across my collarbone, and I focus on doing everything I can to not react to him. To not encourage him, even as liquid heat circulates through my belly, pooling at my core.

"I know what you're good for," he whispers so softly I barely hear him. It's the whisper of a beloved, a lover, the devil.

Lightning fast, he lifts me over the edge of his desk, my belly on top of his ledger, my hips pressing painfully against the solid edge. I gasp at the quick movement, and the sound of my thundering heartbeat in my ears drowns out everything around me for a moment. Not wanting to antagonize him further, I remain still. I don't wiggle, and I barely even breathe.

"You're learning, Celia." My name rolls off his tongue like a curse. "Put your hands out and grip the other side of the desk."

Knowing to fight him is futile, I slide my hands up and curl my fingers against the solid wood edge of the desk. Fear uncoils in my chest, and I quake, waiting for what he might do to me this time. All his threats of raping me, is now the time? Did he reach his limit?

Tears build in my eyes, but I refuse to let them fall, quickly blinking them away. My breath comes out through my nose in shallow pants. I can get through this. Whatever happens, I can get through this. This monster of a man will not be my demise.

He can have my body, but not my mind.

I feel his fingers beneath the shirt, long, thick fingers that slip into the waistband of my underwear. With little effort, he drags my panties down my legs and jerks them off my feet. I remain locked in place, afraid to even twitch and incite his wrath.

The scrape of metal against metal tells me he's unbuckling his belt. My shivering increases until my teeth are chattering.

When his fingers sink deep into my hips, I lie my cheek flat against the wood and try to stop the sob from ripping from my throat.

What else can I do?

To my utter shock, he gently presses his hard cock along the seam of my ass, sliding upward so the crown butts against my crack.

Ever so gently, he surges forward. He's not entering me or parting my legs at all, but that doesn't mean he won't. The threat remains, fear rising higher as he uses my body how he sees fit.

I can feel the heat of his thighs against my own and the fabric of his dress slacks against my calves. The hardness of his body is suffocating, making it difficult to suck in enough air. No matter how many times I breathe in, I feel like I'm not getting the oxygen I need.

After a moment, he angles himself differently, downward between my clenched thighs, right where my pussy is. Like a bow, my entire body anticipates what's coming, my muscles tighten, and my chest aches only to realize a second later, he isn't entering me, just sliding between the natural curves of my body. The head of his hard cock nudges my clit, and I bite my lip to hold back a whimper. When he does it again, a quiet sob escapes my lips.

"What was that, *stellina*? Something to say?" He tsks, his voice husky.

When I don't make another sound, he places his right palm on my bare back, right above my ass, adding another anchor to our bodies. His touch is soft, warm, a caress if I could have ever expected him to be capable of such a thing.

"While you are staying here, your body belongs to me, every inch, every hole. When you are not busy scrubbing the floor, I get to use all of you, any way I see fit."

His words are cruel, and his touch is confusing, making this whole situation worse. I feel helpless and violated. I try to shut my mind off, to go somewhere else, but I can't get away. He is too overwhelming, too close, just... too much.

I inhale deeply when he surges forward again and again. My body loosens the tiniest bit with every drag of him against me, hoping this is all he is going to do to me.

Once he finds his rhythm, his enormous hands lock around my hips, gently lifting me off the desk. I sigh with relief. He seems content with this, not forcing me open or pushing for more.

This is okay. I can handle it.

Condensation spreads out in a fan from my lips where my breathing has taken a mind of its own. I can only focus on keeping my hands and teeth clenched and my eyes closed.

He increases his pace, squeezing the outside of my ass to force my thighs closer, my body hugging him tighter. My heart races, and I have to force myself deep inside my head to think of anything but this.

With a grunt, he stills, his heavy breathing fanning out against the back of my neck. Wet liquid pours down my inner thighs. I'm still quaking as he lowers my feet to the floor and finally releases his hold on me.

He steps away, cleans himself off with a handkerchief, and then pulls his pants up. His demeanor is impassive, like nothing happened at all. While I remain flayed out across his desk, much like a prized bear on the floor.

"Go get cleaned up and dressed. Sarah left some things for you. I have things to prepare for the auction."

His dismissive words are a slap to the face. Actually, I would rather get slapped in the face than treated like this. The sting of a hit will fade, but this dreadful feeling in my chest will stay with me long after the mark disappears.

I peel myself off his desk, refusing to look down at his cum, which I feel trickling down the inside of my thighs. I've been used in the worst possible way. I'm unable to meet his eyes, so I stare at the floor, waiting for it to swallow me whole. The last thing I want is for him to see exactly how much what he did affected me.

I don't look up until I hear his retreating footsteps down the hall. It's then that I raise my head. I'm shocked when I see Sarah standing in the hall, an impatient look in her eyes. Oh my god, did she see us? Even if she didn't see the act, she sees me now, and it doesn't take a genius to figure out what happened.

Another wave of shame overcomes me. Logically, I know I have nothing to be ashamed of. I didn't want this. He forced me. Still, I'm the one feeling ashamed.

She leads me to my room without a word. Once inside, I lock the door and rush into the bathroom and strip off my clothing. I turn the water all the way to hot, letting it burn away the shame. I grab the washrag and scrub at my legs. I scrub and scrub until the skin is an angry red.

All I can think is that I have to remove his mark from my body because I already know I can't remove the one he left in my soul.

8

NIC

*S*oo enters my office sometime later, a phone outstretched toward me.

I glare at it and then him, so he gets how fucking much I don't want to deal with whatever mess is on the other end of that line. "If that's not ten million dollars or the best piece of ass in the entire city, get it out of my face."

The man simply stares at me down the line of his arm. He doesn't say anything, doesn't even react. He merely stares, pissing me off even more with his silent glare.

Finally, I snatch it with a grumbled, "Fuck you."

"What?" I let the annoyance leak into my tone as I bring the cell to my ear.

I'd place the name to the voice any day. Not that I didn't expect him to call, eventually. Marco-fucking-Gardello says, "We need to meet."

I sit back in my chair and breathe to keep from crushing Soo's phone. As cathartic as it might be for me, he'd get pissy about it. "First, you don't make demands of me. *Ever.* You're the one so far in debt to me that when I finish taking it out of your ass, there won't even be a piece of you left for police to identify you."

His panicked inhale cuts through the line. *Good.* Maybe he'll show a little more respect. "It's about the girl."

The girl whose pussy I can still smell all over me. Instead of mentioning that, I decide to play dumb and ask, "What girl?"

"Diavolo, don't blame dumb. You know what girl I'm talking about. My fucking fiancée," he whispers harshly.

I can't help but smile. Yes, I'm fucked up, but knowing how up in arms he is over his fiancée, one would think if he really cared about her, he wouldn't have gambled with her life the way he did.

"You mean the girl that barely even makes a dent in the balance you owe? That girl?" I pause and wait for him to say something, but he must have at least one working brain cell because he doesn't respond. "What, did you think one little woman would wipe away years of bad choices?"

"No, but I didn't consider how much of a fuss her family would make with her gone. Nor did I know the extent of how much money I had to lose when we didn't actually get married."

The loose grip I hold on my anger slackens. He wants to meet to discuss the girl, then we will meet. Not saying he'll leave the same way he came, but that's not my problem.

"Fine, you want to meet, let's meet. Parking garage on Seventh. Bring some money, so it's not a wasted trip on my part, or say no now, and I'll send Soo out instead to have a little chat."

Panicked, he responds, "Yes, of course. I'll be there."

I hang up and hand the phone back to Soo, who is hovering near the edge of my desk. "Let's go talk to this fucker."

As I stand, I roll the sleeves down on my dress shirt and button the cuffs. I leave my jacket as there's no doubt in my mind I'll be beating the shit out of this idiot before the meeting ends.

When I pass the door leading to Celia's room, I pause. I turn, grab the doorknob, and check that it's locked before continuing down to the car.

Soo must have texted one of the guys, because the black SUV we usually drive sits idling in front of the house. I skirt to the passenger side while Soo climbs behind the wheel.

His fingers loosen and tighten on the steering wheel as he pulls out onto the main drive, then to the street. I've known Soo for the better part of my life. He was there for me when I had nothing. He's not just my second in command, he's like a brother to me. Knowing him as long as I have means I know when something is bothering him. However, he's a grown man, and if he doesn't want to tell me what is worrying him, I won't bother pushing.

It isn't until we get closer to the meeting point that he finally opens his mouth. "I don't like this."

"I assumed, considering how you're wearing the leather out on the wheel there."

He grunts and settles into his seat. Relaxing is not his strong suit, and he only ever does it around me. "I don't trust that kid one inch. What kind of man sells his fiancée?" He doesn't have to explain further. Soo is a vicious man but prides himself on having an ample amount of honor. He would die a million deaths before dishonoring his loyalty.

He would never betray his people. Lucky for me, at the moment, I'm the only family he has.

I reach into the glove box and remove my *Desert Eagle*. As expected, it's clean and loaded. "Are we playing the morality police now? Especially when that fiancée is about to make us a lot of money?"

Another grunt, and I can't tell if it's because he doesn't agree with me or if he wants to keep from arguing about it further. There's no way he's growing soft. The mere thought makes me want to laugh. We've both done far worse than sell women at private auctions.

"I've got some of our guys on standby. If he makes a move, I'll put a bullet in his brain."

We arrive at almost the same time. Gardello slides his shiny sports car in between two slots like the complete douche he is. Soo doesn't bother turning ours off. I scan Marco from head to toe as he approaches. Slicked back hair, perfectly tailored suit. There are no visible weapons on him. He carries a bag which he tosses at Soo's feet once he's closer.

"There. I brought some money."

I wave my arms out in front of us. "Let's talk. What do you want?"

He charges forward and halts abruptly at Soo's menacing step forward to meet him. "I want my fiancée back."

Of course, he does. I glance at Soo with a little grin, then step forward to meet Marco. Even if he were carrying, he wouldn't be able to move fast enough to get a shot off.

Marco swallows so loudly I can hear it. "How much do you want for her?"

Wow. I guess he has some balls, after all. I step away from him and slip my hands into my pockets. To anyone else, I might appear to be considering his offer. Only Soo and my men would know it's keeping me from wrapping my fingers around the fucker's throat, until he can't breathe. Until I squeeze his worthless life from its worthless shell.

I stare him down unflinchingly. "You, who owe me millions already, want to pay me to take back the woman you gave me as payment? Is that correct? Because that sounds like the only person making out good on that deal is you."

Marco drags his eyes from me to Soo and back again. No doubt, just now realizing he won't be able to charm his way out of this garage, and certainly not with his requests fulfilled.

As expected, he gives us both a lazy smile. "Guys, listen. If I don't marry her, my parents are going to pawn me off on this other woman who is a fucking cow. I wouldn't even be able to take her out in public. Know what I mean?"

Soo shrugs and glances at me. "I don't know what he is talking about. I like girls with a little meat. Something juicy to grab onto."

It's all a game, an act to put Marco at ease before one or both of us strikes.

Marco steps closer, thinking he's finally breaking through. I, however, am imagining how his brains will look splattered all over the concrete. "She's cute enough, don't get me wrong, she's just not my type."

The smile slips for a second, but then returns. "What can I offer you?" Marco asks, his good ol' boy smile back on his face. "There has to be something you want. Another son or daughter of the five families? I know them all. Hell, grandkids, aunts, uncles. Everyone trusts me. I can bring you anyone you want. Tell me what or who you want, and I'll get it for you."

Seconds drag on, and when I don't answer, Marcos' lips thin out, his patience no doubt worn. What did he think? I'd show up here and roll over for him? The impunity alone means he's getting shot before I walk away. He just hasn't realized it yet.

"I already have what I want." I shrug. "I'm not sorry to say, Celia is off the market. She won't be any good to you anyway. But you should know, the little sounds she made when I slid into her were heavenly. She whimpered and screamed my name over and over again until I made her come."

His face contorts and flushes red. Even his ears are tinged with his anger. "You... you... fucked her?"

I can't bite back the smile that pulls at my lips. "What did you think I was going to do with her, stuff her, and put her over my mantle?"

Soo nudges my chest with the back of his hand. "You stuffed her, all right."

We share a chuckle between us and then focus our attention back on Marco. His fists are curled tight at his side, and I give him about three more seconds before he pops and says something I can truly pummel him for. Not that I need a reason. It just makes sending body parts home in a bag a little more explainable.

"You still want her?" I ask, all mirth stripped from my voice now. "Say I do entertain this stupid idea of yours, what happens if I'm not done with her?"

"Done with her?" he whispers. As if only now considering the dark and depraved acts a man like me might inflict on a woman.

"How about if she's filled up with cum and has been passed around by my men? Would you still want her back then? Would you even be able to look her in the eyes when you stand at that altar and promise to protect her?" I lean in until I can whisper into Marco's ear, "Because, me, I don't think you'd have the balls. Especially if I let it slip how she got into my hands in the first place."

Soo chimes in, "How are you going to sell that to her, I wonder? Or better, how are you going to sell that to her parents?"

He swallows and doesn't meet my eyes. "I thought you were joking. I guess you really did it..." he trails off, mulling over what he is going to do next. "What the fuck good is she now that she's ridden who knows how many dicks? No, I don't want that little slut. Keep her and good riddance. I'll figure out a solution to my problem another way." He shakes his head, and his eyes lift to mine. The anger in them radiates outward. "You know I fucked her first."

I might have believed him had I not felt the awe and surprise in her body when I slid between her thighs earlier. And it wasn't just because she expected me to do more to her. She'd been so close to her own orgasm, I could have nudged her over with the tiniest pressure. Not to mention how tight her little body squeezed my fingers when I tested her myself.

No, Marco wishes he had her, but the dumb fuck hasn't touched her. If I'm right, which I am, I bet he hasn't even copped a feel.

I shrug. "She said she was a virgin. I'm inclined to believe the lady."

"Lady?" Marco spits, his anger barely controlled now. "That whore is lying. She's been all over my cock since the first night we met. I've been in every hole she's got. Plus, a couple of my boys wanted a little taste too. So, if you think you can sell her for a hefty price tag, I'll make sure everyone knows she's nothing but a whore."

Strangely, he's struck a nerve. A nerve I didn't even know existed. I step forward, the distance between us almost eliminated. This fucker has no idea how close he is to death. "The whore you were going to marry? What, today, wasn't it?"

Marco narrows his eyes.

I'm so close to him, I can see the red veins cutting through the dingy white of his eyeballs. Not only does the man have no self-preservation instincts, but he's also shown up drunk or high, or both.

"If I have to marry someone, it might as well be someone I can at least touch. And I wanted to make sure she'd be open to some of my tastes after we married."

"Like your taste for poverty?" Soo interjects.

I snort and continue my stare down with Marco.

"Oh," I tell Soo. "No, it's the money Celia would have brought him when they married. Her trust fund. That's what Gardello is missing, not her pretty little pussy."

Soo inclines his head in response.

The chill in the garage is turning my fingers to ice. I push the cold to the back of my mind. I won't show weakness in front of this dipshit. Not while he's digging his own grave, and so sweetly. The scent of liquor wafting off Marco is finally reaching me. I'm ready to go home.

I drag my gun from the waistband of my pants and hold it out to him. "I'll tell you what, you take this, shoot yourself, and I'll wipe your debt."

His disbelieving gaze bounces between Soo and I. "Shoot myself, where?"

I look over at Soo as if weighing my choices. "How about in the thigh? It's a meaty body part. If you don't hit an artery, you'll walk out of here alive."

Marco's mouth flops open and closes a few times. "I—what about something else?"

"Well, fuck, Marco. Do you want an itemized list of options to pick from? This isn't a fucking game. I made you an offer. Do you accept?"

He shakes his head once, as if he still isn't certain about his choice. Then again, more firmly.

"Great," I say. Then I raise the gun and pull the trigger, shooting him in the thigh.

He falls to the ground, clutching the wound as he squeezes his eyes closed and breathes through his nose. "I brought you money. I gave you my fiancée. We should be square now. I've basically given you my entire life." He grits his teeth to get the words out. I bet his leg hurts like a bitch. Too bad it's going to get worse.

Suddenly, I'm hit with an idea. I motion to Soo. "Get her here. I want her to see the kind of man she almost married. Maybe she'll be a little more grateful for her situation." Mostly I want to see the pain in her eyes, the tears falling down her cheek.

I want it all.

Soo thumbs out a text message and keeps his eyes trained on Marco. He gives me a nod and slips his phone back into his pocket.

I crouch down in front of Marco, who is rolling around on the ground like a turtle on its back. "Now, when *my* girl gets here, and make no mistake, *she is mine*, we can have a real chat."

It doesn't take long for another SUV to pull up. As soon as the vehicle comes to a stop, a small figure climbs out of the backseat. Her legs are bare, her dark hair mussed. At least one of my guys was smart enough to shove her into a coat, even if it is three sizes too big for her. Only her ankles are visible above her bare feet. *Good.* Marco doesn't deserve to see a single inch of her creamy white skin.

She takes a hesitant step forward. Her eyes dart around until she finally spots Marco. I anticipate her next move, and when she rushes toward him, I catch her around the waist and pull her into my chest. Digging my fingers into her hips, I grind my crotch into her plump ass, reminding her I'm still in charge.

"I brought you here for one reason only," I say. "Watch and keep your mouth shut. If you're lucky, you won't be next."

She shudders in my hold, but says nothing.

"Good girl," I whisper only for her before I shove her toward Soo. He grabs hold of her arm, but keeps a few inches between his body and hers.

Turning my attention back to Marco, I stalk forward, towering over him. "Tell her about our deal, Gardello."

He shakes his head, his eyes frantic, his neck scraping on the concrete. My patience is wearing thin. I don't have time for games. I'm going to teach both of them a lesson. Lifting my gun, I shoot him in the other leg.

Celia lets out a whimper and presses a hand to her mouth. Tears pool around the edges of her big brown eyes. I expect to find fear in them, but surprisingly, I only see sadness and disappointment.

"Let's try this again. Tell her about our deal," I encourage as I point the gun at his right bicep.

A loud groan escapes his mouth, and he flops around for a couple of seconds before the words rush out of his mouth, "I drugged you at dinner and sold you to Diavolo to pay some of my gambling debts."

For half a second, Celia just stares at him. A single tear slips down her cheek. "Why?" she whispers, like his fucking response means shit.

Still, I want her to know the kind of man he is. I want her to know everything—all the lies, secrets, the pain, and blood that's been shed. I want her to know the truth.

"Answer her." When he hesitates to answer, I crouch over him and shove the barrel of the gun into his bicep. "Answer. Her," I grit out, my anger flaring.

Marco's beady eyes refuse to meet hers. "Once we married, I planned to kill your father and take over as leader of the five families," he says in one long exhale.

I glance over at Celia. She's now dropped her hand and completely wiped the emotion from her face. A mask I appreciate since it resembles my own overtakes her doll-like features. She drags her gaze to me now. She's looking at me like I'm the monster in this story, but she doesn't have the slightest clue.

Tipping her chin up, she squares her shoulders. "Why did you bring me here? Why did you want me to know?"

Instead of answering her, I dig the gun a little harder into his arm. "Tell her the rest. The part I know you've been holding back."

Marco squeezes his eyes closed and huffs. "You disgust me. Once we married, I planned to pass you around to my guys. Let them break you in, turn you into a biddable wife. Once they did, we'd get your disgusting scar fixed, and maybe you'd be worthy of being seen in public with me."

I expect her to cry, fall to her knees, or at least yell at him, but all Celia does is stare at Marco. She opens her mouth, but no words come out. I don't give her time to collect herself. I don't give her the chance to say her piece. I shoot Marco in the shoulder and enjoy the cry of pain echoing through the air.

When I turn back to face Celia, I find her gazing at the man she was supposed to marry. Her mouth is hanging open, and her eyes are wide, but again, there is no fear, no pain, no agony that I hoped to find there.

"Your presence here is no longer needed. I only had you brought so you could see what a worthless waste of space I saved you from. Now that you have, we can start working on you paying me back. That's for another day, though."

Soo shoves her toward one of the men, who corrals her into the car without touching her. She doesn't fight. She doesn't even try to say anything. They pull away, and I step over Marco's body. He's stopped twitching and rolling like the slug he is.

"And you," I grit through my teeth. "I don't care how much money you owe me. I'm collecting now with your life."

Marco stays silent. He doesn't even flinch. Part of me had hoped he would at the very least beg for his life. Pathetic.

I position the barrel against his forehead. "By the way. Celia is still a virgin, even now. How else am I going to auction her off to make up for the money you owe? Fucking idiot."

Marco blinks, and I pull the trigger. My question needs no answer. I don't feel a single sliver of remorse for killing the fucker. I haven't felt remorse in a long time. What I do feel is anger. Anger at the way Celia reacted. I wanted her to cry, suffer, feel ashamed. Instead, she just stood there with her head held high, like she didn't give a fuck. My need to rip her apart and put her back together again means I need to find another way to hurt her.

I don't care how it happens; I will have my revenge.

9

CELIA

*M*y ears still ring from the gunshot, a sound that lingers in my mind and will probably do so for a long time. I watched the bullet whizz through the air and embed itself into Marco's skin. His pained cry should probably have bothered me more, but after the words he said, his pain didn't touch me. My sympathy for him withered away with the hopes of him coming to save me.

If I'm being honest, I wasn't really that surprised by what he said. I knew what our relationship was from the start. We weren't going to fall in love and pop out a few kids, but for some stupid reason, I got it into my head that there would be some type of respect between us. A mutual understanding about the ridiculousness of our lives. From that, I could have built something. Now there was nothing to build. I'm at rock bottom, grasping at anything I can to pull myself back up.

As much as I try to block it out, I can't forget the way Marco looked at me. Even in pain, the disgust had been there, plain as day. Anguish ripples through me. I feel so stupid. Why hadn't I seen it before? Maybe I just didn't want to. Maybe I wanted to hold on to the sliver of hope of having a better life after I left my parents' home.

I don't know what Nicolo did to him after they carted me away, but something tells me it's not good. He was already in bad shape when I left, and Nicolo definitely isn't the forgiving type. Death will be kinder to him than Nic ever would be.

Time ticks away like a bomb waiting to detonate. I pace across the room, checking the door again, hoping by some miracle that they left it unlocked this time. It's not, but I spend a moment pressing my clammy forehead against the cold wood and grip the handle tighter, willing it to open for me.

The door handle rattles under my palm, and a gasp escapes through my parted lips. Like a skittish newborn calf, I skitter away until the bed comforter brushes the back of my thighs. I expect *him* to walk through the door, but when I see that it's just the housekeeper, Sarah, I let out a sigh.

As always, her hair is pulled back into a tight bun, her features set in a scowl. She refuses to meet my eyes as she sets a tray on the bedside table. "Some water and a late-night snack. I'm sure he'll be up to talk to you soon."

Her words make me flinch, dread bleeding into my veins. I don't want him to come to me with bloodstained hands and gloat. All he is going to do is rub in my face that even my fiancé thought I was trash.

"Could you at least not lock the door," I ask her as I take a step toward the door. "I know this place is guarded. So I won't try to escape. I just want to walk around the house. No one would even know it was you. It can be our secret."

She snorts. "That's unlikely. Considering I'm one of the few who has the key to your bedroom. He would kill me for it without a second thought."

I knew it was a long shot. Still, disappointment engulfs me as she walks out without another word. A shaky exhale escapes my lungs. I don't know why I thought she would give me the chance to escape. I belong to *him* now, and everyone in his little private fantasy world bows to his whim, too afraid of what might happen if they step out of line. Either that or they simply don't care.

The simple wood tray she set on the side table draws my attention. It's loaded with a couple bottles of water, and a plate of fruit, with various nuts and cheeses. What the fuck kind of place is this? Do they think I eat like a Disney princess... nibbling on berries and fruits like it will actually sustain me? What I wouldn't do for a double bacon cheeseburger right now. And fries. And a coke. *Two cokes.*

Saliva builds in my mouth at the thought. I may never have the luxury of those foods again. No, I can't think like that. Like a gnat, I swat the thought away, and in no particular order, I eat the only food I have. I keep shoveling the food into my mouth until there's nothing left. I'm not surprised when I finish chewing through the last mouthful with a grimace that I'm still hungry.

I wash down the offending combination with one bottle of water. I'll save the other in case they forget my existence again for a while. I remind myself to be grateful, that I'm not in that cell in the basement, that he hasn't hurt me beyond the humiliating way he used my body. There is still hope, and I'll hold on to it until the day I die.

My gaze moves to the window. The sun is setting, and the room grows dark with every second passing. I let my eyes drift closed, willing sleep to come, but all I see is Marco lying in a pool of blood. The image feels so real that I snap my eyes open as fast as I'd shut them. With a racing heart, I stare out the window and take a couple of calming breaths.

Even with my father being who he is, I had never seen so much violence, not until the day Nicolo kidnapped me. My father always told me that women were made to sit on the mantle and be pretty. To speak only when spoken to. Mob business was never discussed in front of me, and I had never seen anyone killed. I'd heard rumors about what my father did and knew that he wasn't exactly a good man, but I had no idea how dark and depraved he was.

The rattling of the door handle garners my attention, and I turn away from the window and its promise of a chilly sunset evening.

Expecting Sarah, I march across the room and give her an earful regarding the diet she has me on. "Have you ever heard of protein in—"

But it's not her tall willowy frame that ducks into the bedroom... it's *him*, the devil himself, and instantly, I cut off my tirade.

I can't help but gape at him and hate myself for retreating even more. Especially because he does no more than step into the room holding a box. Fear... fear and something else that I can't quite place settles deep in my gut while I wait for him to give me his next order.

"Protein?" he asks, a brow raised in questioning. I can't tell if he cares or if he's just asking so he can mock me later.

"Yes... Sarah keeps giving me fruit and nuts. I need more than snacks to survive."

His blue eyes narrow, and his gaze sweeps over me from head to toe. Suddenly, I feel naked. I'm still wearing his shirt, and I pull the tails down with trembling hands to make sure I'm decent. It doesn't matter what I wear; he seems to look right through me.

"People survive on less. Quit being a spoiled brat and be glad I feed you at all."

His verbal lash startles me, and I jump a little, not quite expecting that would be his response. I feel like cowering, but I don't, won't, *can't*.

I square my shoulders and meet his gaze again. "I want real food. Burgers, fries, eggs, and bacon. Anything other than trail mix."

The corner of his lips lift the barest amount. It's like he thinks this is a fun game or something. "Is that all?"

"Is that all?" I huff. "Is it really that insane to think that I might want an actual meal and to not eat cubed cheese and almonds every single day!" My voice raises an octave, and the skin of my cheeks heats.

Instantly, his lips flatten, the smile wiped clean from his face as he crosses the room, stalking toward the bed. I know right away I should have kept my mouth shut. My limbs remain locked in place. Like an antelope in the sights of a jaguar, I wait for him to come in for the kill.

"Have you ever heard the phrase, don't bite the hand that feeds you?"

My throat constricts, but I say nothing. I'm not about to dig myself a deeper hole.

"Since you don't want to respond, I'll assume you have, so I'm sure you understand in that pampered head of yours how this works. I give you fucking food, and you eat it. May that be nuts and fruit or a steak and baked potato. I'm in control, not you." The sternness of his voice tells me the conversation is over. Sensing that, he sets the box on the bed and then slips his hands into the pockets of his black slacks. I do my best not to stare at him, but I can't help it.

I notice there is no blood on him this time.

Either he's getting better at staying clean, or he just has an endless closet of clothing to tap into after he murders someone. I'll bet it's the latter since he seems like the type to bathe in the blood of his enemies.

"Get dressed," he orders, and after a second, gestures to the box. "Clothes for the princess."

Imaginary red flags wave in front of my vision. This has to be a trap. He is bringing me clothes? I hover where I stand, uncertain and afraid. He's still lingering so close to the box I'd have to squeeze between him and the bed to get to it. Touching him isn't high on my to do list at the moment.

The way he's looking at me, the set of his too arrogant shoulders, it tells me he knows exactly what he's doing. *Fine.* Fuck him. I've already struck out on one battle I'm not about to strike out again. I stride to the other side of the bed, snag the box, and drag it toward me.

I refuse to look up at him as I slide the lid back and peel apart the thick white paper inside. It's hard to hide my surprise when my eyes land on the contents—a dress. Black, thin, and so short, it might as well be a tube top. He can't actually expect me to wear this?

Picking the dress up, I notice how stretchy and cheap the material is. Something I imagine a hooker or stripper would wear. There's also a pair of towering black high heels to complete the getup. The last thing I find in the box is a small syringe. Shit, he's going to dress me in barely there clothes and drug me.

I lift it up to the light. "What's this? Drugs?"

"Get dressed, and I'll show you." His voice is dipped in poison and laced with honey.

I put the dress and its accessories back in the box and glare up at him. "This isn't exactly real clothes. I was thinking maybe some yoga pants and a nice comfy T-shirt."

God, why can't I keep my mouth shut?

He continues his study of me, his expression unreadable, and then, in the blink of my eyes, he walks around to my side of the bed. My lungs burn as I suck a ragged breath between my lips. Yep, I should've definitely kept my mouth shut.

Running away isn't an option, not when I'm stuck between the bed and the wall. Without another place to go, I hold my ground and turn away, so I don't have to look at him this close to me.

His strong hand comes into view, and he tilts my chin up, forcing my gaze to his. I can see a wave of slow anger rising within the icy depths. Why does he feel the need to touch me?

"You can wear this fucking dress to dinner, or you can wear nothing."

Would he really do it?

I'm half tempted to push him, but afraid of the outcome and what it might do to me. *What he might do.* I know well enough that he would enjoy my discomfort through the entire thing, and that's enough to push me in the direction I need to go. I take the box off the bed and maneuver around him to go to the bathroom to change.

"No," he growls. "Dress right here. You have five minutes, or I'm ripping off that shirt and throwing you over my shoulder. The choice of what you wear to dinner is yours."

Funny, he thinks anything he says is actually a choice of mine. From the second he kidnapped me, he's been giving me these "choices" more like not-so-thinly veiled threats.

Soaking up all my anger, I fling the box to the hardwood and slip the buttons of his shirt through the holes. I watch his face intently as I strip and quickly shuffle through the tilted box to retrieve the dress. It slides over my skin like it has been made for me, hugging tight to every angle and curve my body possesses.

"The shoes," he prompts.

His face is still unreadable, save for the hard cut of his jaw that's clenched tight as he watches me. Something tells me he'd be even more handsome if he didn't have such a damn scowl on his face.

The fucking four-inch spike heels, which look like they were pulled out of some lame-ass porno, take me a little longer to get into and even longer to stand upright in.

He approaches once I catch my balance, the syringe in hand. "This is for you."

I glare. Even in the heels, I only reach his chin. "Will you at least tell me what it is you're injecting me with?"

"Birth control," he explains as he pulls off the cap, exposing the thin needle.

He gives me a stern look as he grabs my arm, telling me without words not to move. Little does he know, I want this shot if it means I won't get pregnant. Having a baby by a man who buys a woman at an auction seems like the worst possible idea ever.

I remain still as he injects the needle into the flesh on my upper arm. There's a slight sting, followed by a burning, but it's far better than having a baby with a monster.

"Good girl. I like when you listen to me." The wicked tilt of his lips should clue me in that I'm not going to like what he does next. "Before we go, you forgot something."

Puzzled, I cock my head to the side and stare at him, a bit confused. What more could there be? Dropping his hands, he fists the edge of my dress. I'm still wearing the plain cotton panties he'd given me, and I think I know where this is headed. Gripping the edge of my panties, he easily peels them down my legs, kneeling as he gently lifts one foot at a time to remove them.

"I didn't say you could wear panties tonight."

I swallow thickly and to my utter shock, not completely out of fear. Staring down at him, the hard lines of his face and the flare of his wide shoulder away from his neck entice me in ways that I never found attractive in Marco. It's not just his body. It's the damn arrogance wafting off him like he owns the world and damn well knows it.

He pushes upward again, trailing his fingers from my ankle all the way to the cusp of my thighs. I try not to flinch as he eases my legs open enough to cup my center.

"What are you doing?" I whisper.

I'm trembling now, and if he doesn't stop touching me, I'll fall over and break my neck.

"Whatever I want."

I jerk away, but he is faster than me and snags my hip with his other hand, holding me in place. "Be still. I won't hurt you until you make me."

Goosebumps pebble my flesh when he slowly parts my folds and slips his index and middle finger inside me. There is no build up, no foreplay. His touch is gentle, but the intrusion itself is rough, consuming like he's trying to claim a part of me. The sensation overwhelms me in an instant. Fear, hate, and loneliness all swirl together into one unwanted feeling.

My muscles tense, and a slight sting follows as he fingers me, touching me in a place no other man has before. What starts as an unwanted touch becomes everything. With every shallow stroke of his finger, a match is struck, igniting, and threatening to consume me in its flames. I close my eyes and tip my head back, forgetting everything else around me.

I'm so consumed by it I don't question Nicolo as he shifts, his hand slipping from my hip. Not until that same hand comes down onto my bare skin, filling the air with a loud smack. I hear it before I feel it, and I yelp at the sharp pain that burns against my ass cheek, but that pain quickly fades away as he continues to fuck me with his fingers while circling his thumb around my clit.

Another slap hits the same spot, right at the crease of my ass. He rubs the pain away before delivering another blow. And I like it. I like the pain that's followed by pleasure, the burning in my skin, and the tightening in my core. His hand comes down on my ass a few more times, and I ride his hand, enjoying the curl of his fingers inside of me and the way he rubs my clit.

"You like this way too much," he murmurs as he pulls away.

His fingers drag across my clit as he removes his hand and stands up. I open my eyes just in time to take in his smug grin.

He holds his fingers up to the light before bringing them to my mouth. "You act like you're so terrified of me, but your body betrays you."

I am afraid of him. Just maybe not as much as I should be.

His eyes swirl with lust as he shoves his fingers past my lips. "Suck, taste how much you want me."

I squeeze my thighs together and gently lap at his fingers with my tongue. My muskiness invades my senses. I never thought I would find this anything but disgusting, and I hate to admit it, but there is something erotic about tasting yourself.

Our gazes collide as I swirl my tongue around his thick digits. His own eyes are dilated, and the animalistic look in them tells me he's ready to part my thighs and taste me for himself.

When he's satisfied, he pulls the digits out of my mouth and leans in, so his lips are only a fraction away from mine. His hot breath fans against my lips, and I lick my own, anticipating something that I know will never happen.

His eyes dart from my lips and back up to my eyes. "You can pretend all you like, *stellina*. Yes, in some ways, you may hate me, but you don't hate the way it feels when I touch you. In fact, I'm thinking you like it."

Intent on not drawing more of his ire, I keep my mouth shut. Even as curses and feelings and words rattle around in my brain.

"You're looking a little pale," he muses, his gaze roaming my face with an edge of concern. "Let's go get you some *protein*."

He holds his arm out, expecting me to take it as if we're headed on a date and not a forced march for his pleasure. If I had more balls, I would tell him to go fuck himself. Well, that and if it wasn't for these ridiculous heels he is making me wear and the fact I'm afraid I might fall and die.

"I'm only taking your arm because if I don't, I'll probably break my neck," I explain as I loop my arm in his.

He grins. "You act like I'm giving you a choice."

All I can do is shake my head because any response from me right now may result in my untimely death. On our walk downstairs, I see his house is still shiny and big and not at all like the hard man who has been using me brutally.

The dining room is as elegant as everything else. A long table bisects the room, candles dot the surface, as do trays of steaming food. Enough for an army of people. My mouth waters as we walk the length of the table, the scents of roasted meat and vegetables overwhelming even my anger and arousal.

He sits at the head of the table like a king might and leads me to stand beside him. I stare at the table and find that there aren't any more chairs. I glare, wondering what kind of game he is playing while he arranges his napkin over one of his muscled thighs.

"You can stand and watch me eat or if you're hungry—"

As if on cue, my belly lets out a long, loud rumble that I know even he can hear. He snorts. It's not a laugh but more of a grunt, and he pats his other knee. "You can sit on my lap."

The idea enrages me. "I'm not a child," I say, the leash on my rage growing thinner by the minute. My stomach grumbles once more, the smell of the delicious foods doing a number on my ability to fight him.

When he faces the food again, clearly intent on eating it all, I surge forward and position myself on his leg, my own clenched together between his thighs. In this position, my dress isn't long enough to cover my pussy, which is now rubbing against his slacks.

It's not as uncomfortable as this dress feels. It's so fucking scratchy all over. It's tough for me to remain still.

"Was that so hard?" he whispers into the shell of my ear and slides a piece of steak from a tray and onto his plate.

Deliberately, he cuts it into tiny bites and then spears several on the end of a fork. To my surprise, he hands me the fork, allowing me to feed myself. Before he pulls away, he clutches my fingers tight around the handle. His grip bites into my flesh, and I wince.

"If you think to stab me with this, you will not like the consequences." A deadly menace laces his tone.

I nod once and shove the food into my mouth. Of course, Sarah, the bitchy housekeeper, makes delicious steak. It doesn't mean I hate her any less for her involvement in holding me hostage.

We continue eating for several minutes. As I clean my fork each time, he skewers more food, steak, asparagus, and tender potatoes on it. Carefully passing me the food to not force or spill on me. He's gentle and almost kind, but I can't forget the monster he really is.

We've decimated two plates of food when the door at the end of the dining room creaks open. I freeze mid-chew and stop to monitor the man entering the room.

His ripped black jeans and expensive white button down are at odds with the tattoos covering him and the riot of hair going in all directions like he's just gotten up and ran his fingers through it. His menacing gaze and down-turned lips make him unapproachable. The clatter of the fork against the plate jerks me back to the present.

My first instinct is to run, the fear in the pit of my stomach tightening. I don't realize I'm shaking until Nicolo grips my hips tightly, pulling me closer and whispering into my ear.

"He won't touch you."

The man drags a chair from the side of the dining room to the table and parks himself to my left. The table is large, and there is a good amount of space between us, but not enough for me. He's close enough that it wouldn't take much to reach out and grab me. The idea makes me tremble more.

"Lucas," Nicolo warns, obviously sensing my fear.

The man—Lucas—glares back at him and drags food onto his own plate without a word of acknowledgment to either of us. All I can do is sit there, a shaking mess, and stare at him.

He eats loudly, almost sloppily, like an animal feasting. Anticipation of the unknown has me on my toes, and eventually, he reaches out, his fingers snagging the edge of my dress where it cuts across my shoulder blades.

"I didn't realize you were dressing up your whores now," he addresses Nicolo, completely ignoring my presence.

Nicolo growls at him, actually growls, like a dog protecting its bone. Without warning, he lifts me off his lap and sets me on my feet. My legs almost collapse under me as I teeter in the heels. I grab onto the table just in time to keep myself from falling.

Nicolo brushes past me, motioning for me to follow. I do so on unsteady legs while pulling my dress down as much as I can. The two motions combined don't mix because before I know it, I'm stumbling. Of course, it has to be as I pass the man I'm trying to avoid at all costs.

Lucas twists in his chair and reaches out to cup my waist. If this was anyone else, it might have seemed like he did it out of kindness, but the menacing look in his eyes and the way his fingers dig into my flesh says differently.

He catches me, his hands gripping my upper arms tightly.

"Don't touch her," Nicolo orders.

Before Lucas can respond, we are marching out of the dining room. Nicolo's hand clasps around mine as he drags me back the way we came. I can barely keep up and nearly trip ten times in the process.

When we make it to my room, he shoves me inside. I stumble again and land sideways on the bed. Realizing the predicament I've found myself in, I scramble to sit in case he gets any ideas of following me inside.

"I'll be back for you tomorrow. We have some work to do to get you ready for the auction," he says, standing only partially inside, leaning against the doorframe.

I stiffen but keep my chin held high and my glare solid.

He continues as if my response is irrelevant, and I guess it is. As long as I'm here, I'm at his will. He can bend me however he sees fit, and there isn't anything I can do about it.

"Behave tomorrow, or I'll give you to Lucas to play with, and he's not as gentle with his toys as I am."

He doesn't give me the chance to respond. The last thing I hear is the click of the lock as he twists it into place.

10

NIC

*S*oo comes strutting into my office and tosses a stack of paperwork down on my desk before I've even had my coffee. I scowl at him, but he takes it good-naturedly, as always, and throws himself into a chair in front of my desk. When he tosses his boot-clad feet upon my desk, I shove them over the edge. His feet hit the ground with a thud that leaves him smiling at me. The fucker sure knows how to be annoying.

I shuffle around the papers to put them in order. "What the hell is all this?"

He lays his hands across his belly, relaxing deeper into the chair. "It's a list of everyone who has paid the auction deposit. Rumor mill is churning, Nic, and everyone is whispering that you're auctioning off a woman soon."

The conversation takes a sudden turn of interest, and I toss the papers to the corner of my desk to deal with later. "Well, they're not wrong. Anything out yet about who the woman is?"

"A few whispers, but I squashed them, since I know you want it to be a surprise. Also, to deter anyone from mounting a rescue at the last moment."

I nod. "Good, keep it that way. If you need to, circulate your own rumors to lead them in another direction. I don't want a single soul outside this house to know who is going up on the block that night."

As if trying to read my mind, Soo narrows his eyes, studying me. "So you're actually going to go through with this?" When I don't reply immediately, he continues, "Once we do, there's no going back."

"Second thoughts?" I prod.

He laughs and holds his hands open. "You know me. I live for this shit. Bringing down cesspit hierarchies is one of my favorite weekend activities." His smile clears as he continues, "Just be careful, okay?"

I don't insult him by asking what he means. Already, the girl occupies my thoughts. Every time I touch her, I tell myself it's the last time, and yet, five minutes later, I'm craving another taste. Soo is right. I need to be careful and watch all our backs. The moment I slip up, she'll take advantage. It's what her *kind* does.

"What are your contacts on the inside saying?"

Another lazy grin slips onto his face. "Right now, the disappearance of your girl has died down in favor of Gardello's disappearance."

Shit. Killing him had been a rash decision. I'd long prided myself on being in control, at least with matters which would affect the outcome of my goals. Marco disappearing could toss many wrenches into our plans.

"What's the word then?"

Soo's lips spread wide, and I roll my eyes. "They are saying Celia and Marco ran off together. That they eloped instead of waiting for the marriage."

I snort. "How does that play out? They were supposed to get married before Marco disappeared, and Celia had left first."

"I don't know, man, they're trying to rationalize and save face. All the houses have their guard up."

An idea pings forward in my mind, and I surge across the desk and snag the paperwork to shuffle through. "Any of these dickheads from the families?"

"A couple lower-level members, no one high up on your list," he says. His gaze tracks over every single twitch as I leaf through the printed stack.

"Any chance of someone in Gardello's family showing up? Better yet, can you make it happen?"

"Can I make it happen..." Soo mocks. "It will only take a little enticement. Probably a little something from Lucas to draw in a few individuals wanting what he is offering, but maybe not what you are."

"It doesn't matter." Once the papers are stacked neatly again, I look over my desk at him. "We just need them to see her, to realize that no one is safe, and even a princess of the five families can fall into hell."

"And after that?"

I shrug. "After the auction, we'll be in the open, and it won't matter as we'll be breathing down all their necks."

He tips his head and lays it back over the curve of the chair to look up at the ceiling.

As if waiting for a lull in the conversation to enter, Lucas shuffles into my office and slinks into the other chair in front of my desk. "Are we having a family meeting?"

Soo tilts his head to glare at him, but it's half-hearted. "We were just discussing the auction. You've got good timing; we need to get some info on what you plan to provide for refreshment."

Lucas shoves his hands into the front of the black hoodie he's wearing. "You make it sound like I'm the bitch here, slinging drinks."

I lean over the desk, ready to ply his ego with what I know he wants most: power. "Actually, we need to ensure a few people are there and no one knows your customer base like you do. Do you have anything special laid away?"

"Like what?" he stares at me, not blinking.

"Like something to lure out more prominent members of the five families. It's time to invite them to come out and play."

He licks his lips and takes a long, gusty inhale. "Yes, I have a few things that might interest them. Mostly a special blend of cocaine from Belize, which I know several of them have been begging me for over the past few months. What do you want me to say?"

I shrug. "Say what you usually say, but make sure they know they can't get the goods unless they are in attendance that night. We need one prominent member of each family to be present."

"Even Ricci?" Lucas asks, studying me as intently as Soo did a moment ago. "What do you think will happen when he realizes his precious princess is on the auction block?" More venom than usual laces his tone as he speaks.

"He'll be a little more difficult to lure out of his compound, but I think we can manage it between the three of us. Maybe tap that little 18-year-old he's been fucking for the past few months on the regular. I'm sure she'd love to earn a few bucks and get him off her regular list. He might pay her well, but no woman should have to suffer his ugly mug indefinitely."

"And his daughter? What are your plans for her?" Lucas asks, still gazing at me.

His interest in her annoys me. Why does he care what happens to her? She's none of his concern. I scowl and lock eyes with Soo as I speak, as he basically asked me the same thing. "Sell her to the highest bidder, of course. If someone from the five families buys her, that will be even better. Maybe they will tear each other apart while we make our move."

"I don't believe you," Lucas sneers.

"Lucas..." Soo warns.

I hold up my hand, stopping Soo from speaking for me. "What are you trying to say, little brother?"

"I'm saying I can tell you're getting attached to the girl. Are you going to be able to keep her a virgin so you can get your money's worth, or will you jeopardize our cut to get your dick wet?"

I don't even think about my reaction or if it will make me appear weak. Instead, I surge out of my chair and lean over the desk, intending to keep my tone even, but it drops toward menace as I speak. "I'll do whatever I damn well please, and you'll say thank you for it whether or not you get a cent in exchange."

Lucas waves a hand in the space between us. "Look at you. Even now, she threatens your control, and she's not even in the fucking room. What are you going to do when a room full of men want to touch her? Want to play with her? Want to fuck her?"

I have his hoodie balled into my fist before I even realize what is happening. We stare at each other, his scowl no doubt matching mine. He digs his fingernails into the back of my hands, and I can feel the blood pooling against my skin. "I'm in charge here. You questioning me isn't going to lend me more control, is it?" I growl into his face.

His reaction is to stare me down as if his silence and my labored breathing prove a point. With a shove, I release him and take a step back. It isn't the girl turning my vision red, but my dipshit brother who enjoys pushing every button I possess.

"Why are you trying to start a fight with me?"

He shoves me back hard enough that I hit the chair. "Because she's about to be your downfall, brother, and you can't even see it coming. You're fucking blind. Maybe I should save us all some time and take care of our little problem that's down the hall. I bet she won't even put up a good enough fight to make it interesting."

The red haze clouding my vision wavers, and I swallow it way down to maintain control. "Leave her alone. I won't tell you again that she is the centerpiece of my plans. If she doesn't go up for auction like planned, then all this will have been for nothing. I won't let you ruin this for us."

His face doesn't shift, doesn't betray a single thing, save the rage it usually sports. "And you hinged all your dreams of sweet vengeance on a little girl? Yeah, fucking great idea."

I shove him back again, and he hits the chair and tumbles into it. "If I have to explain the hierarchy here one more time, you're going to be out on your ass. Do as I say and don't worry about anything but what's in your lane."

The defiant jut of his chin and the clutch of his palms against the leather are the only warning I get before he walks around my desk and launches himself at me. His head and hands slam straight into my gut. Expecting it, I shift enough to the side, so he makes minimal contact. Soo lurches to his feet as I hold on to my brother's scrambling form. He flails and punches at my midsection until I squeeze him into a headlock under my arm. Frustration and anger mount, zinging through the air.

"I don't want to fight you, brother. Calm the fuck down, and I'll let you go."

"Fuck you," he wheezes, renewing his effort to cause damage.

My lungs burn, and my ribs ache, but I hold tight, waiting for him to still again. A few more half-hearted punches, and he stops, sagging in my grasp.

I shove him toward Soo, who grabs him by the nape of his neck. Lucas isn't having Soo touch him either, and instead, shoves out of his hold to escape the tangle of furniture altogether.

Soo rounds to stand between Lucas and me. Something Lucas doesn't fail to notice. "Hiding behind your little bodyguard won't save you."

Soo shoves his hands into his jeans and shifts on his feet like he doesn't have a care in the world. "You want to fight with me? You better know your brother won't be able to save you."

Soo can outfight both of us at the same time, and Lucas knows it. I sit on the edge of my desk and rub the sore area below my armpit where I'd squeezed his stupid hard head. He's a stubborn asshole, but he's my little brother.

Lucas stays in a face-off with Soo until finally he balls his hands into fists and glares at me over Soo's shoulder. "You think you can order me around and throw me away when you don't have a use for me anymore?"

I grit my teeth, my jaw aching. "Are you fucking kidding me, Lucas? Didn't we just have a conversation right fucking here outlining how important your role in this entire night will be?"

We stare at each other, Soo still standing between us. I shove at his shoulder, and he shifts out of the line of fire. I don't need a protector. "If you want to be a part of this, then you need to stop fighting me about every tiny detail. I make the rules, I make the plans, and you follow them. If you have a problem with it, then walk the fuck out now and don't bother showing your face here again."

"Is that right? Will you kill me?" he asks, all menace and malice.

I shake my head. "No, I won't kill you, but you'll likely wish I had when I let Soo finish with you."

Lucas drags his gaze to Soo, who wears his easygoing smile like we're talking about the weather and not torture and death.

"Bring my baubles to reel in the members of the five families? That's what you want from me?" Lucas asks.

I nod. "Yes, and to stay the fuck away from the girl because if you don't, brother or not, I'll cut your balls off and feed them to you."

He flexes his fists, as if he's imagining another showdown with me. Soo would intercept him in a heartbeat. The only reason he didn't the first time was that no one was expecting his dumb ass to go off his rocker.

"You sure are putting a lot of effort into protecting her."

I let him hear the edge in my tone. The one grown men usually piss themselves when they hear. "So you say."

Lucas isn't fazed. He looks death in the eyes and smiles. "You can't protect her forever. Before the auction, during the show, and after... she's going to come face to face with her own version of hell on Earth, and you'll be right at the center of it. How do you think that's going to make her feel?"

I don't even entertain the idea. I narrow my gaze. "Get to the fucking point. I don't give a shit how she feels. She's a means to an end."

With a long sigh, Soo throws himself back in the chair, sensing the fight leaving Lucas.

"Any other complaints you want to register?" I ask. "Because we aren't doing this again. Brother or not, you come at me again, I give you to Soo, and I have your body thrown in an alley to be picked over by pigeons."

He shakes his head and gives me one long, lingering glare. When he walks out, I slump against the desk and rub my side. "Fucker has strong hands."

"You shouldn't have let him get a hold of you. What were you thinking?"

I shrug. "I don't know. An attempt at keeping the peace a little longer. He's plowing headlong into an explosion. I guess I'm hoping to minimize the damage when he detonates."

"Were you serious about me taking him out?"

I shake my head. "No. If it comes down to him or me, then I'll do it myself. He's my brother, after all."

Soo watches me carefully, and I refuse to back down from whatever assessment he makes. "Fine. I'll keep one of my guys on him and ensure he's doing the job you gave him. If not, I'll put a backup plan into place and bring him to you. I don't like that he keeps gunning for you, though. What if it's a gun next time?"

I shake my head. "Lucas likes things personal. If he were going to kill me, it would be with a knife. Up close and messy."

Soo shakes his head and pushes out of the chair. "I'll leave you to your family drama. Just watch your back, all right?"

I cross the room and snag a tumbler from the bar. Liquor lines the shelf above it. I choose a bottle at random and fill the glass. It isn't even ten a.m., but I don't care. Lucas is driving me to drink as if I were...

I cut off the thought as anger sizzles through me. The glass in my hand is the buffer to the world I'm craving. Instead of drinking, I throw it across the room and watch it shatter as it slams against the fireplace mantle.

I'm not my father. I'm not Lucas. And I sure as shit deserve every bit of respect I've scraped together in this life. If Lucas doesn't learn that lesson soon, he's going to find himself in the cold, or worse, dead.

Could I really do it? Kill my little brother? I want to say no since we've both already lost so much in life, but my need for revenge outweighs everything else.

My eyes catch on the liquor that runs down the wall in amber rivulets, and I watch its path until the droplets fade away. Then I sit down behind my desk again, gather the paperwork I'd been studying, and get back to work like nothing ever happened. An illegal auction in our city takes careful planning, especially when every law enforcement agency in the country is already on my ass.

An illegal auction to sell one of the five families' little princesses will take every single bit of cunningness I have to pull it off. And I can't wait to leave every one of those bastards trembling in their beds, wondering who my next target will be.

11

CELIA

*I*t seems my lack of fighting at dinner helped my case. When I wake up, my door is unlocked. A quick dash in the hallway proves my freedom only goes so far. Goons guard every exit I find on my trek from the bedroom to the kitchen.

My wardrobe options now include one dirty button-down shirt and one scandalous black bandage dress. I opt to wear the shirt to eat breakfast; I call it a win when I sit at the counter in the kitchen and find a plate heaped with scrambled eggs.

So overjoyed, I don't even glare at the kitchen staff while I shovel food into my mouth. As expected, it tastes delicious, and I'm equally happy I didn't have to cook them myself. A girl can only handle so many burnt meals.

"Chop, chop! We need to get on with the house chores," Sarah quips, walking into the kitchen.

I shovel the remainder of eggs on my plate into my mouth and wash it down with the last of my orange juice.

"Okay..." I move from my seat and take my dish to the sink.

Sarah gives me a look as if she can't believe I would touch a dirty dish or fold a single towel. I'm sure some hate doing house chores, which is why they hire maids and such. Plus, it's not like I have anything else to occupy my time here. At least it gives me a better glimpse of the house and any possible exits.

Sarah shows me into the laundry room. It looks like something that belongs in a hotel instead of a private residence. How many people live here? So far, I'd only seen the kitchen staff and his cast of guards.

Sarah loads me up with stacks of fresh linens and draws me a very rudimentary map to the rooms I need to change.

I can't remember the last time I changed a set of sheets, but I'm not telling her that. I trudge back up the stairs, a little shocked that there isn't a guard tailing me. The first room I enter looks very similar to my room. The only difference being the color palette. The bed is already made, but I throw back the covers and quickly change out the sheets. Now armed with a stack of clean sheets and a bundle of dirty sheets, I'm not sure what to do. I decide to take them with me to the next room because leaving them behind seems redundant.

In the next room, I enter slowly, so I can study the layout. It's obvious someone lives in this room, and by the clean lines and dark tones, I have a feeling I know who it belongs to. His presence isn't advertised. There aren't any framed photos on the dresser, but the entire room holds his intense energy like a box sealed tight. As if it leaks from his body to soak into the walls.

Would he notice if I stole a couple more shirts? I eye the closet but decide against entering it. No doubt, he would consider it a debt between us if I took any. And I don't need to dig myself a deeper hole with this man. I need to find a way to escape.

His bedding is tucked tight, as if a soldier or a doctor made it. I fear messing with it, but I still have several more rooms to finish before Sarah hunts me down with more chores. The deep navy blue covers match perfectly to the subtly patterned sheets beneath. I peel back the layers and replace the sheet with fresh white ones.

I told myself I wouldn't snoop if I found Nicolo's room, but faced with the possibility of gaining any type of information about him, I can't resist. His furnishings are devoid of clutter. A small box containing a couple of watches and an array of cufflinks sits on top of his dresser. Inside, his clothing is perfectly folded and organized in immaculate rows. Did he do this or the staff? It takes control to an entirely new level.

I skirt the edge of the bed and fuss with arranging the already perfect covers. His bedside table has a gold locket sitting so far back on its surface, I didn't even notice it until the overhead light glinted off it. A delicate chain wound in a perfect loop cups a little gold heart locket. On the top of it, the initials DAC are engraved. Gently, I trace my finger over the letters that are engraved into the worn metal. It's as if it has been rubbed and buffed multiple times over the years.

A family heirloom, maybe?

It's delicate, and my fingers tremble as I flip it open, only to find nothing inside the little heart frame. Disappointed, I click it closed and suddenly feel as if I've violated his privacy. I shove the guilt away as quickly as it comes. The man is holding me prisoner, for fuck's sake.

The chain slides between my fingers and gets tangled. I gently pry it loose, careful not to pull the delicate links, when a voice behind me says, "What are you doing in here?"

I jolt so hard I drop the necklace onto the side table and stumble into the edge of the bed.

Turning, I press my hands to my chest to stop my heart from leaping out of my chest. The mean one, Lucas, is standing in the doorframe, leaning against it casually. How long has he been watching me? I don't bother to ask because I truly don't care. I don't want to have a conversation with him.

Turning my attention back to the locket, I scoop the necklace up again, hoping he didn't see me looking at it. That's all I need, for him to tell Nicolo I'd been rummaging through his belongings.

I clear my throat and answer, "I was just changing the sheets. Sarah drew me a map of the rooms I'm supposed to hit."

His eyes narrow in a suspecting way, like he knows I'm full of shit. "You were looking at something. What was it?"

Fuck. I clutch my hand tighter around the locket and try not to fidget too much to draw his attention to it, but it's pointless. He already knows. Fear trickles down my spine like a slow-moving creek while anticipation builds in my gut on what his next move will be. In the blink of my eyes, he pushes off the door and stalks across the polished hardwood, snagging my hand mid-motion. My heart skips a full beat, and my lungs seize up.

His fingers squeeze tight around the pressure point in my wrist, and I let out a loud yelp.

"You're hurting me!" My voice cracks, but the words do nothing to deter him.

"You're hiding something. Drop it," he growls through his teeth. The pressure on my wrist becomes too much, so I have no choice but to release the secret tucked into my palm.

Instinct tells me to explain myself, so I lick my dried lips and tell him, "It's not what you think. I wasn't stealing it or hiding it."

Deftly, he catches the necklace to keep it from falling to the floor. Then he shoves my aching arm away as if my skin has burned him.

His big fingers dwarf the piece of jewelry, and I watch him study it, all while easing backward and away from him. This man is unstable, and I don't want to be within his reach if he lashes out.

"It was our mother's," he says, lifting his gaze to mine. His dark eyes are large and unblinking, as if he fears never seeing it again.

I'm pretty sure he doesn't want an audience, so I tiptoe toward the door but barely make it a few steps before he pounces on me and drags me back by the same—no doubt bruised now—wrist. "I didn't say you can leave."

"I just wanted to give you some privacy," I whisper. It's all I can manage through the icy chill that now owns the space.

"Is every single word you utter complete bullshit, or do you tell the truth on occasion too?"

I attempt to jerk my hand back, but he maintains his tight grip. The hard edge of his tone is one I recognize from him accosting me twice now. Even as afraid as I am of him, I don't want to be seen as a pushover. I stand tall and straighten my spine.

"What do you want me to say? I don't want to be within two feet of you because I know you're counting the seconds until you can kill me. I'm pretty sure the only reason I'm alive right now is because Nicolo intends to use me for some purpose that may, or may not, include selling me to make a lot of money."

He shifts and gently places the locket on the bedside table, letting the locket hit the dark wood before slowly lowering the chain on top of it to obscure the engraving. It's an act of patience, of mercy, of love. So at odds with his collage of tattoos and menacing demeanor. I don't even know Lucas, but I do know he is violence and rage wrapped up with a tight bow.

When he faces me again, he looks a little more composed and less like he wants to plunge a knife into my gut just to see what's inside me. "My mother was murdered."

Shit. "I'm so sorry for your loss." The platitude slips from my lips so easily I wince at the end. Lucas's dark features remain the same, and he reminds me of a thunderstorm barreling right for you. You're prepared for the rain and mayhem, but you never know the true destruction until the wind settles.

"Really, I *am* sorry. Even more so if you loved her."

He cocks a questioning brow. "You don't love your mother?"

I shrug. "I don't even know my mother, not really. She never gave a shit about my sister or me. We were the half-assed fulfillment of a marriage contract." I don't know why I'm telling him this. He doesn't care about my family, my mother, or me. All he cares about is making me pay for something my father did to him.

When he doesn't respond, I gently try to pull my hand back, but he doesn't budge. I try to remain calm, but it's hard with the mammoth of a man before me. "I really should get back to work. Sarah is bound to come hunting for me any minute now."

His eyes remind me of Nicolo's, if a little unsteady, not crazy so much as the window to a broken soul. I stare into them, despite my fear, and tug again. "Can you let me go now, please?"

From one second to another, his gaze hardens. He twists and lifts my arm toward him, dragging me closer, almost up onto my tiptoes. "Your father killed my mother. He did it in front of me when I was only a child." His voice is a whisper of animosity. A growl of contempt focused on me.

A rock of emotion has formed in my throat, and I swallow around it and try not to let the tears that are building fall. "I don't believe you. I know he isn't a good man, but I can't imagine him being so cruel..."

Can't I?

Oh, my god, what if it's true?

He leans into me, his breath fanning against my lips. The spicy mint scent is too close, too intimate, for all the anger he hurls at me. I cringe and try to turn away, but there is nowhere to run, nowhere to hide.

"Are you sure about that, little girl? Do you even know anything about your dear old dad? No doubt he keeps the gory details out of your precious little head. Why bother the womenfolk with things they have no right knowing, right?"

Well, he's not wrong. It doesn't mean I want to congratulate him on knowing my father better than I do. Anger rises, mixing with the guilt and sudden sadness. "Fine, do you want me to apologize for your mother's death again? I'm sorry." I really am sorry. Even if I had nothing to do with it, I am sorry for his mom dying, but the anger twists my tone into sarcasm.

He tilts his head to watch my expression, rather like a dog waiting for a trick from his master. I try to jerk my hand free again, but he only tightens his grip. I bite the inside of my cheek to stop myself from wincing. My fingers are going numb, and a sharp pain shoots up my elbow with every one of his movements.

"What do you want from me?" My voice cracks, and I'm utterly defeated. I'll be beaten to death by this one or raped by his brother come the end. My options keep getting better and better.

"I want you to admit your family is nothing but scum. I want you to know what kind of kingdom you were born into." He spits the words at me, his face mere inches away from mine.

"You don't think I know that already? My family sucks, and I'm the same as them, apparently," I shout, grabbing onto whatever bravado I seem to have tucked away inside. "I get it. You want revenge. You want to dish out punishment for my family's sins. If so, I'll pay the price. I already have, but that's apparently not enough for you." With my free hand, I shove him back, and finally, he releases my arm.

I'm caught off balance at the shift in weight and tumble back toward the bed. Lucas reaches out to snag my arms, maybe to keep me from falling or something else entirely, I don't know. What I do know is that I can't let him get a hold of me again. Without thinking, I lash out with my fingernails, dragging them across and deep into the flesh of his forearms. Everything happens so fast. With a hiss, he shoves my hands back, and somehow, we both tumble onto the bed. Me flat on my back, and him towering above me.

I shove at his firm chest to get him off me, feeling like things have taken a bad turn when I hear a booming voice from across the room that causes us both to freeze. "What the fuck is going on in here?"

Lucas recovers first, shoving off the bed and putting much-needed distance between us. "Nothing. I was just having a brief chat with our guest."

I'm shaking now, my limbs rattling, no matter how strong I'm trying to be. I can feel Nicolo's intense stare scanning me from head to toe. Once he's had his fill, he turns his attention to Lucas, giving him a glare. "Looks like you did a bit more than talking."

"Aww, don't be such a poor sport, brother. We were just having a little heart to heart. I wasn't stealing her precious virtue or anything."

Nicolo doesn't even blink. "Get the fuck out." When his brother doesn't make a move, he repeats his order. "Are you deaf? Get. Out."

Lucas rolls his eyes but doesn't say another word as he walks out of the bedroom and disappears into the hall. With him gone, it's just Nicolo and me alone in the room. It's my turn to scramble up, to get out from under the rage I see building in the set of his shoulders and the hard crinkle around his eyes.

"I... I was just changing the sheets. I'm done now, so I'll go." I force out the words, keeping my eyes trained on the floor.

I don't want to provoke him, and honestly, after dealing with Lucas, I am done peopling today. Before I can take a step forward, he stops me, his hand taking the same wrist his brother had crushed so easily in his grasp. His touch is gentle, but even the softest touch hurts enough to cause black spots to appear in my vision. I bite my lip to stop myself from crying out, but the sound escapes, and Nicolo shoves me back, surprise coloring his features.

"I'm sorry, I have to get out of here." Tears slip from my eyes and down my cheeks, and my nose is already stuffing up.

Rage fills Nicolo's devilishly handsome features. "What the fuck is going on? What were you talking about with Lucas?"

I shake my head. "I wasn't in here with him. I was changing the sheets, and I guess he saw me from the hallway and came in to talk to me."

"Why are you crying?" he demands, like the reason isn't obvious.

I throw my hands up, my injured one protesting the movement. "I don't know. I'm tired, I want to go home, and I want some damn clothes of my own."

He scans me and clears the look of disgust from his features. The man in control of every facet of his life. He stares down at me from his imperial mask. "Get yourself together. You'll get proper clothing when you earn them, but you won't do it by sniveling when you're only doing basic chores."

He's impossible. How can he not understand why I hate all of this? My mouth flops open, and I shake my head at him. There is no point in getting angry, but I can't help it. "You might be worse than your crazy brother if you don't get why I'm not content to change your sheets and make you breakfast while I wait for you to sell me at some godforsaken auction."

His eyes narrow at me, and he takes a menacing step forward. Of course, my courage only goes so far, so I skitter backward toward the door. If I made a run for it, he'd probably chase me down to assert his dominance again. I've seen it a hundred times before. Men who need to be in charge of every tiny thing, and when the barest hint of control slips, it's as if the entire world has crumbled around them. My sister called those kinds of men narcissists. And I don't doubt for a minute that Nicolo fits that bill. Thinking about how much she would have hated Nicolo makes me feel better, strangely. I miss my sister so much.

He faces the bedside table, and I know he spots the necklace out of place from where Lucas returned it. "Did you touch this?"

If I lie to him, Lucas will probably rat me out, so I nod slowly. "Yes. But I only looked at it. Then your brother came in and took it from me. I promise I was only looking at it. I wasn't trying to steal it or invade your privacy."

I can't tell if he believes me or not. His face is so carefully blank. Long seconds pass with him just staring at me, the gold chain clutched tight in his massive fist.

"Get out of here. From here on out, Sarah can change my bedding. You don't need to do it. Find some toilets to scrub instead. And stay out of Lucas's room too. She'll show you which one is his."

As if I wanted to hunt down the crazy brother and give him more opportunities to scream at me. "Okay," I say. "Can I go now?"

He nods, his focus back on the piece of jewelry.

I gather the dirty sheets and the stack of clean ones and flee back to my bedroom. Once I've locked myself in the room, I rush into the bathroom and stare at my wrist under the brighter lights. Can a man break a woman's bone just by squeezing her? It hurts from my fingertips all the way to my elbow. I don't want to cry because once I do, I know I won't be able to stop. The tears will become sobs. And I don't want Nicolo, whose bedroom happens to be next to mine, to hear me.

It isn't a matter of being strong. I just don't want to give him another excuse to enter my room. I'd expected another display of dominance, another grab to my crotch or nude catwalk, but so far today, he's avoided me. A mercy. If only his brother would follow that lead.

A faint bloom of purple has sprouted on my fair skin right below the hard nub of my wrist bone. Shit. It isn't as if I have anything to wrap it with. They've only given me one damn shirt, after all. I also refuse to hunt Nicolo down and ask him for anything. Including medical attention.

I enter the room again and find the stack of sheets. They feel thick, and I'm not sure I can rip them without something sharp to assist me. I opt for trying to tie one around my neck and wrapping my wrist in it like a sling, but I miscalculate the knot, my balancing abilities, and my distance to the side table. I don't see the destruction before it happens, and I go down hard, my wrist smashing into the wood.

Pain shoots up my arm, and a sharp cry escapes my lips before darkness mercifully ushers the pain away.

12

NIC

What the fuck was I thinking? First, by allowing Celia to wander the house at will. And second, by not throttling Lucas when I should have earlier. He's growing more and more insubordinate by the day. I should've known he'd go after her again. And now she's hurt. I have no one to blame but myself, and I don't like it.

It's not like I care about her pain. But if she is battered and bruised before the auction, it'll mean less of a payment. Like her virginity, my clients will want her skin unmarred, a canvas for their own brutal pleasures.

It's not her pathetic attempts to stifle her tears that give me reason to check on her. It's the possibility of her hurting herself. I'll have to lock her in a padded cell until I can pawn her off on some other asshole. Which will screw with my revenge plans. I need her.

Celia is nothing like her father, at least as far as I can tell. He'd never degrade himself by blubbering. She's even tried to pry out some kind of connection between us, despite the fact I'll be putting her tight little ass on a block in front of her daddy's friends in a few short days.

As long as I can keep Lucas away from her until then. I don't trust him not to do something rash the closer we come to the event. Maybe I'll put Soo on him once we get a little closer to the day. He's dying to knock a little sense into Lucas, even if that means hitting his head into a wall a time or two.

Another sob cuts through the wall, and I huff out a ragged exhale. There's no way I'm going to get any sleep tonight if she continues with the crying. She didn't even cry this much on her first night here.

The thought that maybe Lucas hurt her worse than I suspected hits me. I quietly slip out of the room and down to the kitchen for an ice pack. No one else is lingering in the halls. The kitchen staff have already retreated to their rooms for the evening. I find the jar of balm we keep in the refrigerator for cuts and bruises. As well as one of several thick gel packs we keep stocked in the freezer. The balm is our mother's recipe and works quickly to numb minor pains, and I get a twinge in my chest thinking about using it to soothe Ricci's daughter.

I wonder briefly what my mother would think of the man I've become? Would she be proud? Angry? None of that matters because she isn't here. She isn't alive. She was murdered the same day as my father and older brother.

The anger rushing through my veins becomes a slow boil, but when I enter her room and find her sitting on the edge of the bed, my anger dissipates altogether. There's a faint trickle of dried blood running down from the top of her forehead, and she's clutching her wrist to her chest, rocking it slowly against her.

I shut the door, closing us inside before turning around. "What the hell happened?"

Hastily, she takes her uninjured hand and wipes it across her face, most likely trying to hide her tears from me. As if I hadn't heard her crying in here all along.

When her soft brown eyes finally reach mine, they're rimmed red and glistening with tears. "It's nothing. I got into a fight with the table. It won."

Is she seriously joking right now? I hold up the jar of balm and the ice pack. "Let me see it."

She shakes her head and backs up onto the bed to keep me from getting close. "No, I'll be fine. I don't have the energy in me to spar with you, and the last thing I want is for you to touch me. I think you and your brother have hurt me enough."

I narrow my eyes and stalk forward, sending her to the farthest edge of the king-size bed. "To be clear, I own you. That means I can touch you whenever I damn well please. Right now, I want to touch you in a way that helps you. But if you want to be a brat and won't come back over here, I'll tie you down and force it on you, anyway. Then I'll leave you that way until Sarah comes to get you in the morning."

Her red-rimmed eyes stare up at me, and it looks like she can hardly believe what I'm saying.

"If you make me count you down like a toddler, you won't like the repercussions." My words must hit their mark because she gives another half-hearted sniffle and then crawls slowly toward me.

"Good girl. Sit here and let me look at your head." I pat the mattress.

The gash is just past her hairline. "What did you do? You weren't suffering a head wound when you left my bedroom earlier."

She exhales, her chest deflating. "I told you. I got into a fight with the table. It was dumb. I hit my arm and blacked out. When I woke up, my forehead was bleeding. I must have cracked it on the edge before I hit the ground."

Her dark hair sits around her shoulders in waves. It's slightly tangled from her brushing it out of the way and the lack of grooming items. I didn't think she'd be able to make a weapon out of a hairbrush, but I also would not put it past her to try.

I gently tuck the mass of brown hair down her back and ignore the stiffening of my cock. Her sweet scent wafts at the movement, and for a moment, it's all I can smell. Honeysuckle, lavender. Saliva builds in my mouth at the thought of taking her, devouring her from the inside out. She already thinks I'm a monster. Putting her flat on her back while injured wouldn't help things.

Her big doe eyes peer into mine. She doesn't shy away from my gaze, nor is she glaring like she is imagining all the ways she could kill me. At this moment, she is soft, broken, and in need of saving. Too bad I'm not the saving type.

I squeeze the cut together to make sure it's clotting. She winces, but remains still in my hands.

"I think this will be fine. Just be careful from now on. Don't get any ideas about hurting yourself. I'm not taking you to the hospital."

She ducks her chin, a flash of pink racing up her neck. "I wasn't trying to hurt myself, and I'm not usually so clumsy." A moment of silence stretches on between us. Her pink lips part, and her eyes skit away from mine before meeting them again. It's obvious she has something she wants to say, so I give her a moment to gather her thoughts. Truthfully, I don't really care about what she thinks or has to say. She is a means to an end, but I would be lying if I didn't admit conversing with her is the best type of foreplay.

"I don't understand your vendetta. I'm not a bad person. I don't deserve what you're trying to do to me."

I rearrange her hair again, even though it doesn't need it. I want a reason to touch her, and that annoys me.

"And what am I doing to you?" I prompt, taking the time to inspect the breadth of her scalp to ensure she didn't crack it anywhere else.

She huffs like I'm some sort of petulant child she needs to dumb down her speech for. "You're taking whatever revenge you have saved up for my father, and my family, out on me. Your brother has already said as much, plus his sheer animosity whenever we're in each other's vicinity."

I gently curl my fingers and scratch my nails across her scalp now.

She lets out a breathy sigh.

"My brother has no love for your family, that's true."

"And you?" she asks, almost in a sigh.

Should I tell her I've had fantasies where I obliterate her entire family in gruesome detail? Probably not while she's so soft and pliant in my arms.

I trail my fingers to the back of her neck and dig into the bones right where her neck meets her head. Her breathy sighs shudder out of her now, and my cock aches with each sound she makes. Would she sigh and moan in my arms as I sink into her deeply, owning every inch of her flesh, or would she curse me, her nails digging into my skin, drawing blood? Both sound fucking great to me.

"Your brother—" she begins, trailing off in another moan, dropping her eyes closed with each tightening and release of my hands on her.

"My brother?"

"He's so, he's hostile... so evil," she finishes in a rush, curling forward to rest her forehead on my stomach.

I shake my head, even though she can't see it. "My brother is bitter. He's broken and vengeful, but he isn't evil. There's a difference, *stellina*, remember that."

She opens her eyes and shoves off my hips with her hands, then her eyes fly wide when she realizes what she's done and where she's touching me.

I let her go, even though I'd rather spend more time massaging her head to find out what other noises she can make. The ice pack is still frozen, so I get up and retreat into the bathroom to grab a washcloth. I wrap the blue gel packet inside before handing it to her.

Instead of pressing it to her forehead, she places it over her wrist with a hiss. She mentioned her arm, but I'd been distracted. I gently pull the pack away and inspect the bruises. There's not much swelling, but there is a deep ring of purple from Lucas's rough handling of her.

Despite the surge of anger pressing tight through my chest, I keep my face neutral as I gently test the bones. There is no crunching, so likely not broken. "I think it's just bruised. I'll make sure you keep it iced, and you'll be careful when you complete your chores. We can put some makeup over this for the auction, but I don't want this to bruise and swell even more."

She scoffs and tugs her wrist from my grasp, my words pulling her out of this conversation and thrusting her into reality.

I only glare and snag it back by the curve of her elbow. Hurting her isn't on my list of priorities, but she doesn't seem to have solid self-preservation instincts.

Instead of fighting further, she settles on staring out past my shoulder like she can't be bothered with my existence. It's humorous how little she cares for her own safety. Even while injured, she still tempts the beast. If she continues to push me, I'll have to push back, and she's in no shape to match me.

I release her, but only long enough to open the jar and scoop out some chilled balm. She sucks in a breath through her teeth but stays still as I slather the paste around her wrist. The tension between us grows thick, making each breath I take harder. When I finally finish, I gently wrap the ice around her wrist and hold the ends together.

"Why are you taking care of me?"

I don't meet her eyes when I respond. "Profit margin."

"That's bullshit. You could have had one of the staff come help me. Why are you doing it?"

This time I meet her direct gaze and force her to maintain it since she wants to push me so fucking much.

"Maybe I want to touch you without seeing hatred in your eyes."

"I don't think that will ever happen."

"Are you sure about that?"

She swallows loudly and drops her gaze. Another wash of pink treks up her neck and onto her ears. All I can do is smile like the son of a bitch I am.

I shift my hold on her wrist so I can sit beside her on the bed. To my surprise, she shifts her legs around to make room for me—an interesting new development.

"What happens now?" she asks almost cautiously. "Who are you going to sell me to? Where are they going to expect me to stay once they take me away?" There's no fear in her tone, only exhaustion, as if the entire situation has made her more tired than she can bear.

Again, I shrug. "I don't know. That will be up to them. Once you're handed over, and we exchange the cash, then your confinement becomes their problem."

"What if I escape?"

I try to ignore the way my shirt gapes open at her neck, giving me a top-down view of her cleavage. It doesn't work. My cock is still aching for more.

"Try to escape. I expect chasing you down might be fun for the buyer. I know I'd enjoy it. If you were mine to buy."

She grunts and tugs her hand away. I allow it this time, monitoring her every twitch.

The idea of someone coming after her isn't appealing to her. Of course, it wouldn't be. When rich men hunt, they do it for sport. When poor men hunt, they do it as a matter of survival. She'd have a better chance with one of them than with me. I always catch my prey.

"Thanks for your help," she says. It's a dismissal. Yet another prod of dominance from her she might not even know she's making.

I shift higher on the bed and lie down, folding my hands behind my head to feign comfort.

"What are you doing?" A thread of fear enters her voice now. *Finally.*

"I told you. If you keep pushing me. I'll push back. You don't get to tell me when to leave. I'll leave when I'm damn well ready."

She turns to glare down at me. I have to crane my neck to see her face with our height difference. Her heart-shaped face and soft lips draw me in.

"I was saying thank you for helping me. How is that pushing you?"

"You use kindness as a weapon. All your people do. You throw it out like this great precious gift everyone wants to lap up, and when they can't have it, they crave it, they need it, all for them to become subservient to that need."

Her forehead wrinkles, and then she winces, stroking gently at the cut there. "I think you have a much higher opinion of me than I do of myself. And why do you keep saying 'your people' like you don't have money yourself? Look at this house. Your clothes, the staff. That's a bit hypocritical, don't you think?"

I shake my head and sit up again. "No, we are entirely different species of human."

The anger I always have tucked away on a low simmer boils before I can put it in check. "You grew up with money and privilege. In some ways, I did, too, until it was taken from me. I didn't get money or power again until well into adulthood. Your entire life has been one shining example of what the everyday person should strive for. The perfect life for the perfect daughter. Daddy's little fucking princess."

Her anger matches mine, her beautiful face twisted in shock and rage. "You don't know a goddamn thing about my life. My sister is dead. I don't know a single thing about my parents, and I'm a twenty-three-year-old virgin who has been locked in her house her whole life. What of that tells you I've had a charmed existence?"

I shove off the bed to put some distance between us before I do some damage I can't repair with gentle touches and ice packs. "Thank you for that." A low growl escapes my lips. "You proved my point. You want to know why my brother is so mean? He watched his mother die right in front of him. Her throat slit from ear to ear." Somehow, I strip my own grief from my tone. "And you think being a virgin even compares to that?"

She shakes her head frantically, realizing there is no comparison. "No, of course not. I can't even imagine the pain he's suffered."

The pain I've suffered. I don't remind her of that fact, though. Not when her face softens, and all I see is pity.

I stalk toward the door and grip the handle hard enough to rip it from the door. "Remember one thing, *stellina*. Everything that happens to you is most definitely revenge. And what your father did means it's earned a hundred times over. You know nothing about the bastard, but if you did, you'd hate him just as much as we do."

She hops off the bed and rushes toward me, but I slam the door between us and lock it from the outside before she can reach me. I don't want to hear her excuses or see the pity she has for me in her eyes. I want her hate, her anger, her fear. I want to taste it on my tongue and swallow it down like air.

Back in my room, all is blessedly quiet. I take a moment to gain control of myself and stalk back and forth, glaring at the door separating us. It would only take a few moments to sweep her in my arms, get her good and dripping wet for me, and divest her of her lamentable virginity. Leaving her ruined for any other man.

It would give me relief but not the satisfaction her father's crimes demand. *No.* I need to keep my focus with her. Not allow her sweet words or deep eyes to draw me in.

In a few days, I'll be wrapping her in a satin bow and sending a thank you note to her father before I drive a knife into his abdomen, gutting him myself.

Only his death will bring me satisfaction and relief. Celia is a means to an end. Nothing more, and to think of her as anything else would be a grave mistake. One I will not make.

13

CELIA

*C*hores keep me busy, but they also give me a lot of time to think. Mostly about home. About the life I lived and how I might have been blind to everything around me. Too consumed by my own wants and needs to notice anything else. To notice my sister hurting so badly, she'd rather kill herself than marry a stranger. To notice my mother drinking more and more every night to dull her pain. To notice my father, so straight-backed and stoic, that he could be hiding the soul of a monster.

I no longer wear the blinders of a child when it comes to my family life. For years, we'd been drifting apart inch by inch. But the accusations Nicolo laid at my father's feet... I don't want to believe them. In my time here, I've learned enough about my captor to know, at the very least, he believes them. What motive does he have to lie to me? I'm already locked away.

Nicolo must have spoken to Sarah about my chore assignments as she's taken me off sheet duty, and now I wander the house dusting already immaculate fixtures. Is this a chore or someone's fantasy playing out? Setting me loose, half-dressed with a duster in my hand. I shake the thought away. I'm just grateful Lucas hasn't tried to come after me again.

Nicolo's words keep ringing in my ears. *Everything that happens to you is most definitely revenge.* If my father is such a heartless bastard and doesn't care what happens to me, how is my captivity revenge against him? Questions continue to rattle in my head as I drift through the house, being useful to no one.

Then I remember, the actual revenge hasn't even started yet. A shiver races down my spine as I think of whoever is going to buy me. I'm sure they will have vile things planned for me. I should be terrified, and part of me is, but I've known I'd be sold in some way or form my whole life. Not much has changed, only the seller.

Speak of the devil. Footfalls meet my ears as he passes down a perpendicular hallway, and I freeze in the act of dusting a sconce on the wall. My heart jumps out of my chest, and I almost drop the duster at the surprise of his presence.

Just when I think he's gone, he pops his head back around the corner, and I quickly jerk my arm down from the light fixture and turn toward the next one. In the opposite direction. The one I'd already dusted that didn't need dusting to begin with.

What does he want? Why is he watching me?

I focus too intently on the dusting as his footsteps echo off the hardwood on his way toward me. Each step causes the knot of anxiety to tighten in my gut. When he reaches me, I quickly turn and hustle to the next wall sconce, completely ignoring his presence.

As if that were even possible.

He dominates any space he's in, as if the world itself bows to his will. The air feels denser as I suck it into my lungs. The hallway which felt cavernous a moment ago, has somehow shrunk with him so close. This feels like a cat-and-mouse game, except I'm the mouse, and there is no escaping Nicolo. It's either his sharp claws or a mousetrap.

There is a heavy weight on my tongue. Part of me wants to confront him, find out why he's so intent on looming over me all the time. The other part of me, the one that wins, scurries down to the next sconce and decorative table underneath. I would like to make it through one day without a confrontation.

Of course, the click of his shoes alerts me he's followed. I swipe nonexistent dust off the sconce and carefully move the decorative vase on the table to dust that surface as well. All the while, he stands there. I can't see his face, so I have no idea what he's doing or thinking.

When there are no more things to dust, I twist around and risk a glance at him. I find him staring down at me, his eyebrows tucked in tight, the tiniest upturn in the corner of his mouth. As if he finds my games amusing. As if I'm some kind of pet.

I narrow my eyes, toss the duster onto the table, and storm past him. Out of the corner of my eyes, I see a smile spread across his face, which only angers me more.

Right now, I don't have much of a choice in things, but I have a choice in standing here letting him watch me like I'm some type of entertainment.

My door makes a loud, satisfying sound when it closes. That's the best part about high-end houses. The doors sound so much better when they meet the frame with a purposeful shove.

I wait for a little while, thinking he'll follow me in, demand answers for my attitude, or give me another lecture, but he doesn't. One of the maids brings lunch to me later, and I stay in my room to eat. Not risking another run-in defeats boredom in my mind. At least for now. Another couple days of pacing back and forth within the same four walls, and I might go back out begging for chores, but not right now.

If he wants me, then he'll have to come and get me.

It isn't until I'm lying in bed later, legs stretched out in the fresh shirt Sarah brought with dinner, that he hunts me down. I'm already showered; I tied my long brown hair into a bun at the nape of my neck. I considered asking Nicolo for another hair tie, maybe some more personal hygiene items, but I'd rather eat glass.

When he walks in without knocking, of course, he carries two low ball tumblers in one hand bunched together between his fingers. He holds the glasses toward me without a word. While I don't trust the amber liquid inside, nor the man offering me the drink, I take it anyway. I need something to break up the jumble of thoughts in my head.

Especially with him standing there looking so... *disheveled.* Usually, his clothing is meticulous. Except for the night I met him when he was caked in blood.

Tonight is different, though. He's less dangerous and more chaos. Like he's one second away from exploding. His shirt is untucked, the tails hanging out, and his collar is open, revealing hints of black ink beneath. I want to trace the ink embedded in his skin, if only to know what it feels like. I don't know anything about this man. Knowing what he feels like might mend the kind of disconnect I'm feeling.

He roughly swipes his hand through his dark hair, only adding another layer to the mantle of exhaustion seeming to hang off him.

He slumps on the end of the bed, bringing the glass to his lips, and takes a long sip of his drink. If he can drink it, hopefully, I can too. Swirling the amber liquid around inside the glass, the fragrant scent of vanilla and caramel fill my nostrils. I give it a tentative sip. Well, at least it's not scotch. A few ice cubes tinkle together as I take another gulp. After the first couple of sips burn down my throat, the bourbon becomes smooth, filling my belly with warmth. My experience is limited as I usually stick to white wine.

Nicolo sits in silence, and I take the rare opportunity to watch him. For once, he's not crowding me, nor in motion, forcing me to get the hell out of the way. In the light, I notice that there's a faint scar under his right earlobe that cuts into his deep five o'clock shadow. For half a second, I allow myself to think with compassion for this man in front of me, and I wonder... What happened to him?

His voice jolts me from my thoughts, shooting my heart into my throat. "I set the auction date for a couple of days from now." He doesn't look at me when he speaks, and I continue studying his profile while he talks. "You're going to be my centerpiece. I think you'll bring in a substantial amount of money."

I swallow another gulp of the alcohol, letting it burn down all the way into my gut. It takes everything in me not to lash out, but what will lashing out do? It won't help me escape. It won't stop the warmth that fills my veins when he enters the room. It will change nothing.

Instead, I choose to act completely uninterested. "Well, if you say so. How much do you think I'm worth?" I tap my chin with my finger. "A virgin in her twenties with no interest in sex. You know, one of my high school boyfriends even called me frigid when I refused to put out for him. He called me ice queen and told me no one would ever want me."

He shrugs like it doesn't matter. "I doubt your new owner will give you much choice. A wet hole is a wet hole."

I'm half tempted to ask him how he could say such a thing, but then suddenly realize who it is that is holding me hostage.

"The least you can do is look me in the eye when you so casually describe someone raping me."

He turns his head and stares down at my foot, still in contact with his pants. Then so very slowly, he lifts his chin. His dark gaze clashes with mine when he downs the rest of his drink. I watch the column of his throat as he swallows and the way the light dances off his long eyelashes. He's so handsome it's almost frightening.

He is the perfect predator, drawing you in with his beautiful eyes and charming smile. Even the tattoos and scars somehow add to the appeal. He looks dangerous, but there is something about him that twists that feeling into the need to entice him, to have him on your side. Maybe it's the thought of having him protect me. He could... but he won't.

When he finishes his drink, he lowers the glass to his lap, his eyes never wavering from my own. One side of his mouth tips up into a half-smile. "I'm not worried about your frigidity one bit, *stellina*. Like I said, a wet hole is a wet hole."

I sip the drink to give myself more courage. There's not enough booze in the world to give me the strength to go head-to-head with this man. "And how is that?"

He reaches down and trails his index finger over the top of my foot to my ankle. I pretend I can't feel the jolts of his touch zinging through my body.

"When I fucked your thighs the other day, you certainly didn't seem frigid to me."

Oh god. I've tried my hardest to forget that day, even though the memory lingers in the back of my mind every night. Instead of answering, I hide my shaking hand inside the sleeve of my shirt and clutch the drink to my chest with the other.

"Nothing to say to that?" he mocks. "You talk a big game until someone calls you out on it."

I toss back the rest of the alcohol in one huge gulp and swallow it down. It burns, but it's exactly what I need. I stare at the few ice shards remaining before I look up at him. I don't think about my next action. I simply act and throw the glass toward his head.

He bats it to the side with lightning-fast reflexes, causing it to land harmlessly on the coverlet. Disappointment fills my veins. Too bad he didn't drink more; I would have liked to give him a concussion. With a sigh, as if I'm a small child, he grabs our glasses and carries them to the sideboard against the wall opposite my bed. I can only hope that he leaves, but I should know he wouldn't make things that easy for me.

He walks slowly, precisely, a predator testing his prey. I know after what I just did I should be terrified. I should be running for it. But all I can do is lie here and watch the shape of his perfect ass in his stupidly tailored pants.

"Another way I know you're lying." He speaks into the room, his back still to me. "You continue fighting. If you didn't care, you'd submit, succumb, serve yourself up to me in every way I've demanded of you."

He turns, his gaze hot and heavy as he traces the curve of my body on the bed. "Why fight unless you've got something to lose?"

"Maybe I'm just not made for submission." When he returns to the bed, he stands right next to me, forcing me to look up the long line of him.

"You will learn how to submit and if you're truly frigid, I'll take you outside and let you go."

I suck in a sharp breath. I know he must be lying, or his offer comes with a terrible stipulation. Before I can ask the conditions of his offer, he continues speaking.

"If I put my mouth on you, and you don't come, I'll release you. Let you run off home to be a pampered little princess again. But if you come, you'll have earned a punishment for throwing that glass at me."

Fuck. I walked into this, looking straight at it. If he wants me to prove I don't want him, I can do that. He's a fucking monster, and if he wants something from me, he's going to have to take it. I'd rally to my momentary bravery if he hadn't already shown he doesn't mind stealing whatever he wants.

"Come here, Celia," he calls softly, as if he's beckoning instead of commanding. As if he can coax me into participating.

It's the first time I've heard my real name fall from his lips. Nausea rolls through me. It tastes like bourbon and betrayal.

I've kept him waiting too long. It takes him seconds to grab my ankle and drag me closer on the bed, shoving my thighs wide, so wide my hip joints protest. I'm exposed, a fragile, innocent flower, beaten by the sun and rain.

I swallow the yelp which threatens to slip out and try to wiggle away. But his grip tightens painfully enough that I freeze. With my legs open, he moves his hand to rest on top of my kneecaps. His face is a picture of innocence. The same face the devil makes right before he claims your soul.

"Take off your shirt. Show me how frigid you are."

"Fuck you. I'm not doing a damn thing to make you think I'm volunteering for this," I spit at him.

He shrugs, uncaring. "Take your shirt off, or I'll rip it off, and you'll remain naked for the rest of your stay with us."

With trembling fingers, I slip the buttons from their holes. When I reach the last one, I look up at him through my lashes. "You promise if I don't come, you'll let me go?"

His eyes flash as he guides his hand to the shirt and flaps it open. "Let's be honest, *stellina*. You've wanted this since the moment I walked in the door. Hell, I bet you wanted me the first night I brought you here. You wanted me, and you didn't understand why. Didn't understand how you could want a man as evil and menacing as me."

I glare while he grips the edge of my panties and tugs them down. Not wanting to rip them, seeing as he's likely not going to give me more, I lift my hips and let him draw the white cotton off at my feet. It's my only concession.

Naked in front of him, terror swamps me. What is he going to do to me? I'm breathing heavily from my mouth, almost panting, because I can't draw enough air through my nose.

"What do you want?" I whisper. "I'm supposed to be a virgin, remember?"

He takes his time looking me over, touching me anywhere he likes—a thumb over a small brown birthmark on my belly, an index finger across the top of my right breast.

"Yeah, you look like the picture of fucking reticence. You blush from your ears to your gorgeous pussy; did you know that?"

Heat washes through me. No doubt adding a brighter hue to my skin. Whatever. Maybe if he thinks I'm complying, he'll be gentler.

"Let's see just how chilled you are?" He cups me with his whole hand; his touch is hard, possessive. Carefully, he opens me up and slips two fingers along my folds. "Yes," he whispers so softly I can barely hear him. There's a yearning in his voice that tells me he wants this more than he's letting on. It's not just a stupid game for him.

When he pulls his fingers away, they are coated in moisture, and I shudder. It means nothing, just my body's reaction to a biological stimulus.

I watch him as he stares at me, using his hand again, this time dragging his thumb gently over my clit. I lurch off the bed in surprise.

"Settle, *stellina*. I've got you," he whispers.

Then he leans over me, boxing me in, so he can look at my face at the same time he spears me with his fingers again. Twisting his hand around, his fingers still inside me, he uses his thumb and fingers at the same time.

I'm shaking underneath him. He's barely touching me, his throat at eye level, and I lean back against the bed to peer into his eyes. They are heavy-lidded, and he's drawn his bottom lip between his teeth. I brace, but it's too late. He starts slowly and then picks up a punishing rhythm, fucking me with his fingers and using his thumb to drive me higher and higher toward orgasm.

No. I try to shove his hand away, but he slips out of me and stands. My entire body is quaking, caught between the heady pressure he's applied to my body and the pain he promises with his eyes. When he strips his belt off, I flinch. I barely make it to the other side of the bed before he catches me, traps me with the heavy weight of him. Then so fucking easily, he wrestles me back into place and secures my hands tight with the belt to the bedframe.

Tears pour down my cheeks, wet trails, hot and salty over my lips.

"Now, be a good girl, and ask me nicely to make you come, and I will."

He lowers his body along mine, so he can resume his position, his fingers deep inside me.

I shake my head again, thrashing. Pieces of hair escape my bun and fall onto my face. He huffs against my cheek and starts a gentle rhythm again. His eyes are dark, piercing, and I feel like he can see right through me and into the darkest parts of my soul.

"I'm not a patient man. Ask me or beg me to make you come, and I'll make it all better. It's that, or I'll spend all night edging you until you're not only begging me for my fingers but for my cock as well."

I whimper and squeeze my eyes shut. "I hate you."

"Well, get in line, princess. What's it going to be? If you ask, and I don't succeed, you're a free woman."

The need to come pricks against my skin, and I'm consumed. There is no escaping it. I can do nothing but turn myself over to the devil himself. "Please. Please, make me come," I whisper so softly I'm surprised he can even hear me.

His answering groan of approval shoots through me, somehow dragging me closer to coming than I've been since he arrived. He's not gentle when he shoves his fingers back inside me, resuming his lean over my body to watch my face, and I whimper, barely holding myself together. I keep my eyes shut and let the sensations consume every fiber of my being.

The orgasm sparks quickly, and I pant. He sinks down, so he can feel my breath against his ear, his lips whispering encouragement against my skin. "Let go. I've got you. Give it to me. Let me feel that virgin pussy cream on my fingers."

His mouth is filthy. This is wrong. I shouldn't want this, but I can't stop it. I can't stop my body from reacting as it does. He continues pumping his fingers inside me even as my body contracts around him, my legs squeezing him tight to me, and the scent of him and my sex surrounds us, making the orgasm all the more powerful. The little sparks turn into bigger ones until I'm nothing but embers left in the presence of roaring flames.

Everything in me is fractured and remade on waves of pleasure. A scream rips from my throat, and he uses the hand he's been holding himself up with to cover my mouth, smothering the scream threatening to shake the house to the ground. His weight is heavy on top of me, and the movement of his fingers becomes lazy. I'm melted butter in his hands.

The thick length of his cock digs into my thigh, and I envision him stripping back his pants and sinking deep inside of me. *Would he?* Would he claim me, and what would happen if he did? My body pulses in one huge heartbeat, all orbiting his hands as he gentles his strokes against my sated flesh. When he stops moving, a tear slips from the corner of my eye and slides down my cheek, leaving a cold streak in its path. He's right.

I shouldn't fight when I have something to lose.

14

NIC

*N*othing beats the sight of a little virgin after her first greedy orgasm.

I untie her from the bed frame, even though I wouldn't mind keeping her like this.

She swipes a tear away, thinking I didn't catch the soft brush of her fingers against her delicate cheekbones. I don't care. I'm not supposed to care.

I shove back off the bed to stand. My cock is an iron bar standing at attention in my pants, and I need a moment to get myself under control, or I'll risk lying myself back down and plowing into her wet heat.

The feeling of her pussy clenching around my fingers is burned into my memory. Whatever idiot called her an ice queen obviously knew nothing about how to get the little princess going. I'm learning how sweet she can be when given orders, even if she hates herself for loving every second.

Even now, as she stares away from me like she doesn't care, her knees are still quaking from the aftermath of her release. I want to see it again, watch all her control uncoil in a wave of need and emotion.

"*Stellina*," I say sharply.

Her gaze flashes to mine, as if daring me to call her out on her tears. Her pillowy lips press into a firm line before she says, "I guess you won. Go on, gloat."

I shake my head and tug her by the ankle, bringing her closer to me. In our efforts, she'd ridden up toward the top of the bed, almost out of my reach. "Why would I need to rub it in your face? I already know you aren't going anywhere. You seem to be the only one not quite understanding that fact."

She presses her lips into a thin line and glances over my shoulder. Another move of defiance, pretending I don't mean enough to her to maintain eye contact during a conversation. I want to grab her by the throat and force her to look me in the eyes, force her to see the bad that lays in front of her feet.

So I do just that. I use the opportunity to pounce, pressing every firm inch of my body against hers while my hand circles her slender throat.

Her body trembles in my grasp, and I revel in her fear. I speak softly into her face. "I'm not to be dismissed like I'm dirt beneath your feet. You should be grateful you're in this room with clothing and warmth. I could make your stay here a hell of a lot worse, princess."

My eyes trail over her face, and there is no denying how beautiful she is. Maybe, just maybe, if I wasn't so hell-bent on revenge, I would give in to temptation and allow my cock a small sampling, but to do that would be stupid. It would sacrifice everything I've worked hard for, and for what? A piece of virgin pussy? Ha, I think not.

"When I'm speaking to you, you will pay attention to what I have to say. Nod if you understand me."

The erratic beat of her heart pounds against my forearm, where it lies across her sternum, right between her breasts. So full and lush they beg to be tasted. Her nipples are hard little diamonds beckoning me onward. It would be so easy to suck one into my mouth. To flick the tight little nub with my tongue until she is nothing but a writhing mess beneath my feet. I shake the thought away before it can sink its claw any deeper into my subconscious. Not today, maybe when she's had a few more lessons to learn about respect.

After a couple seconds without a wilting stare or backlash from her mouth, I give her throat a gentle squeeze, loving the way it feels in my grasp, and ease off her again, rising back up to stand between her thighs.

She feels around the bed looking for her shirt, but I snatch her wrist in my palm and tug her attention back. "We aren't quite through here."

With a tug of her bottom lip between her teeth, she drags her dark gaze up my body to my face, carefully skipping the still hard swell of my dick in my slacks before returning. She's more curious and needy than she'd ever admit out loud.

Since she doesn't seem brave enough, I gently place her hand around my erection, which's still tucked tight into my pants. The dash of her eyes to clash with mine shoots a sizzle through me. A mere spark compared to the fierce need in my gut. When I release the back of her hand, she leaves it but doesn't move a muscle.

"Breathe," I say and gently brush stray strands of hair off her face. "You can fight all you want with your words, but your body will betray you every single time. It's the way you sucked in your breath just now—" I trace my thumb over her chest bone. She's so delicate. Oh, how easily she would break. "It's the way your heart is pounding so hard I can see it under your skin right here."

She finally forces an exhale and tries to steady her breathing, as if to prove she's not affected by my nearness. Flames flicker in her coffee brown eyes. "What do you want me to say? You win. You can make me come. You can toy with my body." Her tone is defiant, but her hand stays clasped around my straining cock.

"You can move your hand if you want," I offer, instead of answering her. My lips threaten to turn up at the sides into a mocking smirk.

This has turned into a little test of wills between us, one we both know she will lose. She'll say she doesn't want to, and I'll have to prove, yet again, exactly how much I can twist her into craving me. In an instant, she will become the prey and I the predator.

Instead of letting another argument unfold between us, I flick the first button on my pants loose without looking at her. When she drops her hand back to her naked lap, it's hesitant, like she is not sure what to do or how to act right now.

Her entire body stiffens, and I finally allow myself to look at her face, and when I do, I find her cheeks crimson. "Don't act so shy now. You felt my cock before."

Her gulp is almost audible, and it *almost* makes me laugh. Yet another thing she'll pretend she doesn't want while she writhes for it. "Come here, princess."

At first, she resists. I finish unbuttoning my pants and let them hang open. Her curious eyes are locked on my zipper, and I know she is waiting for a glimpse. Once I peel open my fly and drag out my cock, she gasps, and I catch her innocent gaze widening. When I lock eyes with her again, she pretends to have not reacted at all, and I snicker.

"I see everything, every want, desire, and need." I lick my lips. "Don't worry. I won't tell anyone how much you like the look of me."

"You're delusional." She scoots forward on the bed, letting her legs hang over the side while I take a step toward her.

"I'm too tall to make this comfortable. Come here." I gently help her off the bed onto the floor, using her bicep to guide and place her.

It takes her a moment, but then she realizes what I have in mind. Her eyes study me, and I let her get used to the idea. Let her imagine what is about to happen in her head. I hope she doesn't think just because she is inexperienced, I'm going to be gentle.

"Touch me," I grit, my patience wearing thin.

"No." She shakes her head.

"It wasn't a question. I'm telling you to do it, and you will obey. Unless you want to be back downstairs in the cell? I'm sure my brother would appreciate having you unprotected."

I can practically hear her molars grinding together and see the daggers shooting from her eyes. She is furious, but self-preservation wins.

Her temper is only making me harder. The need to sink into her body growing stronger with every thundering beat of my heart. I can't have her cunt, but I can have her mouth. At least this way, I can feel her around me and still get the full price for her.

Hesitantly, she reaches up to wrap her hands around my cock. She's pushed up onto her knees now, her ankles folded underneath her to give her more leverage.

Her first touch is hesitant. She drags her dainty hand from the base of my shaft to the head and back again. I like how she doesn't keep checking in with me as she does it. How every movement seems enrapt and focused solely on what she thinks feels good to her or to me. I don't fucking know. All I know is I don't want her to stop.

I bite back the order for her to taste me as long as I can. "Jerk me off like you mean it."

She looks up at me through thick lashes. "I don't know what I'm doing."

I cup her hands tighter against my skin and squeeze. "You've never touched a cock before?"

A pretty pink flush works its way over the tops of her bare tits and face. "Once, but it was in his pants the entire time. He came before we could do much."

Shame fills her voice as she speaks, almost as if the fucking boy had made her feel his lack of control had somehow been her fault. I can't explain the energy that consumes me in that second to comfort her. Even as the idea of her with her hand on another man's dick enrages me in another way. A way I can't quite focus on now.

"Suck me. I want your lips wrapped around my cock."

She blinks as if coming out of a daze and whispers, "What?"

I lift her chin so I can look down at her. Her lush pink lips only inches from the tiny drops of pre-cum already leaking out of me. "If you put your mouth on me. I want to feel you fight me as you take me into your body. Feel your anger bleed out of you and be replaced with something else entirely."

Her eyelids shutter for a moment as she contemplates my words. I continue, though, wanting more of that fire in her eyes before I take her. "Besides, I made you come, *hard*, if I'm any judge, and now you owe me a thank you, and I believe your mouth will do nicely."

Oh, yes. Color splashes across her cheeks as she grips me tighter. I bite back a groan before it can escape.

"You enjoy fighting me, *stellina*. Every second closer to the submission, you know I'll take, only turns you on more. Lick it... but I promise, if you bite me, you will regret it immediately," I grit through my teeth.

She's panting through her nose, her nostrils flaring wide as she glares up the line of my body. But her fingers still flex around my aching cock, and she keeps tracing her lips with her tongue, obviously contemplating her next move.

After some sort of internal struggle, she presses up onto her knees to get the right angle and gently—so fucking gently—touches the tip of her tongue to the head of my cock. I don't bother fighting the groan this time, letting it roll through me.

Her eyes go wide with shock, and she leans in carefully, taking only the crown between her lips and clamping down softly. I peer down at her, and dammit to all hell, she looks so fucking perfect with my cock in her mouth. The only thing that would look better is watching my cum dribble out of her cunt. I can't think about that, though, not right now, and probably not ever. She isn't mine to keep, touch, or play with.

"Fucking harder." The icy edge to my voice makes her jump. "I'm not one of your little bitch boyfriends who will come from the first brush of a woman's mouth, and believe me, you were playing with boys before. It's time for you to learn what a man will do for you."

She pulls away and glares. "Maybe I will. Once I'm finished with you."

I take her chin in my hand and squeeze it tight. It's more about asserting my dominance than fighting her mouthy rant. "Suck my cock before I simply fuck your face. Which I'll do anyway. I'm only giving you a few minutes to get used to me first. Don't test my generosity."

Defiance and fury reach a new high, and I revel in her misery as I shove her face away. Once she resettles between my feet, she takes hold of me again with more force than before, and I grab the back of her head and take her soft hair into my fist and pull her toward me.

She drapes her mouth over me again and slides her tongue along the underside of my shaft as she presses forward.

I hiss out a breath. "Yes."

With my control stretching taut on thin threads, I keep hold of her head and let her express her frustration with her mouth. Despite my warning, she scrapes her teeth against the crown of my cock gently, making stars shoot from behind my eyes.

"Watch your fucking teeth, or I'll pull them out one by one," I warn. "Use both hands."

She immediately clamps both of her hands onto the base of my cock and tries to find a rhythm between them. Her inexperience makes it all the better for her enthusiasm, despite the fight in her eyes.

"Meet your mouth with your hands, and you'll find the rhythm you're looking for," I offer.

She rounds her gaze up to glare at me but follows my instruction and catches the pattern she chased unsuccessfully before.

I'm fighting the urge to shove deeper, harder, faster, to use her mouth and throat to come. My knees are shaking with the effort to keep myself in check and standing up straight. It won't last long, but I can give her these few minutes.

I tighten my grip on her hair and study her from this angle. The soft slope of her nose leads down to her plush lips. There's even the slightest dusting of freckles across the top of her cheekbones I hadn't noticed before. It's something she's always hid under makeup when in public. Her eyebrows are strong over her big eyes. Never overdone like the girls Soo picks up and brings home occasionally.

But I love the silky weight of her hair in my hands the most. I flex my fingers through it and take another fistful. She whimpers against me, and I realize I've shoved deeper into her mouth in my reverie. And fuck, it feels good.

I grip her hair tighter and pull her deeper onto me, so much so that she has to release her hands. At first, she gags, and I let her pull away just enough to get her bearings back.

"Open your throat," I say, my voice deep and grating. "I'm going to fuck your face." Her eyes reflect a sliver of fear, and I almost feel bad for what I'm about to do. "Be a good girl and take my cock how I give it to you."

Her eyes are shooting daggers at me, but she knows this is going to happen whether or not she likes it. Almost imperceptibly, she gives a little nod, even with her lips spread so obscenely.

"Good girl," I whisper. "Put your hands on your thighs."

She doesn't respond for a moment, then slides her hands down to her thighs, pulling her torso better in line with my legs. Fuck, when she surrenders, she does it almost as beautifully as when she fights.

I surge my hips forward, and the motion is hard and fast. As the mushroom head of my cock hits the back of her throat, her hands go up to shove against my thighs. She clamps around me like a vice, and I don't even bother stopping the groan which emits from deep within my chest. "Fuck, that's good."

Again, I retreat and shove forward, taking it slow to begin. I look down at her through a lustful haze and see tears leaking out of the corner of her eyes and down the apples of her cheeks. Her fists are clamped around my legs so tightly I can feel her fingernails digging into me with each punishing stroke I take into her mouth.

"You want this as much as I do," I tell her and surge forward again. Each entry and retreat into her hot wet mouth is a slice of heaven. A tiny bit of her, that's all mine. "You want to be my toy, my little whore. You want me to use you, even if you are not ready to admit it yet."

With my patience shredded, I set a brutal pace, surging into her so hard and fast my balls slap against her chin and neck. She doesn't seem to notice, or maybe she does, but knows there is nothing she can do. Her eyes squeeze shut as she lets me use her mouth again and again.

I wish I'd given her some makeup. So I could watch mascara and eyeliner track over her cheeks. Evidence of her submission after I shoot my cum down her throat.

She wiggles between my feet and readjusts her hands on my legs, squirming as I use her hair and the back of her neck as an anchor. My balls draw up against my body, and I pump into her wet, warm mouth faster. I'm on the cusp of my release. My toes curl in my shoes, and my muscles tighten before a lightning bolt of pleasure zaps through me.

"Take my cum. Be a good slut and swallow it all."

I growl as I explode, her throat constricting, milking the semen right out of my fucking balls. She obeys, her little throat bobbing as she swallows around the thick head of my cock. A loud groan of approval escapes my lips, and I ignore her hot gaze on me. Once the aftershocks of my orgasm recede, I carefully release my hold on her head, and she pulls her mouth away. The skin around her mouth is flushed red, her cheeks are stained with tears, and yet, I've never seen a more beautiful woman.

I carefully tuck myself back into my pants and crouch down, so I can look her in the eyes from where she is sprawled out on the floor.

"You keep fighting me with every word you throw my way. But next time, remember your body knows exactly what you want and what only I can give you if you obey so sweetly."

I reach out and pluck one of her puckered nipples. A shocked gasp fills the air, and she slaps my hand away.

All I can do is smirk. "See, you liked that, and yet, you push back against me. Even knowing I can make it feel so good for you."

She looks away almost shyly and swallows again, clearing her, no doubt, raw throat. "It's because you take without asking. You just take what you want, so I'm forced to give in even if I don't want to."

I study her, the vehemence in her ravaged voice. I knew what her body wanted even if her brain didn't. She was too caught up in the hate she had for me to admit it.

"How is it taking when I can so clearly see you want to give it to me? The only thing telling me no," I trace my thumb down her swollen bottom lip, my cock hardening again at the reminder of what we've just done, "is your mouth."

She throws her chin up, a mask of defiance in place now, and it only makes me smile. Every inch of her is screaming for me to throw her across the bed and shove myself inside her so deeply that she won't know where I end, and she starts. To take and fuck her into complete submission. It would be easy, too easy, and yet, a voice in the back of my head holds me back. She's a temptation I cannot afford, a casualty of war. My fight might be with her father, but in the end, hurting her will be the same as hurting him.

When my own body starts responding again, I stand and grab my belt from the bed to avoid temptation.

Little Celia hasn't figured it out yet, but even her pleasure belongs to me. Until I let her go, I'll take it every chance I can get.

"So that's it? You use me and leave?" she whispers.

Who does she think she is?

"Yes, that's exactly how it is." I sneer. "Besides, you came harder than you ever have in your life, guaranteed. Don't act like I took something from you that you weren't prepared to give me."

"I don't want you. I don't want to be trapped here." She stares down at the sheets, a visible shiver rippling through her. "You don't understand. My father doesn't care about me. Why do you think he was marrying me off? If you're trying to hurt him, taking me won't do that. Selling me won't bother him."

It's funny she thinks I care. That she thinks anything she says to me will change the outcome of what's going to happen. She's taken a perfect evening and destroyed it.

"It's not about bothering him or him being hurt about losing you. It's about control. It's about taking something that's his and crushing it in my fist. It's about watching him squirm and putting a bullet between his eyes."

I turn and walk out of the room, slamming the door shut and flicking the lock into place before I do something stupid, something that I won't be able to come back from.

She doesn't understand that this runs deeper than anything she could ever imagine. This isn't just revenge, it's blood for blood, and I'm going to make certain when our time together ends, she sees that.

15

CELIA

*E*ven hours later, I can still taste him on my lips. Not just the cum, which he unceremoniously dumped down my throat, but *him*. The slightly spicy but clean taste of him. Worst of all is that I want more, even after what he did to me, how he used me, and the things he said afterward. I still want more of him, and I don't know how to stop the want.

All night, I laid awake in bed thinking about him. About the way he touched me and how I reacted. I didn't understand how he could degrade me and make me come at the same time?

I sit at the countertop in the kitchen, shuffling eggs around the plate that Sarah shoved my way the second I walked in. They taste fine, but I'm not ready to let go of everything else yet. Even if it's just in my mind since I brushed my teeth last night.

"Salt," someone asks.

I blink and realize Sarah is staring at me. I also realize she's noticed I'm shoving my eggs around my plate. She slides the salt and pepper shakers across the granite countertop to me. "You're distracted this morning."

My mouth pops open, and I feel like I've been caught with my hand in the cookie jar. "I'm just tired. Plus, according to his majesty, it's almost time for me to leave."

Sarah gives me a sort of hum noise. Either she knows I'm leaving soon, or she doubts I'm leaving soon, and I can't be certain which. I study her for another moment and wonder how she fits into this world. She doesn't look like she belongs with a bunch of criminal masterminds. How much blood had she cleaned up while Nicolo rose to his power?

Considering she supplies my food, I decide not to ask such a pointed question. I focus on my plate again and eat as much as I can. I've gotten into a rhythm here in the house, but Nicolo intends to ship me off again soon. I don't know if my meals in the future will be more regular.

A hard lump builds in my throat, and I shove my plate back across the counter toward Sarah's turned back. It's not the idea of leaving here that worries me, but who I'm leaving with and what they will do with me. My captor hasn't exactly been gentle, but neither has he truly hurt me because if he did, he wouldn't be able to sell me.

When Sarah turns away from the sink and back to me, I try not to fidget under her reproving look.

She doesn't comment on the food, though, and points toward the hall. "You're on firewood duty today. There are some gloves and a stack of wood in the foyer. Just put a few in each room that needs it."

The last time she sent me wandering through the house, things didn't go well. First with Lucas, and then with Nicolo afterward. But I didn't dare to argue. Sarah doesn't budge on the jobs she gives me.

I head down the hall toward the foyer. It's beautiful in dark hardwood and blackened stainless steel. Another touch of elegance Nicolo presents in his surroundings, but not his person.

I frown at the enormous pile of wood and then at the guards near the door. It's not as if I have a choice. I slip on the gloves and make a quick stack of firewood in my arms. I decide to take the furthest room first and work backward toward the foyer. Which will put me in Nicolo's office. The one he's likely occupying right now.

Before I force myself to rethink my plan, I head up the stairs and down the long hallway, past my room and toward his office. The door is open as I approach.

Nicolo sits behind his desk, scribbling in his ledger. The moment I enter, his eyes lock onto me, and I can feel the weight of his gaze as I cross the room to a small box where a few pieces of wood sit.

When I glance up again, he's back focusing on his work. I blink and settle the pile of wood on the floor in front of the fireplace, strip off my gloves, and wait for him to say something. Long minutes pass as I watch him, but he doesn't look up at me again or so much as twitch in my direction.

It's not as if I expect a thank you note for taking his cock down my throat last night, but a little acknowledgment would be nice. I huff out a breath and force myself to smile, even if it probably doesn't meet my eyes. "Good morning."

He doesn't even pause in his writing at the sound of my voice. An ache roots itself in the center of my sternum. I wouldn't call it pain exactly, but it's not comfortable. I feel dismissed, like a toy that's been played with and tossed to the side.

"You're not going to speak to me?" I ask as I reach down and stack a piece of wood in the box. "After everything that happened last night, you could at least acknowledge me." I don't bother to hide my anger toward him.

Again, he doesn't respond. I sigh and toss another piece into the box so it thumps around inside loudly. But the noise doesn't seem to inspire a response. I decide to continue talking as if he has responded to me. If anything, he'll get annoyed with me.

"I'm fine. Thank you for asking. I didn't sleep well, but my face is a tad sore, as is my neck because some asshole had to get his jollies off with my mouth." No way in hell I'm letting him know how much I enjoyed it. The sheer power of being on my knees for him, watching as he unraveled all that tight control he keeps bottled up.

"Breakfast was great, and Sarah—as always—gave me an excellent chore to do today, which I assume is at your instruction. Thanks for that. Carting firewood around, half-naked, is super fun in case you were wondering."

I grab the other piece of wood and wait to throw this one in the box while I stare at him. Hoping he'll at least say something. When he doesn't, I huff loudly.

This time, he slams his pen on the desk and glares at me over the ledger. "Things here haven't changed," he says, his voice deep and menacing.

I swallow a tingle that starts in my fingertips and races through me.

"Just because I used your body last night does not make us friends. Why would I care how you are today? You're a pretty distraction that will soon be out of my hair once I sell you. Last night, I was testing the merchandise." He drops his chin to resume his work.

I blink, the fear receding in an ebb of something darker, something stronger. "Testing the merchandise?" I intone, tasting the words on the edge of my anger. "You made me come."

"Only to prove a point. You think I care if you come? I don't give a—"

I clutch the last block of firewood in my hand and launch it over the desk at him.

With his fast reflexes born from survival, he dodges the wood, which thumps to the ground behind him. But that little expression of the boiling rage inside me does nothing to quench it. I march across the room and slap him so hard, pain stings through my hand and up into my elbow.

Some of my anger shifts back into fear, and I take one tentative step away from him. "You are a fucking bastard. I'm not some animal to be locked up and sold for profit. I'm a human being, something I thought was getting through your dense skull."

His eyes spark before he grins down at me. "*Stellina*, you mean nothing more to me than a piece of ass to use before you make me a lot of money. That's it. I've never pretended otherwise. If you have, you do whatever you need to do to get through this, but—" He stands and towers over me.

I take one more step back, but he reaches out and snatches me toward him by my neck, squeezing tight with his fingers. "If you ever hit me again, it will be the last thing you do. Auction or not, I will end you."

He drags me into him and then turns me to face the desk. I can't do anything but flail, trying to find something to grab onto, something to help me escape. When he shoves me over the top of the desk and presses into my ass, fear and desire intertwine again, and I fight back, reaching out to scratch, kick, and hit anything to get him off me.

But he doesn't budge, not even when my fingers claw into the arm that he brings around to trap me underneath him. His torso is pressed down into my back, and my breasts hurt from the counterpoint from his desk below.

"Let's get a few things straight here, princess. Sex means nothing to me. Sometimes I use it to clear my head. That's what happened last night. It also made a point, showing you that you aren't the frigid bitch you try to play in front of others." He grinds his hard cock against me, shoving the air out of my lungs in a huff. My brain is cloudy with fear and the memories of last night.

"The next thing you need to learn is how to keep yourself alive because right now, you're doing a shitty job of it. Do you know what Soo would have done if he'd walked in when you threw that wood? Did you consider what would happen if you actually hit me? Of course, not. You act on impulse and not logic. A fucking fatal flaw in most pampered princesses. No one taught you how to keep your mouth shut and your head down to survive." He growls the last word into my ear and then traps my hands above my head in one of his.

"A word of advice on that front. Don't attack the man who has the power to break you. Did you even think about the fact that I'm the one who will choose who you get sold to?" He uses his other hand to curve down the side of my breasts and then hip to delve under my shirt. When he cups my pussy, I squirm against him, trying to break free of his hold.

He continues whispering like a lover in my ear. "I could pick someone I know will be so very gentle with you. Or I can pick someone who I know will delight in torturing you until there's nothing left of the stupid fucking princess he purchased."

I shiver under him, and it has nothing to do with his possessive hand over my core and everything to do with the devil of a man threatening me like he means it.

He does everything like he means it.

When he grinds his dick into me, I stop struggling and remain still, hoping not to excite him further. All I need is for him to teach me yet another lesson. "I told you last night, I love it when you fight. But there's a difference between fighting for your life and fighting for your plea- sure. This is the difference. Do you see it now?"

I fold my lips together and nod as much as I can, with my cheek pinned between him and his desk blotter. How could I have ever thought things had changed between us? It wasn't as if I expected him to be a different person, but maybe... I thought by giving in last night, I'd earn a measure of respect.

No doubt he'd mock me for my weakness and find a way to use it against me if I ever confessed such a thing. Arching into me, I can feel how much he enjoys it by the way his body shakes around me. His furious breath in my ear, the vice grip he's got on my wrists. The next time he slowly slides his pant-covered dick along my panty-covered ass, I push back into him. He lets out a hiss against my earlobe. "Are we done fighting, *stellina*? You got a little taste of my cock last night, and now you want more?"

I want to shove the fountain pen a few feet away from me into his eyeball, but I keep that to myself too. "I'll behave," I say instead.

"Mmm..." He arches again, and I whimper. Ashamed of the noise, I clamp my mouth shut.

So fast that it takes a moment to register, he flips me over, bringing us face to face. His hips press into me much more intimately now, and I have to fight to keep myself from wrapping my legs around his hips to bring him closer.

"A moment more of your time, and I'll let you get back to your chores," he says, glancing down between us at my puckered nipples against the fabric of his shirt.

Then I hear a sound I don't recognize, a small snick. When he brings a shiny blade to the side of my cheek, I flinch away from him.

"Ah ah ah, little one. Careful, one touch, and this will cut your pretty skin so easily." He traces the point down my scar, slow and steady, until he reaches my lips.

The fire in my veins turns to ice. Terror washes away the lust in a crystal-clear fog. "You won't kill me."

He continues tracing the contours of my face with his knife. The sharp edge pierces my skin the tiniest bit, and one drop of blood slides down the side of my cheek. He lifts the knife and surveys his work. It's barely a paper cut, but he seems satisfied by it.

His eyes lock on mine, and I try to wiggle away. "I don't have to kill you to keep you in line. Remember that. Pain is a powerful motivator for anyone, especially a princess who has never had a real taste of it."

He leans in, so he's almost touching my mouth with his. If I lift up an inch, I'd be tracing the words with my own lips as he says them. "If you want me to be the one to show you the true depth of pain, then keep acting like a spoiled brat. Otherwise, do your chores, follow my orders, and you'll be just fine."

I don't know what to say so he won't hurt me, nor do I know what to say to get him off me, so I remain silent this time. All the fight in me is tempered for the moment. It isn't as if he'd make it a fair fight, anyway.

"I think we understand each other," he finally says and shoves away from me.

Sucking a full breath into my lungs, I try to calm my erratic heartbeat. A chill washes over me at his absence. When I look up, he's already walking out the door, buttoning his suit jacket like he didn't just threaten me.

"Clean up this mess," he calls back.

With my face flushed, tears trailing down my cheeks, stinging along the slight cut, I climb off the desk. At first, my legs wobble until I stand tall and get my bearings again. I want to rush back into my room, to hide there for the rest of the day, but I'm stronger than that. I won't let him push me into a corner.

Quickly, I clean up the mess on the floor, even scooping up the tiny bits of wood near the stack shed when I'd sat it on the floor originally. Once everything looks immaculate again, I glance over at his desk.

On the edge, it's sharp point gleaming in the morning sunlight, is the fountain pen he abandoned when he got angry. I quickly snatch it up, cap the end, and shove it into one of the gloves I'd been using to handle the firewood.

Before I can betray myself, I rush out of the room and hide it between the mattress of my bed and the bed frame. It's not a great weapon, but it's something. And even if the last thing I do is drive it into Nicolo's eyes, I'd die happy.

16

NIC

*T*he sound of Beethoven blasting at a ridiculous volume tells me exactly where Soo is hiding out. He's been conspicuously absent for the last couple of days, and it grates on my ever-unraveling patience that I have to hunt him down to work out plans.

As my biggest warehouse, and where most of Lucas's trade goods are kept, it's a place Soo frequents. His studio apartment is set up in the back of the warehouse, near the loading dock that leads out to the river. He enjoys seeing the water through his windows at night.

Unlike most warehouses, this one is lined in concrete and steel with rich rough cedar lining the floors and some walls used to separate holding areas. It makes the entire building smell like a forest, and the entire place echoes the moment anyone so much as breathes inside it.

I march across the planks to Soo's little holding. He's already lowering the volume on Symphony Number Five in C Minor as I approach.

"Rough Day?" I ask, stepping into his sanctum.

He's decorated his little place in maroons and golds. There's a solid couch in one corner, where he usually sleeps. More wood and stainless steel make up a small kitchen to the side. There's a bathroom in the back with a similar color palette. But near the door, against a glass wall showing the entire warehouse, is a bank of computers Soo wields effortlessly to conduct his business. And mine.

He shuffles over and hands me a bottle of water. "The usual. Seen Lucas?"

I shrug, not wanting to admit to yet another argument between us, resulting in Lucas running off to sulk. Or dismember someone. I guess we'll find out soon enough. "I'm sure he's around here somewhere. I'll send him to come find you when he shows his face at the house again."

Soo nods and hops up onto his counter. His bare feet dangle over the edge. His gray sweats and white T-shirt tell me he is about to go to bed, and I've interrupted. Not the first time, and it won't be the last. He's grown accustomed to my strange hours by now.

"We need to discuss plans," I say. "Some things have changed since our little run-in with the Gardello kid."

Soo nods and crosses his arms over his chest. There's a faraway look in his eyes, and I let him have a moment to think. It usually pays off.

"You still want to go through with this plan? Once the five catch wind of your auction and the Ricci girl is actually sold, things are going to hit the fan pretty quickly."

I skirt the edge of his workstation and plop into the rolling chair in front of it. "Of course, I want to continue with the plan. Why the fuck would I bother with a plan if I didn't intend to see it through?"

"That's not what I mean, and you know it. Shit changes and plans adapt. We both know that fact well."

I run my hands through my hair and focus on dulling the sharp edge of my anger that rose to the surface at his chiding tone. "The goal has never changed. This is war, and I want Ricci face down in a puddle of his own blood before I'm through with them all. I don't care about the other fuckers as much as I do him. Got it?"

Soo holds his hands up in surrender, his water bottle tucked tight into one. "I'm not saying you don't get revenge for your family. All I'm asking is if you still want to carry out your plan the way we have been heading? As of right now, we might have to move things anyway, if only to remove suspicion from you until you pull off this auction. There are already rumors going around about Celia and the Gardello heir. Some of his brothers are saying he wouldn't have run off with her. We were counting on that story until we were ready for our big reveal."

I give him a non-committal noise and roll myself forward to brace my elbows on my knees. "Give me a few hours, I'll think of something on that to cover our asses."

"He's not my only concern," Soo adds.

I glance up at him and the wary look on his face. "Oh, come on. What the fuck else? Did I come over here to talk plans, or you playing therapist now?"

Soo huffs and sits his water bottle down. His way of giving both of us a minute to think about our next words. "Again, that's not what I mean. But, I have noticed you've been spending some alone time with the girl. You're growing attached."

I can't sit here and listen to him accuse me of... what? "Are you asking me a question or making an observation? What?"

"Maybe I'm drawing your attention to a problem which needs correcting before you carry on with your business."

I shove out of the chair, cross his kitchen to the bar, and pour myself a glass of amber liquid, not even looking at the labels. Sufficiently fortified, I turn back to my friend. My best friend, I remind myself. "There's nothing for you to worry about. Everything will continue as planned. The girl will get sold at auction in a couple of days and be the catalyst to bring down the rest of those old bastards."

Soo nods, but I'm looking at the back of his head, so I can't see if he believes me or not. It doesn't matter. He'll do what I say until I tell him otherwise. He's always been reliable in that regard, unlike my wayward brother, Lucas, who looks at my plans and somehow interprets them to mean something completely different from what I lay out.

"Did Lucas get the supplies to draw in our special guests?" I ask as I come back around to take my seat again.

Both of us relax at the new subject. "Yeah." He nods toward the warehouse. "It's all stacked in the back. Did you have a plan for how you want the auction laid out?"

I swig back a sip of the whiskey and consider his question. I've planned the actual auction thoroughly. But when I get to the part where all those men are staring at her, touching her, something in me boils over in a rage. If I can keep them from touching her, I can handle it, but my carefully forged control can't handle someone else touching something that belongs to me: the girl, my guns, anything. I'd feel the same no matter what merchandise I'm offering.

"Yeah, we'll start at midnight. She'll be blindfolded and in a dress. No one touches her but me until the auction is over and they remit payment. I don't want any of those old fucks getting ideas about things until they've paid for the right."

Soo nods. "And afterward?"

I smile. The afterward is the part I'm looking forward to. "We clean the house and burn it down. They'll come hunting, but they won't even realize we've snuck in their back doors and are waiting for them when they come home. I can't wait to show that bastard Ricci pictures of his little princess all trussed up and ready for sale. And then the pictures of his friends and business partners, the ones doing the bidding for the privilege of taking her."

Soo leans back on his hands on the counter. "Now you sound like yourself. Once they rip each other apart, we'll swoop in and clean them out before you can finish things off. I already have my contacts in the police on standby, ready for the eventual body count, or..." his mouth lifts in a grin, "the missing persons reports."

"And now you sound like yourself," I concede. No one can hide a body like Soo can.

The dust of the tension settles between us, and I toss back the rest of the liquor and set the glass by his keyboard. Immediately, he hops off the counter, snaps it up, and takes it to the sink.

Under my glare, he settles on the counter again. "What? It's sensitive equipment."

Even though I don't want to talk about it, I level him a look and nod a few times. "I'll admit, killing the Gardello kid probably fucked our plans up a bit. I know we were counting on him running around blowing money a little. Drawing out the Romeo and Juliet angle between the two of them so their families would start making moves sooner. Are they doing anything yet? Have your spies picked up anything?"

He shrugs. "No, they've been quiet. I think we seriously underestimated the indifference they have for their offspring. Like I said, the only ones causing a stir are the Gardello brothers. And I honestly think they were hoping to get a cut of whatever money was coming his way after he married Celia."

I consider this news. "So, it's about the money, not the man himself? Can we throw some money at them another way? Throw them some winnings at one of our casinos. I know they frequent The Rainbow Pearl more than the others at the edge of town."

Needing to stretch my legs to think, I stand and pace a circle around his kitchen. "If we can get the brothers out of the picture without killing them outright, then it will give us a little more time to put things in place. After that, it won't matter anyway because they'll be tearing each other's throats out to save their own skins." Soo remains quiet while I pace, since I'm talking to myself more than him right now. "Do it that way, then. The oldest brother is the one who would have wanted some of the cut. Let him win a little and see if that gets him off his questions." I halt and swivel back to face my friend. "Or…"

"Or?" he prompts.

I quickly unhook my cufflinks, stuff them in my pocket, and roll my sleeves up.

Soo raises his eyebrow in a silent question.

"What if we scrap the plan entirely and go at them from a different angle?" I say.

"We've been working on this one for a long time. Did you have something else in mind?" His faith is unwavering, and I clap him on the shoulder. A show of gratitude, the only reassurance I can provide him.

"It's not about the girl. In case you're thinking of going down that road again. But what if we don't target the heads directly? We head straight for their children just like we have with Ricci."

Soo hops off his seat now and heads to his computer. In seconds he's got screens of security cameras up and others containing spreadsheets and notes. "Marino has three children. Greco has two—twins. Ricci, we have covered. Gardello has five…" he smirks, "four now. And Bianci just has himself and therefore no one to target to get to." He spins to face me in the chair. "What are you thinking?

I continue my pace across the floor, letting the data flow in and assimilate. "Marino is an easy target. His daughter is too well protected. He actually cares about her safety, unlike Ricci. We should target his oldest son: Dominic. He's being groomed to take over. The Grecos are a little different. The twins run the family together, and the rumors are…" I break off, trying to think of the word. "Disturbing. From what I've heard, the twins crippled their own father and run the family together, together."

Soo nods. "That's what I've heard too."

I shake my head as we don't have time to deal with that clusterfuck. "Gardello we can still hit with the casinos, but what if we do it the other way? Force them to shell out their money instead of winning. It might keep them all occupied for a while. Every brother has a substantial debt racked up. Bianci is the wild card. I need more time to think about how he plays into things. Technically, my fight was with his father. He rarely involves himself with the family businesses anymore."

Typing in a furious stream, Soo speaks up. "I have something to help with that."

I pause and face him. When I have a plan, he always has what I need to wrap things up in a tight little bow. "What's that?"

His lips curl up into a grin, and he jabs his finger at one monitor. A woman in a slinky red dress sitting on one of the Gardello brothers' laps is displayed on the screen. "This is one of my spies on the casino floor. One of the paid girls. She gets a little extra on the side when she picks up anything I might want to know about. The other night she was working with Dominic Marino, and she caught him mentioning a meeting with one of his brothers. It looks like the families are about to have a reunion."

I curl my hands up and drop my head. "And why didn't you lead with this little tidbit?"

"Probably because it wasn't relevant until you threw years of careful planning out the window to start over?"

And that's where my side of things comes in. Soo covers minor details, whereas I can see the bigger picture much better than he can. "It was relevant. It doesn't matter what the plan is. The families meeting for the first time in over twenty years is a big fucking deal. And it's the first meeting without the fallen Costa family."

Soo observes me. I see him studying my every twitch, looking for clues as to his next move based on mine. "What does it mean? Where I come from, meetings of the families happen all the time."

I lean against the counter and cross my arms to tuck my hands into my armpits. "It means things are about to change. But it also means we need to be in that room. Did your spy have information on when this meeting was happening?"

Soo shakes his head. "I can put her on it. She's trustworthy. Shove her into the fray with all our targets and see what other information she can get."

I nod and let out a long sigh, an ache blooming in my temples. "We need to know when. It'll happen at Ricci's since he's the head of the five. Put a watch on his house and his wife. She'll be preparing a menu. You might get information out of a caterer or staff. That woman does nothing herself."

"There's one thing that you need to decide next," Soo says, his attention back on his keyboard and the workstation.

I watch as he pulls up his dossier on the families, pictures included. My prey all lined up in a digital row. If only life made things so orderly.

"We need to decide if we take them out one by one or pull a mass strike on all the bastards at once," I say and Soo nods. "The reunion meeting is the perfect chance to do it, but it will also be risky with the amount of security each family will have in place both before and during the event."

"Not we, though. You need to decide. This vengeance belongs to you and Lucas. Maybe it's time you bring your brother in and let him make some of these choices with you. The blood of these enemies belongs to him as well."

It's always been my job to protect my brother. I've been protecting him from himself for so long I don't know how to stop. But Soo is right.

He belongs at my side when we kill these fuckers, if not pulling the trigger himself.

I shove away from the counter and head for the door. "Thanks for the drink. Set a meeting with your spy. I'll talk to my brother."

The time for vengeance is coming, and if anyone deserves to put a bullet in someone's head, it's Luca.

17

CELIA

I can't decide which chore I hate most, sheet changing, dusting, or firewood duty. All of them pretty much suck, especially when the staff sit around on their asses while I do their jobs. They must be happy to have the break while I'm here. I wonder how many of them know I'll be gone soon enough. Furthermore, the details to which I'll be removed from Nicolo's home. Doubtful, at least the extent of the details.

Sarah hands me a dusting cloth today and sends me back out into the dust-free house like a child being shooed away from her mother's legs. I dust everything I can find and skip lunch to duck into my room. It's not as if anyone is going to drag me out and force me to do anything. They all seem indifferent until I act up. Then Nicolo steps in to take charge, sets me in my place again, and stalks off in a huff.

My cheek still stings when I wash my face, but the tiny pink dot is barely visible now. I still can't believe he actually cut me. No, I can believe it. I just expected him to fuck me while he did it like the true animal he is.

I throw the dusting rag on my bed, only to watch it snag on the edge of a big black decorative box. Oh. Oh no, not again.

Praying, even though I'm not stupid enough to have genuine hope, I flip back the lid on the box and find a silk dress, which won't cover anything at all. Underneath is a black thong, a white paper bag of makeup, and a pair of black strappy high heels. The man has a fetish for ridiculous shoes that hurt my feet. Hasn't he ever heard of sensible flats?

I scowl at the ensemble and shove the box toward the middle of the bed, so I can sit on the edge. A white sheet of paper sits on the bottom of the box, and I fish it out to scan the page.

The bastard has detailed exactly how he wants me to wear my hair and makeup. His handwriting is neat, in thick block lettering made in black ink. I crumple the note up and toss it across the room just to make myself feel better. It doesn't work, of course. Especially since the last line of the letter specifically instructs me to put my scar on display.

If I were braver, and if my cheek didn't currently sting from his reaction to my last outburst, I'd defy him. Show up in the shirt he seems to like to keep me confined to wearing. He deserves it for running around dressing me up whenever he feels like it.

He didn't list what time I have to be ready, and I'm worried if I get ready now, I'll be sitting here in those painful shoes for hours. But, if I don't, and he shows up to find me unprepared, he'll be angry.

I decide to wait until before dinner to get ready. Not to mention, once I slip into that dress, I'll be uncomfortable as hell.

The day speeds by, and I check the clock several times. His demands and outfit sit behind me on the bed, mocking me for my fear and obedience.

Once the time comes, I go into the bathroom and get ready, per his demands. I carefully apply the makeup he provided. All products I used myself, which leads me to believe he must have someone working inside my home. *Home...* something that seems so far away now.

After I finish my makeup, I pin my hair away from my face, so it falls straight and long, coming to rest at the top of my ass.

I groan as I look in the mirror. The dress hugs every inch of my body like a glove. I look fucking naked and cheap in this dress. My hair is too heavy to wear up, so he has to be satisfied with this. I'll have a headache by the end of whatever it is he wants to do with me. Something I haven't allowed myself to consider until now. Why does he want me dressed up like this?

I quickly cross to the bed and dig out the fountain pen I stuffed under my mattress. Damn, there's nowhere in this outfit I can hide it. With an exasperated sigh, I shove it back in its hiding place.

As I'm slipping on the shoes, the door opens, and Nicolo steps inside. He's dressed in his usual black slacks, white shirt, shiny shoes, and an expensive watch. But tonight, he's styled his hair and put on a jacket. The effect is disturbing as he's gone from ruffian to businessman with the addition of a fucking blazer.

With the last strap of my shoe in place, he extends his hand to pull me to my feet. When I wobble, he steadies me, slipping his arm around my waist while pulling me tight to his chest.

"Where are we going?" I ask, focusing on something that isn't his wide chest against mine. Especially when his proximity inspires both arousal and fear.

He doesn't answer but leads me out the door and into the hallway. The guards are gone now, no one wanders the hall, and I don't see a soul until I spot the dark head of the driver in the town car he stuffs me into.

After he settles into place beside me, I shift in the seat to face him. "Really, where are we going? Is the auction tonight? Is this it?" Fear rakes its claws down my insides, igniting a wave of adrenaline.

He levels me with a look. But I can't just sit here and not try to get out of this. "Please, don't do this. I'll do anything. Don't sell me off. You could keep me instead. It would be equally vengeful for my father just knowing I'm gone."

This time he stares out the window, slumped into the seat, all arrogance and male ego. "No, we are not going to the auction. We're going to dinner."

My mouth falls open, and I snap it shut again, trying to sort through any hint in his words, any tricks. "You're taking me out to dinner?"

My statement earns another snort from him. "*We* are going to dinner. I never said I was taking you out to dinner. There's a difference."

I settle back into the seat, a little less worried now. Whatever he wants, I'll do. If being well behaved tonight might keep me off the auction block a little longer, I'll be a fish with wings, if that's what he wants me to be.

We drive for about ten minutes. When the car stops, the driver comes around and opens the car door for us. I scan the nondescript alley and realize we're in a populated area. The casino district maybe, by the lights and sounds.

It's only confirmed once we get inside, and I hear the faint clank of slot machines and the chatter of people off in the distance. Nicolo leads me into an intimately lit room with a round table in the center. On the white tablecloth, four plates are laid out, and two people sit in the surrounding chairs.

The man I recognize as Nicolo's friend, or second-in-command. I can't remember his name at the moment, not with my heart lodged in my throat while trying to figure out Nicolo's mood, his plan, and exactly what he wants from me in this situation.

Nicolo pulls out an empty chair next to the man. "Sit."

I take the seat, and he gently pushes me toward the table, unbuttons his jacket again, and throws himself into the last empty chair. I'm scared to look at the other two occupants of the table and keep my gaze on the plate in front of me.

The woman across from me is wearing expensive perfume and from the tickle in my nostrils, way too much of it. I catch glimpses of curly blonde hair and sleek, smooth bare shoulders from my periphery.

"Pet," Nicolo says.

I glance up and realize he's talking to me. "Serve the food. Start with the beef, end with the sauce."

He can't be serious? I answer the question in my head as soon as it arises. Of course, he's serious. Why am I still surprised at anything he does?

Taking exception at the word 'pet' right now won't help, so I swallow the little pride I have left and do as I'm told, serving food from a sideboard. "Do you—?"

He cuts me off with his hand and motions for me to fill my own plate as they all watch me move back and forth, without saying a word. That's the disconcerting part. I'd prefer them ignoring me than monitoring my every twitch.

When I finish serving, I resume my seat. The woman leans over and whispers, "Thank you." Her voice is deep for a woman.

I look up at her over the plates and blink a few times. She's stunning. Tall, tan, and thin. She wears a red dress that emphasizes her body. Her hair is curly, natural curls, piled on top of her head in a cloud of platinum blonde. I swallow and nod, unable to speak.

Why are we here? I ask myself. Out of the corner of my eye, I watch Nicolo study the woman. Something clenches tight in my chest at the way he's regarding her.

"Do you enjoy your work?" Nicolo asks her.

I assume she's met them both before since she doesn't ask their names.

She takes a sip of wine and smiles. "Of course, or else I wouldn't do it. I like the challenge of it. What about you, Mr. Diavolo? Do you enjoy your work?"

The sultry look in his eyes is layered with meaning, but I can't read it. I glance at the other man. He's also watching the pair of them. But he seems more focused on the woman. His brow furrows as he continues watching.

"I imagine you are challenged in multiple ways," Nicolo says. "And please, call me Nic."

I blink and turn to look at him again. *Call me Nic.* Call me Nic? He stuck his dick in my mouth, and he never once asked me to call him Nic. I can't describe the anger I'm feeling right now, just that I want to stab the man in the side of his head with my fork.

"Do you have something for me?" he asks her.

She giggles and drops her chin, a pink flush climbing her neck. She sets her glass on the table, stands, and plants herself on his lap like she belongs there. Her legs hang off one side, and her dress is so short I'm sure he can see her panties if he looks down... if she's even wearing any.

I freeze in my chair, unable to look at my food, let alone consider eating it. Oh, god. I'm fucking jealous. Of some random bimbo climbing onto the lap of my kidnapper.

Damn it. I shouldn't care. I should be happy he's focusing his attention on someone else.

No. He can't see this reaction. It would be yet another win, another way to torture me in his twisted games.

What the fuck is wrong with me?

She drapes her arm over his shoulder as she leans in seductively to whisper into his ear. His hand curls around her waist to hold her steady on his lap. Tears prick at the corner of my eyes, and I stand abruptly. I can't sit here and watch this for another second.

"Excuse me, is there a restroom I can use?" I ask the other man.

He points to the doorway across the room. "You can go in there. There's no exit, so don't try to escape. You don't want me to be the one who has to come after you." I meet his dark eyes and nod.

Nicolo doesn't even glance up as I wobble my way into the bathroom. I'm just glad I couldn't hear what she was saying to him. I imagine he'll take her back to the mansion and fuck her while I lie in bed next door, listening to the entire thing.

I hunch over the sink and focus on breathing. Obviously, I'd been under the assumption I meant more to him. Something he keeps disillusioning me of, and yet, my brain goes right back there. Maybe I am a spoiled princess if I can't get it through my head that he doesn't want me.

Matter of fact, I shouldn't fucking want him, not when he's planning my demise as we speak. The door opens, and I expect Nicolo to stalk in, demanding my presence. Maybe he needs dessert served over their naked bodies. It's not Nicolo who comes walking in though, it's the woman.

She's even taller up close and comes around to splash some water on her face over the second sink. "Are you okay, honey?"

I nod, staring at her through the mirror. "I'm fine."

When she faces me, she's not the same woman who'd draped herself over Nic's lap. "Are you sure?" she whispers.

I blink. "Are you offering to help me?"

She nods and waves her hand like duh. "Obviously."

I know I'm gaping at her, but I can't help it. She has to be joking. Either that or they sent her in here to test me.

"No, really. I'm fine. It's..." I trail off because I can't think of a convincing lie. "I'm fine. I don't need your help," I finish.

She gives me a nod and dries her hands. "Okay. If you change your mind, just let me know."

She sounds so sincere. Can she actually be serious, or is she simply a superb actress? Of course, even if she is being honest, what could she possibly do? If she did help me, Nic would probably kill her for it, and he would never stop looking for me if I disappeared now.

We head back out of the bathroom together.

Nic turns to me at the table. "What were you two ladies talking about?"

I shrug and give him a little smile. "The usual. Lipstick, hair products, destroying the patriarchy."

"Classics," the other man says from behind his wine glass.

Soo, that's his name. I study him closer. He's Korean as far as I can tell, and he looks good in the navy suit he is wearing.

Nic turns his attention back to the other woman. "As I was saying, Reya," he cups her hand and brings it to his lips, "please let me know if you can help me with my other problem."

She giggles one of those fluffy sounds men seem to think are all for them. He runs his lips across the top of her knuckles and then down her fingers. "Of course, I'll make it my special mission to attend to your request. For a solid tip, obviously."

I can't do anything but watch and burn inside. When I can tear my eyes away, I look at Soo, who's also watching the woman. There's an edge to his gaze. A bite. Not jealousy, but something else. Using my fork, I shuffle the food around my plate and try not to listen to the wet sounds his lips make, nor her breathy sighs in response.

"Celia, go to the door on the right and get us some more wine," Nic orders.

My feelings are wrapped into a tight ball, stuck tight in my belly, churning and twisting into a painful knot. I shove back from the table to do as he says.

The kitchen is empty as I enter. A few bottles of wine sit on the stainless-steel commercial countertops. All of them open and ready for pouring. I scoop one up and stare at it for a moment. Then take a long drag directly from the mouth of the bottle.

I can't stay here. Nor can I go back out there and watch him flirt with that woman. I turned down her offer to help me escape. There is still the strong possibility Nic planted her to test me. That this is all one of his sick and twisted games to break me.

Will he be fucking her when I walk back out there?

I shake the image out of my head and walk to the other kitchen door. It's propped open with a can of vegetables. A nagging at the back of my mind tells me that someone left it open on purpose.

This has to be a test... *but what if it's not?*

What if this is my only chance to get away? To finally be free? I wouldn't have to worry about endangering anyone but myself. If I make a run for it, it's all on me. Still, I know that if I walk out this door, and he catches me, he's going to hurt me—badly. That's one thing he's made very clear through this entire ordeal. If I don't follow his orders, he'll make me regret it. The longer I stand here, the more I gravitate toward walking out that door. My body makes the decision for me, and I know I'll deal with the punishment, whatever it might be. That's if he catches me.

I put the wine bottle down on the table and shove open the heavy door and peer out into the alleyway behind. There's a fence line a few feet away, and on the other end, the fence cuts over into the building, blocking the path. I can't see the other side without walking out there. The organ in my chest squeezes tightly, and there's an ache radiating outward with every heavy beat.

The image of his lips sliding over delicate knuckles. His lips on a woman who isn't me. Those thoughts alone give me the strength to step out into the darkness.

Consequences be damned, I'd be stupid not to try to escape.

18

NIC

The one thing I didn't expect from this evening was the look of jealousy on Celia's face the second she saw our lovely dinner guest.

Honestly, Celia's reaction is the only reason I keep touching Reya. Well, her's and Soo's. They were both on edge and tense, neither of them speaking, just glaring between Reya and me before I sent Celia off for wine. It makes me wonder if Reya noticed the tension as well. Most likely, but she's not dumb enough to say anything.

From what Soo's said about her, I suspect she has much more going on in her head than it seems from the outside. And she likes for people to see her as simply another bimbo. She doesn't feign the heat in her gaze. The rare sex worker who enjoys her job makes the package she presents even more fascinating.

Reya focuses on her plate for a moment, and I sit back in my chair, surveying my second-in-command. His jaw is clenched as he watches his spy. He hasn't touched his food since Celia served it, and he's been glaring over my shoulder whenever I put my hands on her.

If I didn't know for a fact Soo has sworn off women completely, I might think he had himself a little crush. But, surely not. A man doesn't bounce back from his fiancée trying to carve out his heart on his wedding day.

"What do you think, Soo?" I ask, drawing his attention.

He clenches his jaw again and stares through me. "About?"

"Allowing our beautiful friend here to see what else she can learn for us. Maybe keep her on the payroll indefinitely if she turns over some useful little tidbits."

Soo shrugs, eyes skipping Reya completely as he scans the room for threats. A habit he's never broken from his days running with the unorganized street gangs of Korea. "You do what you want anyway. I'm sure she'll be an excellent asset."

I smile at the chill in his tone. Reya glances up at him over her plate, perhaps noting it too. How much time do these two actually spend together? Maybe I don't know Soo as well as I thought. Or maybe he's getting better at keeping secrets?

After she takes a sip of wine, I snag her hand in mine and carefully drag her back into my lap. I don't really care for fucking her today, but the fire in Celia's eyes makes me want to keep touching Reya.

However, the second she touches me, I compare her to Celia. Reya is taller, thinner, more like a supermodel. But I prefer how sweetly Celia fits to my body.

Even now, the only reason I'm hard—and have been all fucking night— is because of Celia's petite frame in the scrap of silk she's wearing.

Reya twines her hands around my neck and resettles against me. Her perfume is too strong, but she's warm, and I'm enjoying the tension on my friend's face. It's not that I want to hurt him, but he rarely shows me even a twinge of emotion. I've seen more in the short time we've been in this room than I've seen on his face in years. Which makes Reya more dangerous to our situation than anything.

If Soo loses control, cities burn.

I lean in and whisper in her ear, "What have you done to my friend here?"

She giggles and glances at him as if we're sharing a secret. "I'm not sure. I don't know what you mean. He and I have a working relationship, that's all."

I reach down and cup her round ass in my hand. It's firm and full, and the reaction I expect from my body isn't the one I get. She does absolutely nothing for me. "A working relationship or a *working* relationship?"

Another giggle escapes her painted lips as she cups my cheek. "Oh, baby, I never kiss and tell."

I shoot Soo another glance, but he's not looking at us, he's sipping his wine, feigning disinterest. Oh, he's interested, more than interested.

I twist her in my lap, so she's facing forward, and I gently lean her over the edge of the table. Her long arms narrowly miss my plate.

"Then if no one else is interested. I guess I could take the edge off."

She tenses underneath me for a fraction of a second and then relaxes, resting her cheek on the table. When she looks up at me from the corner of her eye, she whispers, "Do it hard."

Fucking hell. My cock doesn't even twitch. I should want to do nothing more than beat that fight right out of her and fuck her until she's begging to follow my orders, but I'm not even a little interested.

Speaking of orders, I pause and listen intently, closing my eyes. I hear nothing but the faint sound of slots from the distant casinos. I don't bother helping Reya up, but skirt around her lifted ass and march toward the kitchen. It's way too quiet, and Celia has been gone for far too long. When I reach the kitchen, I find it empty. A few bottles of wine sit on the stainless steel counter, and as I look around the kitchen,

I find a lone bottle on the counter further away, near the wide open back door.

She ran. I can't believe she actually ran.

A smile tugs onto my lips before I even clear the doorjamb. The little brat wants to escape. Then I guess I'll be the one to capture her again.

Then I'll show her what happens when you try to run from the devil.

19

CELIA

My heart is pounding in my chest, and fear zings up my spine. I miscalculated the distance that this place is to the actual casinos on the other side. Nor did I see the massive fence which lines the entire place from side to side, brick building to brick building.

"Fuck," I shout into the chilly, empty darkness of the alleyway.

Light seeps from the still ajar doorway I exited.

If I go back now, no one will know I tried to run.

No, he'll be able to read it all over my face as soon as he takes his mouth off the other woman long enough to notice me.

Wow. I've fallen so far. Jealous of some random woman my kidnapper flirts with. It doesn't matter anymore. I take one last look at the door and head in the opposite direction, up the alley toward a streetlamp cutting through the dark. I hit a fence before I can reach it. My only choices are to retreat inside or keep following the fence until I make my way out of this warehouse maze.

Forward it is. The urge to run beats at me, especially knowing the second he realizes I'm missing, he'll come chasing after me. The farther I get, the less of a chance he has to find me.

I drag my fingers along the chain-link fence, picking my way through the alley. Trash and debris line the fences along either side of me, so it's a tough walk to manage in high heels. I peer behind me but can't see the building I left or the casino on the other side of it. Even the lights are mostly gone. Just a faint brightness in the sky remains from that direction. I keep moving, focusing ahead again, praying I don't run into anyone out here.

A shout comes from somewhere behind me, and panic rushes through my veins. Fuck these shoes. Quickly, I unbuckle the tiny silver buckles at my ankles and rip the shoes off my feet. Then I do the only thing I can... I run.

My bare feet slap against the rough concrete. Each step shoots a twinge of pain into my ankles and calves, but I shove the pain away. I can't slow down. Not with him chasing me.

I need to get out of this maze. When I reach the end of the fence line, it cuts to the left, and I jog, hoping it will eventually let me out. Another bellow of rage reaches me, so much closer than before. The fence cuts in another direction, and finally, it opens up to a vacant lot.

My muscles burn as I push forward through the knee-high grass. Every rock scrapes against the soles of my feet, but none of the pain matters if I can escape. I can feel freedom, see it, almost taste it. I don't know where I'll go after this or how I'll survive, but I will manage.

The bubble of joy pops when an arm clamps around my midsection and drags me into the solid rock of a body. I don't need to look to know it's him. I let out a whimper of defeat and try to shove his arm away. He only adds his other one, squeezing me tighter in his grasp.

I use my shoes as a bat, swinging them wildly toward his face and head. One makes contact, or at least I hope it does by the grunt I catch. When

I go for another swing, he loosens his hold enough to grab my wrists and tosses the heels away into the field. It doesn't stop me from fighting. I claw, scratching at his arms and twisting to do the same to his face.

"If you don't fucking knock it off, I'm going to knock your fucking lights out," he growls into the shell of my ear.

I scream, the sound piercing the night air while I continue to fight, adding my legs to the mix, kicking and shoving my heels into his shins. With every twist of my body against his, my dress rides up to bunch around the arm that is pinning me tight against him. I don't care that my ass is hanging out for the world to see. I just need to get away from him.

"*Stellina*," he warns, his voice an angry hiss of air in my ear.

I'm almost out of strength. The lights in the distance seem so far now, out of my reach. I give him one last kick to the shin and sink my nails into his forearm. True defeat claims me. I've got nothing left, and I sob in his hold. No tears fall, though. It's more out of exhaustion than anything else.

When I don't hit him again, he relaxes his grip around my middle, allowing me to draw a full breath again. He spins me in his arms to pin us together, front to front. His dark blue eyes are calm, but I can tell he is seething by the hard set of his jaw and the way his fingers dig into my back. My dress is still bunched up between us. My legs and underwear are completely exposed to the cool night air. I don't dare pull them back into place for fear of him growing angrier.

"The first thing I'm going to do is spank the shit out of you. And then, depending on how well you endure it, I'll drag you back to my house and keep you in chains until the auction. Are you happy now? You don't have a single thing to say to me?" he bites out an inch from my face.

I flinch away, turning my cheek, so he's not screaming directly at my mouth. He doesn't like that, and his jaw tightens, as do his fingers, digging into my tender flesh.

He shoves me backward, and I nearly trip over my feet. "Stay the fuck there. If you so much as move an inch, I'll knock you out and drag your unconscious body home."

I gulp and pull at my dress to cover some of my exposed skin as he jerks his suit jacket off and throws it on the dirt. Then splits his cuffs to roll up his sleeves. Even in the dark, I can see the ink splayed up his forearms that disappear under the fabric.

He holds his hand out to me, and I drag my eyes between his outstretched fingers and his eyes. When I don't take his hand, he steps forward, snags my wrist, and yanks me into him again. I trip, and he uses the momentum to pull me down to the ground. The rocks in the dirt cut into my legs as he carefully lays me across his knee.

"You've earned yourself a punishment. First, I'm going to spank you, and then we'll get on with the rest of the business."

He lifts my dress back up over my ass. I try to reason with myself. Maybe this is another scare tactic. Maybe he won't actually hit me. That thought evaporates into thin air when the flat of his hand connects to my ass, and I jostle forward across his leg. My flesh burns from the impact, but then the burn fizzles into something deeper, something weighty in my core.

He delivers another smack on the other cheek, and again, I grit my teeth with the impact and ride out the pain into a faint throb that blooms into something else inside me. The next smack is harder, and I hiss out a breath, clawing my nails into the arm clutched tight around my upper body.

"Let go," he orders. I ignore him and dig my nails in deeper, the pain overtaking reason.

He doesn't hit me again. Instead, he flips me onto my back and climbs on top of me, pinning me to the ground. His hips part my legs open around him.

I shove at his chest, and he moves my hands above my head and holds them there.

"Guess you should've thought about all of this before you ran," he growls.

"I hate you." I curl my lip and spit the words at him. I wish they were daggers and had the power to pierce his flesh.

I continue to struggle and wiggle against him, trying to shimmy out from under his body until I feel the hard outline of his cock against my bare thigh.

I freeze at the revelation and suck a ragged breath into my lungs.

He tugs me back into position underneath him, his face even with mine. "Hate me all you want but, if I were you, I'd remain very still, so I don't forget how much I need you to be a virgin."

His words sputter through me, and I fold my lips together to keep a moan locked inside. I'm soaking wet from the spanking, and even now, my no doubt welted ass lies in the dirt, and I don't care. Not when his cock is so close to where I need it.

His exhales shoot sparks along my neck. Even as he speaks, he arches his hips into me, rubbing slowly, deliberately. "Oh, no. I don't reward little brats who don't follow my instructions."

With his face so close to mine, I can see every line, every worry, and maybe a hint of fear. Without thinking of any further repercussions, I press my lips to his, and heat consumes me. I have no idea what pushed me to do it. Curiosity? Fear? Or maybe I'm simply insane.

He freezes against me. He doesn't respond to my kiss, and the hand that was digging into my thigh a moment ago stills against my fevered skin.

I pull away, heat already washing up my neck and into my ears. Of course, he won't kiss me back. He's been vocal about the fact I'm nothing more than a sex doll for his newest client. I close my eyes before the tears slip down my cheeks, and he sees them.

I want him off me, away from my body, so I can think straight. But he doesn't move, even when I lift my hips to dislodge him. The movement only grinds my wrists harder into the rocky field, along with the backs of my thighs and calves. The pinpricks of pain cut through the haze until his mouth descends on mine.

Some men kiss with permission on their lips. Nic isn't one of those men. He kisses me with demand and the expectation that I open for him in every way. And when he bites into my bottom lip, using his teeth to tug my lips apart, I pant and wiggle underneath him to pry my hands free.

He releases my wrists and fists the hair at the nape of my neck. The strands tangle between his fingers to deliver a delicious tug with every flex of his knuckles.

His lips plunder mine, devour from the inside out, all the while his hips rock into mine slowly, rhythmically even, as I thrash for more skin, more friction, more anything to reach the orgasm looming at the edge of my grasp.

Every swipe of his tongue against mine is a claim, a flag planted, his body marking mine as his. And I want it more than anything. Him to take everything and keep me.

The thought punches its way through the lust, and I freeze underneath him. Sensing my tension, he jerks up and stares down into my face.

He cups my pussy through my panties. "Every orgasm, every little whimper from your sweet lips belongs to me. And when you come, crashing into a million pieces, your pretty little pussy gushing against my hand, that's mine too. Every drop of your sweet orgasm belongs to me.

It's not a whimper he wrings out of me, but a full body shudder. He rips my panties to the side and threads his fingers along my wet skin. The wind across the field raises goosebumps up my legs. He takes his time exploring, tracing the contours of my pussy with his fingers as if he is memorizing every inch of my bare flesh.

It feels like forever before he nudges my opening, dipping in only enough to cause me to clench around nothing, my body yearning for more. Always more.

"Such a greedy little brat," he whispers in my ear, his hips bucking against the seam of my inner thigh as he threads his fingers into my body inch by delicious inch.

Another whimper escapes, and I delve my fingers into his hair. It's thick and soft at the nape of his neck. I breathe deeply, sucking in his manly scent. He groans into my shoulder and then shoves the last couple of inches inside me with those fucking clever fingers.

When he anchors himself over me to stare down into my eyes, a curl of unease washes through me.

"We're going to play a game. I'll ask you a question, and if you answer it correctly, I'm going to make you feel so good. You don't answer, and I'll leave you a quivering mess, aching for a release I'll never let you have. Nod your head if you understand."

I nod slowly, avoiding eye contact, so he doesn't spy the urge to shove him off me, to fight his words and the demands of both our bodies.

"Good girl," he whispers along the column of my neck, his lips tracing along every sensitive bundle of nerves there. "Let's start with an easy one. Who do you belong to?"

He punctuates his question by shoving his fingers deeper inside me and twisting his hand so that his thumb grazes my clit.

I shudder. "You."

He rewards me with another slow thrust of his hips and fingers. "Mmm. Very good."

We stay locked together for a few long moments. I'm panting with the need to move on his hand, to feel any kind of stimulation.

And when I'm squirming below him again, he brushes his lips over mine. "Let's try one I think you'll find a little more difficult. Who does this pussy belong to?"

A groan rolls out of me, unbidden, as he rocks his fingers inside me a little faster this time. I meet his thrusts with my hips, trying to pump on him at the same time he pushes inside. He doesn't let me. The moment I pant again, he stops moving, leaving me thrusting, and him simply holding steady. My ragged breathing doesn't even sound like me.

"Yours," I croak out.

"I can feel you squeezing my fingers. So tight, like a goddamn vice. I bet you would feel so good around my dick. I can almost imagine it now, pressing deep inside you and stealing that precious virginity of yours." His words add to the pleasure threatening to consume, and he continues, "Last question. Answer it correctly, and I'll let you come. Easy as that."

A mewling noise escapes my throat, and I slap my hands over my mouth in shock.

He chuckles into my neck then sobers, his tone steel and unrelenting. "Are you going to run from me again?"

His hand stills, and he holds me like a damn grocery bag, two fingers inside me, his thumb pointing up over my clit.

"No. I won't run again."

The nuzzle he gives me is almost worth what he'd just stolen. What little hope and fight I had left fizzles with his grasp. He makes good on his promise and puts his hand to work, pumping into me faster while working my clit at the same time. My orgasm sparks inside me before igniting in a full blaze of pleasure. Light swims in and out of my vision, and I drop my head back into his grip. My shout echoes off the surrounding buildings.

He gently pulls his hand from my body and delivers a sharp smack right over my clit. I arch off the ground with a whimper, this time in pain, as my nerves sizzle from the blow to my sensitive bud.

I glare at him, but he's not looking at me. He shoves off the ground, rips open his belt, digs out the hard length of his cock, and strokes it in one long pull. The groan ripping through him makes me slick all over again.

I'm about to move out of the way and give him some room when he grabs me and shoves me back down on the dirt, thrusting the two fingers he'd put inside me into my mouth.

"Suck them, clean them off while I take care of this," he demands.

I blink, both aroused and appalled, but do as he instructs. Tasting the salty sweetness of my arousal while I watch him.

He strokes himself hard and fast, unrelenting and with no reserve. It takes seconds for the first splatter of cum to land on my thighs, and then thick ropes follow, hitting my panties and dress. It's erotic as hell, and I'm suddenly wet again. When he finishes, his breathing uneven, the spicy, musky scent of him in the air, he leans down and rubs the head of his cock against my clit, cleaning the cum from his body and depositing it on mine.

Then he uses my dress to clean his hands and carefully closes himself back into his pants. Now clean, he shakes himself out and pulls me to my feet by the hand.

"We have to get back; Soo will come hunting soon if we don't."

I blink and stare down at my dress; no doubt my hair is mussed, and my makeup has smeared all over my face. "I can't go in there looking like this."

He brushes his thumb over my bottom lip, fire flickering in his eyes with a lingering promise of something more. "Why not? I want everyone to see what we've done, what you've done."

I meant what I said earlier. I really do hate this man, even if a part of me is mystified by him.

As if he knows I will follow, he starts back to the casino, leaving me to pick over the rough ground, barefoot and seething. I may have gotten caught, but soon enough, I'll be free of this man and his menacing ways.

I want my marks on her skin. To feel the give of her body around mine in every way. Not just her tight as fuck pussy, but her soft hips relenting to my grasp, her mouth taking every inch of me. Her little virgin asshole spread wide around my length.

It's all I can see in my mind as I sit at my desk the next day. Of course, knowing she is naked, tied to the bed in her room, doesn't help. I felt like that was a fitting punishment for her running away, for almost escaping me completely. I can't even think about it, or else I get the urge to take her, mark her, claim her all over again.

The need overcame me last night. I did nothing I regret, except for stopping before I buried myself in her warmth. Even now, something primal in my body demands to take her in ways I've never taken a woman. To the edges, I reserve for my own dark fantasies. The way she'd writhed on the ground, rocks and dirt grinding into her skin, she'd delighted in my cruelty. And she'd savored the reward afterward.

It's not until Soo marches into my office and throws himself into the armchair in front of my desk with a meaningful glare that I push the thought of her soft skin under my hands away completely.

He's wearing black jeans and a gray T-shirt today. Obviously, not meeting with clients or vendors then. His hair is gelled back, neatly away from his face. Like this, he appears younger, more like a college student than the second most powerful man in the city.

Soo raises one eyebrow, a soft frown on his otherwise expressionless face. "What the fuck happened last night? I had to call another car to pick me up. You just disappeared."

"Celia ran and lost part of her dress in the process. I caught her easily enough, don't worry. I was gonna walk her through the building but decided against it. I didn't want to risk drawing the wrong person's attention."

Despite having my back at every turn, Soo has been wary of this plan since its inception. Explaining her race to freedom in more detail would set him on edge when I very much need him to be at his best. Especially as we deal with my rogue brother, the upcoming auction, and the meeting between the five families. Neither of us can allow any distractions. Soo surveys me, his brown eyes sweeping the length of my body, missing nothing. Will this be the time he calls me on my bullshit? Or will he let it ride?

After a heartbeat of silence, he asks, "What happened?"

I shrug. It's pointless to pretend I don't care, so I don't bother. I let him see the anger and fear I felt last night when I found her missing. "When she went to get the wine, she snuck out the back door. But she didn't get very far between the fences and the mess of the construction behind the casino. When I caught her, I taught her a lesson and made sure she understands running isn't an option."

"Are you sure she will listen? We are days away from the auction, and I don't want to stumble across the finish line."

We'll be here all day, going around in circles if I let him continue on with this conversation. "How did things go with your spy last night? Did she hear anything else about the meeting?"

"Don't think I didn't notice the change in subject. Where is she now?"

I wave at the door. "In her room, tied to the bed. Why? Want to go make sure she's okay?" I joke.

"If she is contained, then everything is fine. I don't want this to go south so close to the auction."

"As long as we don't take anymore field trips, I think she'll behave."

"You *think*?"

I slam my hand on the desk and meet his eyes head on. "She'll fall in line."

The grinding of his jaw is the only outward sign of agitation he gives me. I let the silence stretch for a heartbeat too long and sigh. "Your spy? Any news on the meeting? It will be absolutely perfect if it happens the day after the auction. Then I can rub her sale in their faces before I take them all out at once."

The idea of taking out the entire fucking infestation in one blow energizes me. Almost as good as it felt to have Celia under me. To be the one who takes away every scrap of innocence she possesses.

Soo says something I miss, and he levels me with a look, which tells me he knows why my mind is wandering. Then he repeats himself. "She is going to keep monitoring the situation. One of the Gardello boys is fond of her and likes his pillow talk. She doesn't have the exact date yet, but she's going to be seeing him soon and might weasel it out of him with her wiles."

I snort. "Her wiles were definitely lovely."

Of course, Soo betrays nothing. But that wasn't the case last night. He'd watched every twitch his spy made, and then some. When Celia fled, he hadn't noticed that either. Out of character for him. Soo prides himself on knowing every single detail.

"And Lucas, have you heard from him?" My brother hasn't come home the last couple of nights. I'm not worried for him. He often rushes out for weeks at a time on his smuggling runs.

Soo's eyes shutter. "He says he'll be here for the auction, but he's busy until the night of, acquiring the product we need to set the atmosphere."

"But…"

There's always a 'but' when Lucas doesn't provide the entire story, and Soo tries to protect me from the truth about my brother. Like I don't already fucking know.

"He hasn't gone anywhere. He spent some time at the local hospital this morning, and then he went downtown immediately afterward."

Why would Lucas be at the hospital? Unless he had a doctor contact providing some of his product.

"Do you have someone trailing him?"

It kills me I need to even ask. That my own brother has turned into someone I don't recognize most days. Between the anger and the lies, he's falling apart one night at a time, and I'm never able to reach him.

Soo sighs, and I realize he was talking while my mind wandered —again.

"I guess the only thing left to finalize is the guest list. Do you have a list of interested parties? We can't reveal her identity until the event, but I'm sure you've been putting out feelers."

There were several inquiries in my email about the special auction for Celia. All of which I forwarded to Soo since he'd do a background check on every attendee. We don't need law enforcement screwing things up for us when we are so close to our goals.

Soo leans forward, bracing his elbows on the knees of his black jeans. "I do have a list. Several people have already been confirmed and checked out. I also ensured there are at least two extensions of the five families at the event. I know you want to use them to sow discord. It won't take much effort if they are already closing ranks."

I wonder how Celia will feel seeing men she'd lived life alongside, bidding to own her. The image of her in the dirt, my cum on her dress, her makeup mussed, rushes back into my brain. I can still feel her whimpers and every pulse of her cunt around my fingers.

God, I can smell her on my fingers, her sweat and arousal as I tipped her over the edge. She hates every orgasm I give her, and yet she begs by the time I put my hands on her.

A thought strikes me. "Do we have any record of the last meeting between the families? Records, video, anything that can tell us who attended and what they discussed? Also, the when, where, and lead up to the event? Most of these bastards, especially Ricci, are stuck in their old ways. If he initiated the meeting, he might have alerted the others in a similar way as last time. A letter, maybe? Verbal delivery?" I consider what I know about the man. "He wouldn't trust anyone but family to contact the others. And since he has no sons, he'd have gone a different route."

Soo nods, the first glimmer of interest at our conversation in his eyes. "It won't be an email. As far as I can tell, he doesn't even own a laptop. His wife does, so I've hacked his network, but it doesn't help if he doesn't use it. He's also living twenty years in the past with a flip phone, so I doubt he called anyone or sent a text. My bet would be on a letter, likely a fancy invitation meant to show the others he's still just as powerful without his daughters. He needs to re-cement his alliances, show the others he's powerful, despite the two women in his family not falling in line."

I nod. "Some of the children of his original allies are taking over their family seats. He's worried he won't be able to maintain power much longer. It makes him more dangerous, harder to pin down as he'll be suspicious at every turn."

I can see the calculation in Soo's eyes. There's nothing he loves more than a puzzle with a prize at the end. And once we dismantle the five families, we'll own every inch of this city.

As if waking from a dream, Soo shakes himself and meets my eyes over the desk again. "Did you make a plan for whoever buys the girl?"

I smile. I've spent a lot of time on a plan to ensure her cooperation. Every touch, every nudge of her body and mind pushes her further under my control. I'm not worried about her cooperation. The hard part will be ensuring her and the buyer's safety while I flaunt my spectacle in front of her father and all the families. The moment they see not a single one of them is safe, will be the moment I can sweep in and take everything.

"I've given it a lot of thought, actually. The girl is easy enough to control. Last night was a fluke and was remedied. Once she's purchased, and we have the confirmation of sale, I'll have the helicopter on standby to take them out of the city to the buyer's chosen destination. After that, their safety will be the buyer's responsibility. Even if the buyer fails to keep her safe, it will only help our narrative. No matter what, I took something from the five families. Celia will be sold, and it doesn't matter if she dies right after."

As I say the words out loud, my chest tightens uncomfortably. To my plan, it doesn't matter what happens to her afterward. It shouldn't to me either, but thinking of her death has my stomach souring.

"If you say so." Soo shakes his head at me and leaves the room.

I exit shortly after, my legs carrying me to her room without thinking. She was furious when I tied her to the bed. I wonder if she has calmed herself. Probably not. Maybe I can smooth things over for now. And if I can't, well, she won't be my problem in a few days, anyway.

I shove the door open and stalk into her room. She is sprawled out on the bed just as I left her. Completely naked and on top of the covers, her wrists are tied to the headboard and her ankles to the foot of the bed.

"Enjoying your stay, princess?"

"Sarah came in here earlier. Do you know how embarrassing that was? She saw me... like *this*." She tips her head down, looking at her body.

I drag my gaze up and down her naked form, lingering at the junction of her spread out legs. "That's the whole point of this punishment. Be thankful I didn't send any of my men in here. Thinking of... I could still make that happen." I wouldn't, but the sharp intake of air lets me know she believes I would.

When her eyes meet mine, they are red-rimmed and glacial. "You already control me and use me. Do you have to degrade me as well?"

I study her for a moment. Let her glare all she likes. "Yes, all the above and more. That hasn't changed since the very first night you arrived. What makes you think it did?"

She only gives me a sniffle this time, nothing else, even dragging her eyes to stare off out the window. Her dismissal grates on my nerves.

Leaning over the bed, I capture her chin in my fingers and drag her gaze to mine. "You thought because I kissed you and fucked you with my fingers that you somehow became something else... something more than a rich man's toy to me?"

A new fire ignites in her brown eyes, and then she does something I never expected, spits in my face. It only takes a heartbeat for her to realize her mistake. She tries to scramble away from my grasp, but the rope is holding her in place, making that impossible.

I take out a handkerchief from my pocket to wipe my face. It's not the first time someone, even someone like her, has thought so little of me they did the same.

"Let's get one thing straight, princess. I may like how your body fits around mine. I may enjoy the sweet little noises you make as you come, but it will never be enough to make me keep you. You, and your family, stand for everything I'm against. I'd rather take a fucking goat to my bed than keep you to warm it."

She gapes at me, her mouth hanging open now. "You really hate me that much?"

Like a wild animal attacking its prey, I'm on her in a flash, letting most of my weight rest against her until she is completely locked in my hold, her face inches from mine. I lean down and bite her bottom lip hard, relishing in the small whimper that escapes her throat. I want her fire, her hatred.

"And while we're on the subject. You belong to me. Every inch of your body, from your mouth to your asshole, is mine to do with as I please. If you fight, I'll only make sure it hurts worse and that you're not satisfied at the end of it. Are we clear?"

She whimpers, and I squeeze her tighter. "Are we clear, princess? A nod will do for me to ensure you understand."

Instead of answering, she squeezes her eyes tight, and after a heartbeat, she nods once.

I peel myself off her and stand up to straighten my cuffs. "I'm glad we had this little chat. I'm disappointed in how quickly you forgot, *stellina*. How my lesson from last night didn't make things clear. If I have to teach you another lesson, I won't be as gentle."

"Are you not going to untie me?" she asks when I start toward the door.

"I'll be back later." I grin like the bastard I am.

I'm not surprised when I find Soo waiting on the other side of the door, monitoring our interaction, missing nothing. "You good?"

I nod and step into the hallway, leaving the door ajar behind me. Let her hear what I say next, since I know she'll enjoy listening in. "Set the auction for tomorrow night. Get everything in motion and follow up about that meeting we discussed. Once I get her off my plate, I can work on more important matters."

Soo nods and glances back at the door one last time. Then he stalks away, no doubt already calculating and plotting any weakness.

I, too, stare at the door, waiting for her to call after me, either begging or demanding to be untied. When she doesn't, I turn back to my office and take up my place behind the desk. Things are better this way. If she believes me the monster she's built up in her head, she'll better protect herself mentally for the next monster who is about to enter her life.

If she sees all of us that way, then she'll continue to fortify herself. And then, and only then, will she be able to function in this world where the only winner is the biggest monster.

21

CELIA

I don't throw myself pity parties. I didn't when my sister died or when my father told me he was arranging my marriage. I'm a firm believer that crying over something doesn't change the outcome. Right now, I'd give myself a few seconds to feel what I'm feeling and then push past it. I've concluded that there is no way out of this house. I'm resigned to that fact. My escape attempt proved useless.

Still, every second that passes, I wonder how I'll live through this hopelessness that's swamping me? Dragging me under in wave after wave of despair? Nicolo intends to sell me. He hasn't once deviated from that plan, and yet I keep trying to make him see I'm worth more than a paycheck, more than revenge.

I guess it's stupid to hope I'd gotten through to him. When he kissed me last night, I saw stars. Even though it was little more than teeth and tongues tangling roughly, it was the first time I felt him with me when we were together. Every other time, as he so eloquently puts it, I felt like little more than a wet hole. My ignorance of sex stamped across my forehead for him to mock.

It's the ignorance he enjoys when he touches me, and it's his touch that I enjoy so much. I enjoy how his breathing quickens and his heart beats faster against me. He wants me, but he doesn't want to admit it.

The proof of all of that is me being tied to the bed. I still can't believe he just left me here. I'd never been so ashamed as when Sarah walked in. He made sure my legs are open so everyone walking in gets a magnificent view of my most private parts.

At least Sarah was the only person to come in here. I don't even want to think who else could walk in. On cue, the doorknob turns, and the door opens. Like a bunny caught in a trap, I wiggle against the restraints, the rope cutting into my skin painfully.

"I know you're excited to see me, but that's no reason to squirm," Nic's voice booms through the room, and to my annoyance, that calms me. Better him than some random guard, or even worse, his brother.

"I need to use the bathroom," I blurt out.

"Good thing I'm here to untie you. Your punishment is over," he announces and starts undoing the knots. He frees my ankles first. As soon as my legs are free, I squeeze my thighs together, making him chuckle.

"Too late to be shy now," he murmurs while untying my wrists. "As much as I'd like to play with you a little more, I have things to do. Behave, or you'll be right back here."

"Great," I say sarcastically. Rubbing the soreness from my wrists, I sit up and watch him leave the room like it's just another day at the office.

Still angry as can be, I climb off the bed and head to the bathroom. Then I find something to wear and sit back down on the mattress. I lean back into the side of the bed, the ball of my hair pressing uncomfortably against my scalp. My gaze gravitates to the ceiling as I'm trying to come to terms with everything.

There is nothing I wouldn't do for a Starbucks right now.

A snort slips out as I imagine the extra whipped topping on a mocha frappuccino. I don't know why I'm even thinking about something so mundane, especially when there are more pressing matters, like how the hell I'm going to get myself out of this without being tagged and sold like a cow at an auction.

I push the thought of a Starbucks to the back of my mind; such luxuries are a thing of the past. My buyer will have certain expectations of me. He'll realize quickly that I won't sit quietly and let him do what he wants with me.

The thought of escape, of fighting back, pushes a little of the despair away, making the pressure on my chest bearable. I might not escape Nicolo, but that doesn't mean I won't escape whoever purchases me tomorrow night.

The door opens with a slight creak behind me, but I don't bother looking. What more can he do to me now? The click of shoes across the hardwood is stiff, hesitant, not Nicolo's you-should-be-bowing-to-me gait. I glance up over my shoulder to find the other man, his friend, Soo.

His brown eyes are electric as he surveys me from head to toe. "Are you all right?" He's asking like he legitimately cares, which I can't believe for a second.

I don't bother hiding my snark. "Why do you care? Need to make sure the merchandise is intact before you can put me up to the bidders?"

He tracks his gaze up the bruises on my legs with a little frown. "Contrary to what you might think, I don't enjoy this."

"Well, Nicolo does. He seems perfectly content leaving me naked and tied to the bed all day, using me, and selling me. Matter of fact, he's done all of this with a smile on his face. I'm pretty sure he's enjoying this."

"He needs his revenge. Unfortunately, you are collateral in his plan."

"Whatever revenge he gets by selling me won't help him and won't make him feel better when he's finished. I'll just be another mark on his conscience, another scar he'll never be able to erase."

My voice is low and thready. I try to keep the tears at bay so he doesn't truly see how scared I am. "He should have done his research. My father doesn't give a shit about me except for what my marriage could bring him. He's waited years for an alliance with one of the other families, but he's resourceful. I'm sure he's already bounced back and launched a new venture to bring him the connections he wants."

"This isn't about your father caring about you. This is about Nic taking something away from your father. You don't think we know he doesn't love you? It's clear he doesn't but knowing that Nic took something from him is what will destroy him. Knowing he used you for his benefit instead of your father's, that's the real revenge."

My mouth falls open, probably making me look like I feel—a fish out of water. Of course, he knows. Yet, he doesn't care that I'm innocent. I don't know if that makes it better or worse.

Soo studies me, his long muscular legs showcased in tight black jeans. With his hair back, I can see the straight sweep of his cheekbones and the sharp cut of his jawline. He's beautiful, but so is Nicolo, and I'm reminded then that even the devil can look like an angel.

"Do you have any requests? I can get you something, make you more comfortable."

"Why?" I spit. "So I owe you something too? Want to pop by for a hand job later to make sure I live up to the expectations of your clients?"

His posture is rigid, but he doesn't react to my statement. Not even a flinch. "I want nothing from you, Celia. Do you have any requests or not?"

Anger simmers in my veins. I'm tired of being here, trapped in this ivory castle with a man that will never be my hero.

"Sure, let me go. If you release me, I'll leave and disappear. I won't even go home, and then you guys can still pretend you sold me or killed me, whatever you want. I'll never come back, I promise."

The corner of his mouth ticks up the tiniest bit, but his eyes remain flat. "I can't do that. Nic would kill both of us and stick our heads on spikes at the end of his driveway. Not the fate I have in mind for myself. Is there anything else?"

I sob and laugh at the same time. "All I can think about is a mocha frappuccino right now. And pants. If I can have anything, can I please have some damn pants?"

His eyes shoot to my bare legs again, which are stretched out in front of me. My toes are still perfectly painted a lilac purple, despite my barefoot ordeal outside last night.

"I'll see what I can do. Don't do anything stupid again. I don't want to have to hunt you down. And in case you're wondering, I'm very good at hunting."

Without another word, he spins around and leaves. I turn my head to watch him walk out of the room and close the door behind him. What the hell kind of game is he playing? Is he truly being kind, or is he trying to get me into trouble with Nic?

I stare at the door for too long, thinking about the differences between Nic and Soo. Both are powerful, strong men. Nic is more authoritative and a little crazy, so people give him a wide berth. Soo seems like the type that will take you down from the shadows. He's there and gone before anyone sees a thing.

Out of nowhere, an idea hits me, and I hate it the minute it blooms with life in my brain. Nic wants to sell me to the highest bidder, so sure that my virginity and status as a daughter of the five families will bring in some big cash. But what if I'm not a virgin when I walk up on that auction block? The idea is crazy, absolutely insane. Of course, it would be his word against mine. Until the buyer got me home, and my word proved true. Then he'd want his money back.

I tap my finger against my chin, thinking deeper on it. There are flaws in my logic. The only way a buyer could tell he lied would be to touch me.

A shiver runs down my spine, and bile rises up my throat at the simple thought.

Soo might be a good prospect. At least he's pretty to look at, and he has an intensity about him that says he'd make it his mission to please a woman underneath him.

I'd already tried my stumble fuck version of seduction on Nicolo, and while I may tempt him, his control runs too deep. He will use my body in every other way, but he won't fuck me. Even if I want him to, which I hate. I hate wanting him, even more so knowing that he won't give in to temptation and give us both what we want.

The guards and male staff I've seen won't even look at me. It's like they know the second they do, Nicolo will come along with a handgun and a devilish smile.

The last choice is Lucas. He's good-looking enough, but he's broken. Jagged, shattered from the inside out. It's not in the same way Nicolo is, but deeper, harsher, like nothing will make it right again. It makes him dangerous and unforgiving—two things I don't want for my first time.

I slap the heel of my hand against my forehead. *No.* I can't be thinking romantically about this. Losing my virginity is nothing more than a plan with very low chance of succeeding—both in the act and in the results.

With my only options being Lucas or Soo, I'd choose Soo in a second. But I need to be ready to accept anyone who comes my way.

With that grim thought bolstering me, I shove off the hardwood and head out into the hall. The pile of firewood is still there, and Nicolo's office door is open.

The idea of running into him or seeing him right now... No, I can't face him like this. Not without protection. I rush back to the room and find the fountain pen I'd tucked under my mattress. I carefully fold the sleeves of my shirt up so I can hide it inside the bunched-up fabric. It won't do a lot of damage, and it won't hold forever, but it makes me feel safer.

Back in the hallway, I gather the firewood and then enter Nicolo's office. Thankfully, it's empty. I let out a sigh of relief and take the wood to the still mostly full box by the fireplace. Once it's neatly stacked, I turn to leave and collide with a firm chest.

Craning my neck back, I drag my gaze up *his* body. Not the devil, but the devil's brother. Lucas stands directly in front of me, blocking my exit.

He's wearing jeans, a tight black T-shirt, and a scowl just for me. "What the hell are you doing in here?"

I take a step back, but remember my plan, and force myself to at least not retreat any further. "I was just filling the wood box. It's my chore for the day." I add a smile on the end, which only causes his frown to deepen.

He throws himself in the armchair in front of the desk like a teenager called to the principal's office. All his long limbs splayed; his arms crossed over his chest defiantly. "Get the hell out of here and bother someone else."

I try not to flinch at the harshness of his voice. This is not going how I expected it to. I almost flee in fear, coming up with a different plan, a better plan.

His voice makes me jump. "Why are you still here?"

I clear my throat and take a fearful step toward him, but he doesn't look up at me. "I was actually wondering if you had any advice for tomorrow?"

Now he arches his neck to stare at me over his shoulder. "Tomorrow?"

"The auction? Any advice to make sure I end up with someone decent?" The words make me want to vomit, but I spit them out anyway, hoping I sound at least pitiable.

He drags his eyes down my body to my bare feet and back up to my face. "You'll be fine, I'm sure. Just keep your disgusting scar covered. Not that it matters, they can just fuck you from behind, I guess."

I squeeze my hands tight and then release one to touch the top of his shoulder. It's a gentle touch, but the second I make contact, he launches out of the chair and halfway across the room.

"What is wrong with you?" he roars.

I can't stop the shaking, not when he's screaming at me. I tremble, and not in the same way I do when Nic touches me. This is pure, undiluted fear. Even my voice shakes when I answer him. "I'm sorry... I thought—"

"Thought what?" he demands, stalking forward to tower over me.

With him so close, I can see the resemblance to his brother, but I also see something else. His eyes, so full of pain, look familiar to me. I can't place how, but I drag my gaze from his and stare down at the floor. "I don't know. It was stupid. I'll go back to my room now."

I turn to head out, but he snags my arm and drags me back to him. He's not touching me anywhere but the grip on my arm. It's not as tight as the hold he had on my wrist before, but still iron, with no give. "What is stupid?"

Like I'm going to confess my plan to him. Not in a million years, not even if he tries to shake it out of me. "Nothing, you just looked like you were upset, is all."

His forehead bunches up, and he looks so much younger without the perpetual scowl on his face. "I don't need your pity or comfort. The only time I care for a woman's company is when she is on her knees."

That's an opening if I ever heard one. I blink and look down at the floor, knowing what I have to do next. I slowly sink down to the rug in front of Nicolo's desk. "I can do that."

I think more in shock than permission; he lets me get all the way to the floor. Just as he hauls me back up again, Nicolo walks into the office at a slow and steady amble.

Oh, god. I am so fucked.

"Am I interrupting?" he asks, studying us, especially me, still mostly kneeling in front of his brother.

I surge to my feet and gently tug my arm from Lucas's grasp. "No, of course not. I was just putting the firewood away like you asked."

Lucas's expression is unreadable. A cross between you're a fucking idiot, and how did I end up in this situation.

Nicolo turns his attention to his brother, who's already flexing his fists at his sides. "Anything you want to tell me, brother?"

He snorts and shrugs. "Just the usual. Go fuck yourself, and I'll see you at dinner."

When he tries to walk out, Nicolo grabs him by the shirt and flings him back in front of him. I scramble out of the way, so I don't get caught between them. Nicolo and his brother remind me of a bull and a red flag. The outcome can never end well.

Nicolo has his brother's shirt bunched in his hands while he leans in with a growl, "Thought you'd take my girl for a test drive?"

I don't like how the way he says *my girl* slips through me, warming up in places I'd tried to ice over with indifference.

Lucas shakes his head and shoves Nicolo off him. "I don't want a fucking thing to do with her. She'll be gone tomorrow. By the way, thanks for letting me know you set the date, asshole."

Nicolo looks ready to throw a punch, and I cower behind his desk chair, something like guilt slithering through me. I'd dragged Lucas into this, and now he was going to get punished for it. *Shit.* I step out from behind the chair and approach Nicolo. "It wasn't what it looked like. I wanted someone to take my virginity. I was trying to seduce him."

Both men turn to stare at me with slacked jaws. Nicolo recovers first, turns, and shoves his brother toward the door. "Get out."

Lucas shakes his head and walks out the door.

Then Nicolo's focus is on me, and I'm left swallowing my tongue. "I'm sorry. After this morning, I was angry, and I felt like you used me. It was a half-baked plan at best. Lucas didn't show a single bit of interest in me." I know I'm digging myself a grave, but for some stupid reason, I want him to know that his brother didn't show a lick of interest.

Nicolo stalks forward until he's inches from my face. "You're trying to protect him? Why?"

I wave at the door. "It wasn't his fault. I didn't want you to hurt him because of something I did."

A new fire flashes in his eyes, and I reflexively back away until my hip meets the edge of his desk, and I have nowhere else to go.

"You were trying to lose your virginity so the auction wouldn't pay out as much. Was that your plan all along, *stellina*?"

I shrug, refusing to meet his eyes now. When he says it, I feel even more idiotic. "I had hoped it was Soo, I could seduce, but Lucas showed up first."

Now he laughs. He throws his head back and laughs at me. Actually laughs. All the anger I'd been feeling fires through the guilt, and I shove him away. "You don't get to mock me. Not when you're the one who's about to sell me like a pig being sent off to the butcher."

He growls and charges at me again. I quickly fish out the fountain pen from behind my back and uncap it. He won't touch me without my permission again.

"Soo would have wiped the floor with you and left you in a whimpering puddle without ever having touched you. He'd also never betray me because he knows what this auction means to me." He leans in and places one hand on either side of the desk, boxing me in.

I shove at him with my shoulder, but he doesn't budge. All over again, I'm trapped. I raise the fountain pen and jab it as hard as I can into the center of his hand that's placed along my right hip.

He jumps back with a hiss, and I do the only logical thing I can do. I race toward the door, knowing that this might be the moment he actually kills me.

22

NIC

*T*he point of the pen barely breaks the surface of my skin. She could have done more damage if she'd taken the pen to my neck and shoved it in my carotid. But this little star doesn't know how to play dirty. Not like I do.

By the time I rip the pen out of my hand and cast it to the floor, she's running to the door. I don't bother stopping the smile from spreading across my face. I spin and beat her to the door, slamming it hard in her face. She yelps and jumps back. Then turns and rushes around the office, looking for another exit.

"There isn't another way out of here, princess. No point in running when you'll pay the price for your attack, anyway," I croon, waiting for her to realize she has nowhere else to go.

While she races around like a pinball in a machine, I pull out my handkerchief and wipe the blood off the back of my hand. It's barely a scrape considering some scars I have slashed across my skin.

She backs herself into the far-right corner of my office and sinks down onto the floor with her knees pulled to her chest. I shove off the closed door and cross the room. She watches me approach, no doubt waiting for my wrath to descend.

It's not wrath I feel when I look at her, though. I crouch beside her and lift her chin to force her to meet my eyes. "What were you thinking? You'd flee me with a fountain pen, clear my guards, and race out of here to safety? That's naive, even for you."

She sniffs and squares her shoulders. There's my princess. "I didn't have a plan. It was more of a reaction."

I eye the pen still lying on the floor, my blood caking the bent tip. "I wondered where that pen disappeared to. When did you take it?"

Instead of answering, she raises her chin higher and stares over my shoulder.

I grip the back of her head, dig my fingers into her soft locks, and pull her to her feet. If she wants to treat me like a soulless brute, then I'll be one.

I half drag, half carry her to the desk. Her body arches into me, and I smile against the dark hair at the nape of her neck. She likes the abuse, and despite her hatred of me, I feel the tremble in her thighs against mine. If I put my face between her legs, I could smell her arousal and feel her soaked panties.

Turning, I pick her up and sit her on the edge. Fire already roars in my ears in time with my heartbeat. Since laying on top of her and grinding my cock between her silky thighs the other night, she's branded me. I need more, and if she so freely wants to hand it out, then I'll take what she's offering.

"What are you doing?" she asks, her voice wavering.

I rip the top button of my shirt out of its hole while I stare into her eyes. "What does it look like?"

It takes me seconds to rip the rest of the buttons out and jerk the shirt from my pants. She drags her gaze down every slowly revealed inch of my skin. She might think she is above all of this, but I can see the whites of her eyes as she takes in my abs and the tattoos that blanket my torso. I toss the shirt onto the chair and unbuckle my belt, keeping my eyes trained on her.

But she keeps staring at my body like it's the last dessert at the buffet line.

"See something you like?" I grit out.

When she doesn't answer, I release my belt and snap my fingers in front of her nose. She jolts and grips the desk on either side of her hips. Her eyes flash up to mine. "What?"

"It's rude to stare, *stellina*. Tell me what you want, what you were going to offer my brother, and maybe I'll give it to you. Use your big girl words."

She swallows heavily, her voice low and husky when she answers. "You call me princess when you're angry, and *stellina* when you're not."

"How observant of you," I say, stepping forward.

Without thinking, she spreads her knees, welcoming me between her thighs. I give her a little smirk, but she doesn't know what it's for.

Her gaze falls to my neck, and she just looks at me, looks and looks. "Tell me why." It's a demand, not a question.

I'm feeling generous, mostly because I plan to be inside her body very, very soon. "As a princess, you stand for everything I hate, everything I want to destroy. As *mia stellina*, you shine bright, and I want to do nothing but worship every inch of your body."

Surprise flashes in her eyes as she meets mine. I'm shocked that I admitted it out loud. But the words are out, and I can't reel them back in.

"Now, tell me what you were going to offer to Lucas or fucking Soo. Tell me what you planned to do." There is no give in my tone.

She swallows again and grips the desk so hard her knuckles turn white over the ridges. "I told you, I didn't plan anything. I just figured if someone took my virginity, maybe you wouldn't sell me, or at the very least, you'd get a lot less money."

I lean in, caging her, allowing myself one small touch. My hands clench around her hips. "Were you going to ask them, or were you just going to bend over this desk right here and offer your cunt to them? Did you imagine it? What they would look like pulling out their cock and sliding it into your pussy?"

Her eyes are hazy now, her breathing uneven. If I put my hand between her legs, she'd be soaked through her panties. My mouth waters for a taste.

One little taste, and then I can punish her like she deserves.

I work the buttons of her shirt and strip it off her shoulders. She lifts her hands to take it off at her wrists, but I shake my head, twist the material, and gather her hands behind her back. When she protests, I pin her with a glare and slowly sink to my knees in front of the desk.

A small gasp passes between her plump lips. "What are you doing?"

"Whatever I fucking want. Remember, you're mine?"

The scent of her greets me, and I stare up at her with a smirk when she finally gets what's going on and scoots to the edge of the desk, spreading her legs wide enough to wrap her calves around my shoulders.

I squeeze her inner thighs in my hands, pressing my thumbs along the pressure point there. "Greedy *stellina*. You're in trouble, so don't sit up there feeling too smug."

If she reacts to my words, I don't see it; my focus is already on her pussy. I lick my lips and strip her panties down her legs, leaving them on the floor. She glistens for me, soaked already. I want her to make a fucking puddle on my desk, or my face, or both.

I shove her legs wider, as far as she can go, and I shuffle forward on my knees to press my lips to her wet core. God, she tastes good, sweet, salty, and musky all at once. I spear her with my tongue and enjoy the choked sound she emits from above.

My dick is a fucking rock in my slacks, but I can't focus on anything but the velvet skin against my lips.

Slowly, savoring every stroke, I run my tongue up to her clit and nip at the swollen bud. She jerks against my face, and I chuckle. The little princess needs someone's face she can ride regularly, to get used to all the ways a man can feast on her.

I shove the thought away even as it forms. I want to be that man, pulling her across my face in the morning before she's even fully awake just to feel her break, her thighs quivering against my cheeks.

"Harder." Her voice reaches me in my reverie.

I sit back on my calves and stare up at her, incredulous. "Did you just demand I lick you harder?"

Her face is flushed, a dainty pink hue stains her cheeks, her neck, and all the way down to her belly button. "Please."

Fucking hell, if she begs, I might come in my pants.

She does, and I don't, not yet. "Please, lick me harder."

I don't bother hiding my smile. "You are so fucking beautiful when you beg for what you want."

Her eyes drop to mine, surprise and pleasure etched in every line. "You're beautiful when you make me beg."

Fucking hell. I grip her legs tighter in my hands and lean forward to devour her. From opening to clit, I flick my tongue until she wriggles in her bonds above me. And when I feel her hips try to catch my rhythm, I shift focus and lick her clit in sharp little dips. It takes seconds for her breathing to shallow out, and her thighs to shake in my hands. A fresh wash of liquid greets my tongue as she comes, and I lap it up, savoring every drop.

When she stops shaking, her head hangs in front of her chest, her fingers are dug into the shirt behind her back. And she looks goddamn delectable.

I could pull my cock out now and shove it so hard inside her she'd come again. But somewhere in the back of my mind is a warning. Screaming at me to go slow, not to push too hard or too fast. I stand before I can overthink things and grab her panties off the ground.

She stares at me wide-eyed. "No."

I round on her, not bothering to hide my anger. "No? You don't get to say no to me. This isn't a yes, no relationship. I give you an order, and you follow it. If you do it nicely, I'll make sure you're rewarded. If you make me work for it, you'll be punished."

"Is that what you just did by making me come so hard I'm still shaking? Punish me?"

I react before thinking, taking her neck in my hand, not squeezing, just owning, her panties forgotten on the desk now. "Watch your mouth before I make you regret your lip."

She holds my gaze with her own. I know she's goading me. I can feel it. All she wants is for me to flip her over the desk, shove into her, and fuck her until we're both screaming. I can't do it, though. Not like this. Not when it's her choice and not mine.

I lean in further, pressing my erection between her legs. She sucks in a gasp, but I keep my face clear, calm, collected. As if she's not affecting me at all. As if I'm not dying to sink balls deep into her warmth.

"You can't manipulate me, princess. I own you. Every freckle, every wrinkle, every sexy little sigh belongs to me. Say it."

"What?"

"Say you belong to me."

Her eyes narrow. "I'll never say that. Do what you want. Rape me. I won't say it."

I arch my hips into her, and she gasps, dropping her head back, exposing her neck.

"I'm pretty sure if I press into you right now, you'd be screaming my name, not rape. You didn't finish telling me what you were going to give to my brother. Were you going to straddle his lap, ride his cock until you came all over him? Or were you going to take him to your bed, ask someone like him to be sweet and gentle with you?"

Spell broken, she focuses on my face again. "I told you. I didn't have a plan. I figured..."

"You'd shove your tits in his face, and he wouldn't be able to resist? He'd succumb to his brute-like instincts and take you, so you don't have to blame yourself for teasing him. It would be all his fault, right? You're a sweet little innocent princess." Disdain leaks from my tone, and she finally looks shamed for what she attempted.

She wriggles in the shirt, still binding her hands. "Let me go."

I shake my head. "I'm not done with you. I still haven't punished you yet."

Her hair has loosened from the tie on her head and now tumbles down her back freely. I shove a few strands over her shoulders so they don't hinder my view of her perfect breasts. Before I can think too long, I lean in and take one of her nipples between my teeth. A little moan breaks out as I apply pressure and then suck the hurt away. I switch to the other side and do the same.

I'm supposed to punish her, get her back under control, but every time I see that telltale pink flush of her skin, all I can think about is touching every inch of her body, branding her with my own until I'm all she feels, the standard by which she'll measure every man after me.

"Do you still want me to release you?" I ask, lips pressed into her sternum. She arches into me, begging me with her body.

"Mmm... that's what I thought." Regardless of my words, I strip the shirt off her wrists. "Open my pants and touch me."

She dashes her eyes to mine, even as she's already moving to the fly of my pants, dragging it down, my belt buckle clanging against her wrist. Carefully, she shoves my pants with one hand while gripping my hard length with her other. "Do you want me to suck on you?"

Hearing her say those filthy words draws my balls up tight into my body and shoots me to the edge, especially with her fingers gripping me so tightly. I shake my head. "No, don't suck on it. Just touch me while I gain control. Then I'll give you exactly what you asked my brother for."

She drops her hand. "What?"

I grab her wrist and wrap her fingers around my cock again. "Don't stop, or I won't be gentle when I take you."

Her big eyes go wide, and she squeezes me once, sliding her fingers to my base and back up to the crown. I breathe and focus on what I need to do, how we can both get what we want. I know the moment she realizes what I'm about to do, she's going to change her mind pretty damn fast.

"What are you going to do to me?" she whispers, her eyes still locked to her hand as she casually glides up and down my shaft.

I rock into her grip, savoring her tight hold for a moment. Fuck. I want to take her to my bed and do this over and over again until she's so sated she can't move. Until her begging for it turns to begging me to stop, even as her body defies her words.

"Patience, *stellina*, you'll find out in a moment. Are you ready to lose your virginity? Is that something you've made peace with?"

I lean in and trace her lips with my own. When she tries to catch me, I pull back, leaving her chasing my mouth in return. "Kiss me."

"I don't take orders. I thought we went over that."

"Please, kiss me." She punctuates her plea with a firm grip of her palm around me.

"You're playing with fire," I warn, but still give her what she wants, only because I want it too.

I lean in and capture her mouth with mine, nipping her bottom lip with my teeth before grabbing her face between my hands and delving my tongue into her mouth exactly like I did with her sweet little pussy.

She doesn't understand why she wants me as badly as she does, but that doesn't matter. All that matters is that she wants me. She moans against me and starts rubbing me harder.

I pull away and still her hand. "Not yet."

Instead of explaining, I pick her up and flip her onto her belly. At first, she resists, and I carefully arrange her limbs into the most comfortable position.

"Are you ready?" I ask.

She nods against the wood, her forehead rubbing against the grain, her ass wiggling toward me in the air. "Please."

"Settle down, *stellina*. I'm going to give you everything you want."

23

CELIA

I don't know what to do with my hands, my feet, these feelings roaring through me with every proprietary sweep of his fingers. He's not mine, and I hate the bastard anyway, but I can't stop the way my body tightens in anticipation with just a look. Or how my heart suddenly feels like it won't fit inside my ribs any longer.

If love can't sustain me, hope can. If he is willing to take my virginity, he might not want to sell me anymore. It's not much, but I'm willing to take the chance.

I focus on it as I map the pattern in the wood grain on Nicolo's desk. He orders me to stay belly down until he returns, and for once, I'm inclined to listen. Not just because I fear reprisal, but also because I'm boneless from the orgasm he just gave me with his mouth.

He licked me like he'd tasted nothing so delicious. After I came all over his tongue, he kept going, like he didn't want to give me up.

No. I can't afford to think like this. Let him secret away in the back of my mind like some dark prince who might one day save me with the power of his love. If I've learned anything in the time I've been captive, it's that love doesn't exist, not how it is on TV, and no one is going to save me, not even myself.

I should be angrier. I should fight more. Even as I think about it, I reposition myself on the desk in anticipation. I fought, and I lost, and this doesn't seem like such a terrible consolation prize. Especially if he's going to do what I think he is.

I hear his footsteps first. The tread of his shoes as he marches back toward me with his long gait filled with purpose.

When he enters the office, he closes and locks the door. I spot him over the edge of the desk, watching him approach with something in his hand I can't see clearly through the loose fall of my hair all around my head.

He takes a moment to rub his hands up and over my ass, shaping it with his palms, massaging it in his grip. "You are so very fuckable like this. I want to leave you here twenty-four-seven so I can get my fill of you whenever the urge strikes. And I'll admit, the urge has been quite often since that first night."

I try not to shiver under his word or his hands. I can't let him know how he truly affects me.

He rubs his cock along the seam of my ass and then dips it down between my thighs to catch some moisture there. "How does it feel? Tell me."

I clear my throat, sure I'm about to betray every emotion and riotous thought in my head if I speak. "It feels good." Good. If I keep things short and sweet, I don't sound like an idiot begging my kidnapper to fuck her.

His hands dig into my hair, gathering it up so he can lay the heavy mass of it over my shoulder. The gentleness with which he twists the strands together to secure them doesn't go unnoticed. His touch lights me up all over again. I want him inside me so badly I can almost feel it.

When he slides himself along the seam of my ass again, I whimper. "Are you going to spend the entire time teasing me, or are you going to fuck me?"

The words come out before I can stop them, and I thump my forehead onto the desk several times for being so stupid. He hates when I mouth off to him.

"Usually, that behavior would earn you more punishment, but I find I'm liking this greedy side of you when it comes to my dick. To answer your question, yes, I'm going to fuck you in a moment. I'm working my way up to it. Besides, I need to take a few steps to ensure you're properly prepared. As much as you think I'm a monster, I don't actually want to cause you any harm."

My only answer to that is a snort. He's harmed me plenty since I got here. I have a cascade of bruises all down my backside, and I can't say I regret a single one of them. Especially with the memory of his heavy weight on top of me so fresh in my mind.

I wiggle on the desk in the hope it will urge him on.

He swats my ass, and I shudder as the sting of his palm sinks into my skin. "I'll give you my cock when I'm ready. Until then, be fucking patient."

My breath creates a semi-circle of dampness in front of my mouth. I focus on breathing and watching it grow farther and farther with each exhale. It's the only reason I don't jump out of my skin when his finger prods the tight circle of my ass.

I suck in a gasp and peer at him over my shoulder. "What are you doing?"

The glare he returns is full of heat and dark promise. It sets my legs quivering and my heart beating hard. I swallow heavily but maintain eye contact.

"You're tight, and I want to be as gentle as possible with you. I need to loosen you up before we do this."

It takes me a couple of tries to get the words out. "But my ass? You want to fuck my ass?"

His devastatingly devious smile tells me I should have realized that the moment he volunteered to divest me of my virginity. "You want someone to fuck you, so I'll fuck you. But since you've been misbehaving so badly, I'm not going to give you the pleasure of fucking your cunt, yet." His gaze hardens. "And just so we're on the same page. If I see you throwing yourself at Soo or Lucas again, I will strip you naked and dump you with my guards. They'll more than make sure every single one of your holes are filled. Are we clear on that?"

I nod quickly, still watching him. He drops his gaze down my body, and then a stream of liquid follows. Oil, or lube, I think, since I can't see the bottle, coats the seam of my ass, down my thighs, and even the top of my back as he rubs it into my skin.

I'm shaking, shivering. This is not what I wanted, not like this. The idea of him nudging me open with his cock and sliding it back there—I shudder again. It shouldn't fill me with warm, sticky heat.

"You're shaking. Is it because I threatened you?" he says from behind me.

He's rimming that tight little pucker with his thumb, slowly working it inside with each pass. It doesn't hurt, but I'm still scared. I'm not sure what I expected. Whatever hole he uses, it's going to be the first time.

He lays his body over the top of my back, his face almost against my ear. When he takes my earlobe between his teeth, I jump against him, and he moans at the contact. "You brought this upon yourself, *stellina*. You acted like a little slut, throwing yourself at my brother. Now I'm going to treat you like one."

A thrill settles in my nerves, an adrenaline rush with an oh so needy chaser as my body betrays me. I want him. Despite everything, I want him to touch me. I want my captor, and I think that's the worst part of all of this. That I want someone who only sees me as revenge.

"I'll make you feel so good," he assures me. His breath is hot down the shell of my ear and onto my neck. "I'll make you scream my name before the end. I promise you."

Pleasure, I want, but I won't scream his name, no matter how good it feels. I force myself to stay so still my muscles clench tight with sheer control.

"You have doubts," he proclaims. I can hear the smile in his voice and glance up to meet his eyes. It's nothing more than a wry twist of his lips, but still devastating.

He shoves upward, his focus already shifted to my ass again. I whimper as he inserts his thumb, carefully working the slick digit against my muscles. It still doesn't hurt, and a slow curling heat is building in my core again. Damn, I hate when he's right. I hate it all, hate how much a part of me craves him, how every nerve in my body reacts when he touches me. He makes me feel alive, more alive than I have ever felt before.

After a few moments of me regulating my breathing and trying not to whimper underneath him, he carefully adds a second finger to his probing. I exhale a gust of air onto the desk, and it clouds around my face in a halo.

"Doing okay, *stellina*?" he asks, seemingly from far away.

"Yes," I croak out. Adding a nod in case he can't hear me.

His dark chuckle tells me he did. He slides his free hand around my front, shoving my legs wider to delve his fingers into my pussy. A hiss escapes him against the center of my spine. "You're soaked. So fucking wet, it's dripping down my fingers."

He renews his attention to my ass, this time adding a third finger. When I flinch away, he soothes his hand down my ribs. "Relax, just relax into it, and it won't hurt. There you go. Let me prepare you so you can take my cock."

I settle back down on my feet and again try to regulate my breathing. Trying to relax is impossible with the incessant throb of my clit with every brush of his dick between my thighs.

"Please," I whisper, hating myself even as I beg for it.

He gives me another tight squeeze of my ass cheeks. "You're almost there. Then I'll give you what you want. Can you already feel me inside? I can. I'll try to be gentle, but I can't guarantee anything once I fight the tight clasp of your asshole around my cock. You make me fucking crazy."

I jolt in surprise at his admission. He's always been either completely indifferent around me or using my body to get his own pleasure. The idea that someone like me could drive this man, this monster, to distraction leaves me full of pride. This must be how Stockholm syndrome starts. But it can't be; I'm not unreasonably convinced he's a good, perfect man. Nicolo is nothing more than a monster. I guess I'm just the type of girl who needs a monster to make her feel like this.

I don't know if it will be worth it in the end, but for now, with my knees knocking against the desk and his hot, soothing body against mine, it feels too good to stop.

He removes his fingers from my ass, and I follow him backward until he stops me. "Let me lube us both up a little more, and then I'll give you everything."

The word *everything* from his lips sounds like a promise. One he'll keep, no matter the cost.

I wiggle in answer, pressing up onto my tiptoes. We have a height difference, but he tosses me around like I weigh nothing. I want him to lift me up, like he did the other day, and pound into me until I have bruises on my hip bones.

"You're so fucking perfect," he whispers.

I don't know if I was supposed to hear it, but for the second time, I'm clenching my pussy in anticipation, and it's not even the part of me getting all the attention.

The broad head of his cock sliding along my ass drags me from my thoughts. He gently nudges the head of his cock into my puckered hole, and I try to remain still and calm. Inside I'm thrashing, and outside everything is tight and coiled.

He runs a hand down my spine, almost soothingly. "Settle down, or I'm going to come before I'm even all the way inside you. You're squeezing me so tight."

I whimper and dig my fingers into the desk. I can't resist anymore and slide one hand under my hips to catch my clit with my fingers.

Just as I make contact, he grabs my hand in a bruising grip and removes it. "No, I told you I'd make you feel good. If you need me to touch your clit then tell me, and I will."

"Please." It comes out harsh, but it is all I can manage.

He drops my wrist on top of the desk and angles me so he can guide his cock inside my body with one hand and cup my pussy with the other. I'm almost completely off the desk and against him now.

I wriggle back into him and enjoy the curse he spits out. It hurts as he makes progress, too slowly, but it hurts the way it did when he fucked my face, and the way it did when he came on my belly. It hurts, but I want more, need more.

His finger makes a lazy swirl over my clit, and I sink into the sensation. The assault and the coaxing, the edge of pain, and the slow lazy sparks of pleasure washing through me.

When his hips meet my backside, I can't stay still. I feel stuffed full of him, his hard body around mine, inside me, over me. It's too much, and I realize I'm panting, little wet puddles onto the desk in front of my lips.

"You feel so good," he groans.

He pulls out, as achingly slow as he entered. But I don't want slow. I can't take slow. I need more.

"Please, just fuck me," I plead, my face burning in a wash of shame. I'm absolutely begging, and I can't bring myself to care now.

He increases his pace, pulling almost all the way out, and then nudging back inside my tight ass. I clench around him, moving, thrusting, doing anything I can to gather up the sensations and shove them deeper, feel him deeper.

"I liked when you were greedy for my cock in your mouth. I like it even more as you squirm for my cock in your ass. I wonder what you'd do if I put it in your tight little cunt. Would you beg then too?"

I moan at the thought of him fucking my pussy next.

He picks up his pace, both in the maddening swirl of his fingers on my clit and the slide of his cock into my asshole. Each pass is achingly gentle, and I hate every single one, even as I chase him for the next. He's toying with me, punishing me, like he promised.

This time when he pulls almost all the way out of me, he's so focused on where we join, I shove back into him, almost taking all of him inside me in one smooth toe-numbing stroke.

He barks out a strangled sound, his hands bracing on the desk beside my hips to still us both. "You're playing with fire, princess," he growls.

If fire feels this good, then it can burn me to ash.

I settle my hand on my clit again and glance at him over my shoulder. "Just do it! The way I know you want to. I can feel you holding back. Just fuck me, please, Nicolo."

It's me saying his name that's his undoing.

He grabs my hips, one hand on either side, and lifts me so high my feet hang above the ground. Then, even though he's mostly already inside me, he shoves deeper, so deep it feels like he's reached the end of me.

Then he pulls out and sets a brutal pace. I rub my clit harder and faster with each thrust, whimpering, groaning, struggling in his hold. None of it matters as my orgasm sparks inside me, my clit tightening against my finger as I move faster, always faster, and harder.

He keeps going, slamming into my ass hard and deep. I can feel his balls at the back of my thighs and the coarse hair above his cock against my skin. He's imprinted on my body, maybe even joined me in my skin.

With each thrust, he grunts until his own breath is shuttling in and out of him in heavy heaving gasps. "Come for me, *stellina*. Now."

Somehow my body obeys, and I shatter into a thousand brittle shards, my hand slowing on my slit until I can't even see or think straight. Pleasure zings through me, followed by a soft groan from him. I don't understand the things I'm feeling. Why does his deep voice sound so good when he makes those noises?

He thrusts harder still, slamming into me until he freezes with a loud grunt. His fingers dig into my skin with bruising force as he comes, and his thighs shake as he holds himself into my body.

Carefully, almost reverently, he settles me on my feet, holding me tight against him, as he ensures my knees will hold up. I'm not convinced, but he is, and when he lets go, I flop belly first onto the desk.

At some point, I feel a warm towel against my skin, but then it goes hazy. I think I'm lifted and carried somewhere. I drift into darkness, only to wake up a moment later when I'm placed on something soft.

On instinct, I curl up, reveling in the fresh linen scent and silky fabric against my heated skin. Something warm and hard presses against my body, and that's the last thing I notice before sleep drags me under completely.

24

NIC

I wake up with a tingle in my arm, letting me know the limb is stiff and blood flow sparse. Looking down at the sleeping form curled into my side, I find Celia. Her soft, pink lips are parted, and her angelic features are softened in the early morning light. Right now, she isn't afraid, isn't tense, or trying to fight me. She is an angel, and how mocking is it that I'm the devil?

An inky darkness cloaks me as a dull ache spreads through my chest with one glance. My heart thunders against my ribs, amplifying the pain, and I can't ever remember a time when it beat this hard before. *So soft, fragile, and trusting.* That's how she appears, like a sleeping lamb in the pasture while the big bad wolf lurks at the edge of the woods. If only I was a better man, a man that wasn't so dead set on revenge. Maybe things could be different?

I have to squish the thought before it builds into something more. Today her entire world will change, and I suppose, given all these fucking thoughts coursing through me at the sight of her, so will mine. I don't allow myself to dwell on things that can't be changed, and I ignore the pain slicing through my chest.

I shift my legs against hers and realize the blankets are wound between her bare legs. When she fell asleep on top of my desk, I carried her back to my bed, even though I knew I should have tucked her into hers. For one night, I wanted the scent of her hair on my pillows, to fall asleep intertwined with my knee shoved between her thighs.

I gently climb out of bed and study her. She flays herself out when she sleeps like the entire bed is hers. In the middle of the night, she curled up on my chest like a small animal seeking shelter and warmth, and I didn't stop her. Instead, I kissed her forehead and watched her sleep. Watched as she took comfort in my presence instead of wanting to stab me with something or back talk me. It often takes hours for me to fall asleep, and even when I do, it's only for a few hours at a time. With her in my arms, I slept more than I have in years. I don't want to think that it's her that helped me, but it's hard to deny.

With one final glance at her peacefully sleeping body, I leave her in my bed and go to the bathroom to get ready for the day. One steaming hot shower later, and I feel revitalized. Wrapping a towel around my waist, I step into the bedroom to grab clean clothes and find that she's rotated onto her side, the blankets curled up underneath her, one thigh spread over the top lump like she wants to open her thighs around a lover's legs. Fuck. Her shapely thighs wrapped around my head as I eat her for breakfast, lunch, and dinner play out in my mind. It takes all my carefully cultivated discipline to walk out of my bedroom to head into my office.

It still smells of sex, and I'll never be able to look at my desk again without seeing her on top of it. I don't look at where I fucked her last night, but I open the windows to let the chilly morning air refresh the room before Sarah stops in with my breakfast.

I focus on the paperwork and the plan Soo must have left on my desk during the night. It's a stack of papers as thick as my thumb. Each page shows the men and women who are attending tonight's auction. Also, where their allegiances lie and how to sweet talk them. I've never been the sweet-talking type, but I've learned in order to finish this mission.

The thought of revenge, finally, after so many years, seems like a hazed dream. Something I've wished for over and over is finally within my grasp. And I can't let whatever I feel for Celia jeopardize it. I'm a big enough man to accept I have feelings. How can I not when she's everything I want in a woman? So giving of herself, even to a monster like me. It doesn't matter though, she's going up for sale, and then I'll come down on her family and tear it apart—blood for blood. There's no other way. In the end, at least I'll have spared her an untimely death. At least with putting her up for auction, I'll have saved her. I don't know what the future holds for her, but maybe she will escape her new owner?

She's stubborn enough to succeed. That's if her mouth doesn't get her killed. The mere thought of her dead, of her flesh bruised, and her eyes vacant of life sends me into a mental tailspin. Red hot rage bubbles in my veins. I want to kill anyone who ever harms her, even if I have no right to.

I can't think of it. Can't think of what's going to happen to her. When she is gone, she'll be gone from my mind as well. It's the way it has to be.

As if she knows that I'm thinking about her, she comes tiptoeing into my office wearing one of my shirts, an impish grin on her face. She is the image of beauty, sultry and intoxicating. Her dark curls hang down past her breasts, her hard nipples poke under the fabric, leaving little to the imagination. I want to suck one of the hard peaks into my mouth and finish what I couldn't earlier by sinking my cock deep inside her. *No!* Conflict rages inside me like a battle scorn country caught between good and evil.

One thing is certain though, the second she walked into this room, I could feel her. Like she'd straddled my lap and left me panting in her wake.

Once the image enters my mind, I wave my hand at her to approach. "Come here, *stellina*. I want to touch you."

She crosses the room with her chin tucked, as if she isn't sure how to act today. I draw her into me and lift her over my legs, so her thighs rest on either side of mine.

"Good morning," she whispers.

I cup her ass and drag her into me, wishing her naked skin slid across mine in this position. "Go get some breakfast and then go back to bed. You'll need your rest. I rode you hard yesterday."

A flash of pink washes into her cheeks, and I can't help but see it in my mind, all the way to her belly button.

"Are we going to do it again?" There's a note of hope in her tone that I don't have it in me to squash.

"Not right now. I have to get some work done. Busy day today."

She wiggles in my lap suggestively, and I still her hips in my hands. "Are you sure? We could go back to bed right now? I'll—"

"As much as I would enjoy spending the morning in bed with you, I can't." I try to keep my tone gentle. Knowing that the moment she realizes I'm still selling her, she'll start hating me again. I'll deal with it, but it doesn't mean I want to hasten the moment.

She slumps and then quickly scrambles off my lap.

Sarah walks in a beat later and deposits a tray of food on my desk, staring between us. "Everything is ready for tonight. Just let me know who is doing the driving and who you want as servers."

I glance at Celia, who stares between us in confusion. "What's going on?"

Sarah clears her throat, casts me a look, and leaves. The woman always has impeccable timing, both for good and bad situations.

Celia puts her hands on her hips and then grabs a piece of toast off the plate. "I'm eating. Tell me what's going on before I imagine the worst."

With no other choice, I shrug and answer, knowing this is it, the moment she shuts down and closes me out again. "Today's the day. The auction is tonight. My staff are preparing, just like they do for every single one of my events."

Her hand holding the toast freezes, hanging inches away from her lips. "The auction?"

I lock down all the warm and tender shit that I let run rampant through me for the past day and meet her eyes with the stone-cold expression I give every other bastard on the street. "You knew this was coming. It shouldn't be a surprise. At least now you can get back to existing outside of these walls."

Her eyes fly wide, and she throws the toast onto the plate. "Did you just say 'get back to existing' like the moment I walk out of your little party, I won't belong to another human being? Like they won't use me and throw me away the second I bore them?"

I keep steady eye contact with her and lean back in the desk chair. "You want out of this house, and you'll be getting out tonight."

Some part, deep down, hates the hurt flashing across her face and how she keeps trying to master it and failing.

"We had sex yesterday. I'm not a virgin. Can't you find some other woman to put up for sale, another virgin even?"

Now who is lying to herself? "You're telling me you'd be fine if I went out, plucked another virgin off the street, and sold her in your stead? You wouldn't feel one bit of guilt for me doing that?"

"Then cancel the event altogether."

"I can't, and I won't. Did you really think last night would change anything?"

She stays quiet for long enough that I don't even need an answer. I grab the piece of toast she'd been eating and shove it in my mouth. If only to keep from getting up and offering comfort. Something I don't even do for my own brother.

"I guess I should have made things more clear yesterday. What we did was fucking, and it was more of a punishment to get you back in line than anything else."

Her eyes narrow, and she stalks forward. "And me waking up in your bed, was that part punishment too?"

I surge out of the chair. Something more than anger, more than my need to dominate my emotions, bubbles up inside me. When I meet her anger with my own, she stumbles backward until I press her into the wall. "Listen, princess, you mean nothing more to me than revenge. Yesterday was nice. It felt good, but don't think a little sex is going to sway me from my goals. Nothing on this planet has that power. Especially not you."

She trembles against me, her chin held high despite the sheen of tears coating her eyes. "Well, thank you for clarifying that for me. I see now that I mean nothing to you, despite the evidence to the contrary. I wouldn't want to put a dent in that masculine pride of yours." She shoves me away from her, and I allow it, if only to put some distance between her body and mine.

I watch her carefully, waiting for another outburst, but she picks up the mug of coffee and takes a sip. Using the food as an excuse, I shove the tray toward her. "Take it with you back to your room. I'll have someone bring you some clothes later today so you can prepare yourself."

"Prepare myself," she whispers against the rim of the mug. "Exactly how am I supposed to prepare myself to be sold to another person? How can I get ready to no longer have control over my own life? Any tips for that?"

She carefully replaces the mug on the tray and then lifts the napkin wrapped silver and throws it at my face. Of course, since I'm within a foot, she makes a direct hit, the butt of the knife leaving a sting on my cheek.

I leave the utensils where they've fallen and glare. "Do it again, and I'll drag you to the auction naked tonight. I'll let every man there inspect you himself with his hands, his mouth, even his cock if he's willing to pay the right price."

She hisses out a breath. "You wouldn't."

"Why not? I'm already done with you."

I went too far with that last comment, my anger riding me. I don't know why I can never stay in control around this woman. But I can't apologize. I've already shown too much weakness to her.

She lifts the apple from the tray like she might take a bite, then chucks it at me hard enough it makes a thud against my chest. I stare down at the apple, and then back at her, my mind a desolate wasteland where thought used to be. I snag her arm in my grip before she can run away.

"No, you're not going yet." I walk her to the desk, lift her up, and lay her across it.

She struggles and shoves at me, futilely. "No, get off me, you asshole."

I pin her arms above her head, and her body with my own. "You don't give me orders. I'm the one who gives you the orders. When you can't obey them, you get punished."

"What are you going to do? Fuck me? Lock me up? Sell me?" she mocks.

I pull her hands together in one of my fists and capture her chin in my hand. "You're done talking for the day. I don't want to hear another word out of you."

She gasps, stilling over me. Her next words are soft. "I know you care about me. I can feel it every time you touch me. Like a tongue to a 9V, it sparks through me so obviously I can't ignore it."

"You don't know anything about me, and I know nothing about you. What we did was fun, but that was it. Leave it alone now. It's time to move on."

Her eyes are wide and bright, tears hugging the edges. I feel like I've kicked a puppy with the way she's looking at me.

She arches her neck toward me and presses her lips to mine, tears streaming over her cheeks as she stares into my eyes. I let her kiss me and refuse to move or even breathe as she molds her lips to mine. I don't react, even as hard as it is for me not to. I stand like a statue, showing my cold indifference.

"It's not true," she whispers.

Before she's out of my hands, I need to kill any notion in her we can ever have a future. As long as she thinks it's possible, she won't stop trying. I dig my phone out of my pocket and scroll to the last picture. It's of her dead fiancé, lying on the concrete in the parking garage where I shot him.

I hold the phone up, so she can see the image. When her brain processes, she reels away in shock.

"This is what happens when you think love is real. People die. For some idiotic reason, you agreed to marry this fool. And he took that weakness for himself. Your fiancé wanted money more than he wanted a wife. When he drugged you and sold you to me, I thought it was enough to cover a percentage of his debt. This is what happened when he pushed for more, trying to see how much he could weasel out of me." I close the phone and toss it on my desk. "Also, I didn't like his face. Don't mistake me for a kind man. I'm not. You're here to make me money, and if you can't do that, you're expendable. Do you understand?" I put more bite in my tone than usual, for both our benefits.

When she nods, I turn to the tray and what is left of my breakfast. "Get the fuck out until I come find you tonight."

She doesn't leave right away, and I shovel some eggs into my mouth, pretending she doesn't exist or that the very scent of her hasn't worked its way under my skin.

The air around me stirs as she walks to the door. I don't look at her when she goes. The second my office door closes, I throw myself into the armchair in front of my desk and focus on piecing myself back together again.

When I told her love is a weakness, I meant it. The only good use for it is manipulation. Nothing works better than a person's love for another to ensnare them. Even idiots like Gardello are susceptible. He just didn't love a person; he loved money more than anything else. Which ultimately led to his downfall.

Soo finds me still in the chair a little while later. "Everything good?"

I nod and stand to go back to the other side of my desk and get back to work. She's distracted me long enough, and I need to ensure everything is settled before tonight. If even one thing falls through the cracks, the entire event can be ruined.

Soo stands in front of my desk, a look I don't like on his face.

I snatch up a piece of paper that had fluttered to the floor in my fight with Celia. "What's your problem?"

He shakes his head. "Nothing. You seem worried, is all, and if I'm being honest, you're not usually one to show any type of fear or concern."

His assumption of me being worried or afraid is annoying. "Well, I don't know. Today is the event we have been working toward for years, Soo. I'm entitled to fuss over the proceedings. They are mine, after all. Just do your part. Did you get the clothes for her?"

He waves at a black paper bag by the door. "Everything she will need is in there. Have you considered what you'll do if she refuses to get ready?"

I shrug. "I don't give a fuck. If she won't put on the clothes I've provided, then she can walk into the warehouse naked. I'm sure the buyers would love that even more than the dress."

The thought of all those men looking at her bare flesh makes me want to punch something.

I stare down my second-in-command. "Fine, a new proposition, then. If she fights you on getting dressed, tell her that I'll come in and dress her myself. And once I've put her in the slinkiest, sexiest thing I can find, I'll tie her up in ropes and walk her into the warehouse hogtied. Let's see which she will prefer."

Soo dips his head, a smile playing on his lips. He just might enjoy fighting with her. And I hate him a little bit for it.

25

CELIA

*T*he bastard wants me in ribbons. A stylist showed up at mid-day, and while I endured her attentions as she fussed with my hair, waxed me to within an inch of my life, and expertly applied makeup, so I didn't even look made up, I hated every second.

Once she leaves, I slip back into the shirt and wait for whatever costume Nicolo has prepared for me. A maid skirts into the room carrying a dress bag a few moments later. She places it on the door to my closet.

"Thank you," I tell her, even if the dress and this place leaves me with a sour taste in my mouth.

As soon as she retreats from the room, I climb off the bed and walk over to the closet, pulling the zipper on the bag down to inspect the contents. I'm not surprised to find it's a deep red, almost wine color, and barely what I would call a *dress*. The front of the dress has a panel that is little more than lace, and the back is open, save a thin ribbon criss-crossing from the top of the barely-there skirt to where it ends just under my shoulder blades.

Jesus, I can't wear this. I might as well wear nothing.

As I stare at the dress, I can't figure out how I'm going to get into it. A knock draws my attention to the door just as Soo comes walking in. I grab the dress off the door and carry it over to the bed.

"Glad the dress made it to you," he says. "Can I help you?"

I glare at him and wave at the red scrap of clothing. "You call this a dress? I've worn underwear with more material than this thing."

Soo approaches and stares down at it. "Nic picked it out personally. He wants you to wear it, so you can either put it on, or he has other ideas in mind. And as you know, he has a vivid imagination." His tone is bland, and I can't tell if he cares or not.

He continues before I can think of something both witty and cutting to reply with. "Sorry I missed you yesterday. I stopped by your room to give you those pants and coffee, but you were ...detained."

I snort, and my cheeks flood with heat. "You mean I was fucking your boss."

He picks up the dress and deftly loosens the straps carefully and almost methodically. "He's not my boss. He's my best friend. We're partners."

Once he finishes, he kneels at my feet to help me into the material, but I retreat. "No, thank you. I can get dressed on my own. I don't need your help."

His arched eyebrow and deadpan look tell me exactly what he thinks before he even opens his mouth. "You're about to be sold to someone who will most certainly keep you without clothes for his pleasure. Why are you worried about me?"

To be honest. I'm not. I'm stalling, trying to buy time.

He comes to that conclusion himself. "If you aren't ready, Nic will just drag you out the door naked. He doesn't care one way or the other. Let me help you into this, and you can make both our lives a little easier tonight."

"Why would you think I care about making your life easier? As you say, I'm about to be sold. I don't give a shit about any of you."

He spreads his hands in the material pointedly, urging me to put it on. "I'm very good at reading people, Ms. Ricci, and I know for a fact you're lying your ass off when you say that. You might wish you don't, but you do."

I step toward him just to get him to shut his mouth. We manage to get it up my torso and the thin spaghetti straps over my arms without too much embarrassment. Then he sets to work on the lacing in the back. It takes him minutes to do what would have taken me an hour.

He gestures at the bathroom. "Do you want to take a look?"

I shake my head. "No. I don't really care. Do I get shoes this time or what?"

"Barefoot, I'm afraid. But don't worry, no one will let you step on anything."

Nicolo's second-in-command is much more formal today. He's wearing tailored slacks, a black button down, and his hair is perfectly braided at the back of his head. With his matching scowl, he looks like a scarily sexy assassin.

When I've finished adjusting my dress, I stand awkwardly. "What now?"

He rips a long red ribbon about two inches wide from his pocket and gestures for me to spin around. "I'm sorry, but it's protocol to ensure you don't know where the house or the warehouse is."

I do as he says, only because he's been the nicest of the men in this house. "Can we set up some kind of signal system? I'll pick a winner, and you make him bid."

He finishes typing the ribbon and gently rotates me to face him again. "Sorry, the winner will be all about the money he'll pay."

"What if some old warty dude buys me?"

Soo adjusts a few straps on the dress and arranges my hair to fall over the front of my shoulders. Since I can't see him, I assume he's primping me for a reason. "We don't know any old warty dudes if that makes you feel any better."

"Marginally."

I assume the little huff he makes is a laugh. It doesn't matter, because he tucks my hand around his forearm and leads me out of the room. The drive to the location feels fast, but I can't tell if it's actually fast or if I'm simply terrified, and my brain is tricking me about the details to calm me the hell down.

After Soo helps me from the vehicle, I hear Nicolo talking nearby, and then he comes over to join Soo and me.

"Any problems?" I assume he is asking Soo since he made it clear this afternoon that I'm ornamental and shouldn't be expressing my opinions to him.

Soo answers and lays a comforting hand over mine where it's wrapped around his arm. "No problems. Have you seen Lucas yet? He wasn't at the house."

There's a tension between the two men that seems to crackle along my skin. I keep my face down, not that it matters, since I can't see. But when someone brushes my hair away from my face, Nicolo, by the subtle spicy scent of him, I shiver. He tucks the hair behind my ears, putting my scar on full display to everyone.

"Let's go," he says, his voice low and deep.

He doesn't take my arm, though. Instead, he wraps his hand behind my neck and drags me beside him like a dog on a leash. I try to twist out of his grip, but his hold is too tight. Any more pressure, and he'd start cutting off my air supply.

"When we get in here, you don't speak to a single soul. Nod if you understand," he whispers harshly as the cold concrete below my feet gives way to smooth wooden planks.

"Don't do this," I plead one last time but am only met with silence.

The noise of lots of voices speaking at once greets me, along with a sweep of warm air. Then Nicolo's hand tightens, and the voices slowly die down to a dull murmur. I can't make out any specifics, but no doubt many of them are talking about me.

When someone brushes a hand along my arm, I jerk away, stumbling right into Nicolo's side.

"No one touches her until she is bought and paid for," he says, loud enough his voice echoes through the room.

There are some groans and protestations, but they dribble off, and then silence reigns. I'm drawn up onto a low stage or platform and left to stand elevated for inspection. I plead with every god I can think of that no one will go against his order to touch me. Any moment, I fear vomit will come spiraling up from some hidden depths. Of course, it doesn't.

I shouldn't love how protective he sounds or the tight hold he keeps on my neck. It's almost soothing to feel owned by him. The devil you know, right?

I can't afford to disillusion myself. He walked me through a warehouse full of people who want to buy me. As far as I'm concerned, this place can burn to the ground with everyone inside it.

He leans in and whispers, "Behave."

I put on my fakest worst smile, and not bothering to lower my voice say, "Fuck you."

His hand tightens on my neck for a flash, and then he shoves me away, releasing me completely. I guess I hit a nerve, but what does he expect? Me to sink to my knees and let him fuck my face again? After everything I've endured, even after the things he said to me, I know he has feelings. He's just trying to hide them so no one else sees, especially me. Nicolo might not want to believe it, but he cares for me. And he hasn't realized yet, but he's killed any chance for me to return his affection now.

Air swirls around my legs, and a whisper of a touch across the top of my foot shoots me backward into him. There's a scuffle in front of me and the sound of someone being dragged off.

"What part of 'don't touch' do I have to make clear?" he says, his voice low and menacing. It's the voice I heard the night we met, more monster than man.

Numbers start flying around me. Thousands of dollars turn into hundreds of thousands. My knees wobble, and I fear my legs will give out. But I don't want to show that kind of weakness in front of these people.

There is a shuffle behind me, and then Nicolo draws me back to sit on his lap. I have to turn to keep my legs closed as the dress leaves me completely on display. His hand feels just as possessive around my waist, clasping me into his body. The memory of him on top of me, of him holding me naked, threatens to swamp me, but I shove it out of my head. We're done with that now.

It's all I can do to keep my head up and not let the tears fall as the auction winds down when someone shouts from the back.

I don't hear him, but by the way Nicolo tenses behind me, he does. "Say that again, and I'll drag you out of here. In the years I've been moving product, when have I offered something fake? Tell me," Nicolo demands.

The other voice is closer now, the heavy scent of his cologne making my nose itch. "Look at her, Diavolo. How are we supposed to believe you didn't fuck her while she was in your care?"

Now's the time to speak out. I can tell them all I'm not a virgin, and maybe they will stop bidding. The second I open my mouth, Nicolo's hand clamps across my lips, and my head is wrenched back into the curve of his shoulder. "You say a word, and I just let them have you. Understand?"

I move my lips until I can dig my teeth into the fleshy part of his middle finger. He doesn't react to the bite outwardly, but his hands tighten around my face and waist.

"If you don't want to bid, then don't bid. It's your choice," he tells the man calmly.

There is more shouting, and Nicolo settles again, using his thigh to part my own instead of allowing me to keep them closed. I try to maneuver sideways again, but he spreads me wide open. No one can see my nudity since I'm so far up his thigh, thankfully.

The bidding is down to two men. Their voices rise and fall as they throw out numbers. Then one of them yells two million dollars, and the other falls silent.

I hear Soo say from across the room, "Sold for two million."

The word *sold* blasts through me. Sold. Sold?

Sold.

This can't be happening. Through the haze of sweet cigar smoke and the grating sounds of laughter, I hear it again. Sold. It's like my stomach's bottomed out into my toes. I can't draw a full breath in. I just can't believe he actually did it. All this time, some tiny part of me hadn't released the hope that I'd be saved or that Nicolo would, by some miracle, change his mind.

He didn't, though.

Sold. The word still echoes in my ears.

Nicolo pulls me to my feet, and I stumble forward, my legs like jelly, as he leads me away. We enter a room, and he yanks the ribbon from my face and grips me by the throat.

"Did you fucking bite me?" he growls into my face.

The cold wall is at my back, and no one else is in the room. I expected my new owner to be here, but maybe Nicolo just wants one last run with his toy before he hands her off.

I throw up my chin and glare. It's all bravado. An act as my breathing seesaws in and out of me, each one heavy and jagged. I'm three seconds from hyperventilating. But I refuse to let this beast see me break.

"Yes, and if you put anything else near my mouth again, I'll do the same." Before I can stop them, the words come tumbling out despite my breathlessness. "You disgust me. You talk about revenge and family honor, and here you are selling a defenseless woman to a bunch of disgusting pigs. I can't believe, for one minute, I let you touch me, that I actually thought…"

His smile turns predatory. "Actually, I'm selling you to one pig, and what did you think, princess? Finish your tirade since it'll be the last time we speak."

My gaze narrows. "I thought maybe that you had a soul. Obviously, I was mistaken. You're the devil, a heartless, cruel, asshole, devil. You are no better than my father."

The smile falls from his lips, and he shakes his head. "Soo will be in to take you to the car. Have a nice life, princess."

I say nothing as he walks out, slamming the door behind him. It's obvious he's angry, but so am I. If only he had changed his mind, we wouldn't be here right now.

Some of the righteous fury fizzles from my blood. A tremor takes over, and a wave of nausea follows. *Oh, god.*

I double over, bracing my hands on my knees. It's hard to breathe, and my head is swimming against the heavy pounding of my heartbeat. How did this happen? I was supposed to convince him to keep me. I'd completely misjudged his intentions, hoping that he would give up the revenge and money for something more.

Stupid. I was so stupid. The creaking of the door as it opens causes me to glance up and jump back. I'm half expecting Nicolo to come walking through the door, but I know better than to hope for such a thing. Instead, a familiar face saunters into the room.

I'm not dumb enough to relax, not around *him*. "What? Didn't get your turn, so now you're here to take it before you miss your chance?" I spit the words at him.

His hands are shoved into his pockets, and he surveys me with wariness. Gone is his usual brooding venom. He steps toward me, slowly, like a wolf hunting its prey, but I hold my ground despite the roaring fear in my blood and the shaking in my hands.

When he remains silent, the knot of fear in my gut tightens. "What do you want? Surely you didn't just come in here to stare at me?" Despite the words coming out in one piece, they give away my defeat. "Please, just leave me alone."

Again, he says nothing. Hell, he's not even looking at me, keeping his gaze firmly over my shoulder.

These are my last few moments alone. Who knows what will come next. I don't want these last moments to be in his presence. Wanting him to go away, I spin around and give him my back. What can he do to me that hasn't already been done, anyway?

It doesn't matter. None of it matters.

"Is that any way to talk to your big brother?"

Big brother?

"What the—" I don't get to finish the sentence because, in the next instant, something hard hits the back of my head. Pain flares bright through my neck, shooting stars behind my eyes. The strike sends me to my knees, and my vision blurs as the floor comes into view. Is this how it ends? After everything I've been through?

"Sorry, this is going to hurt."

My last thought before everything goes black... he has to be lying. There is no way that he's my brother.

To be Continue in Devil You Know

ABOUT THE AUTHORS

J.L. Beck and C. Hallman are an USA Today and international bestselling author duo who write contemporary and dark romance.

For a list of all of our books, updates and freebies visit our website.

www.bleedingheartromance.com

Printed in Great Britain
by Amazon